"THE AREA IS FAR FROM STABLE,"
PRICE STATED

"The Taliban might have been kicked out of power and the Northern Alliance put in charge, but up in the mountains you'll encounter hostile groups. If Mahoud is on the run, you'll have to contend with them."

Brognola held up a hand. "This is for both teams. Listen up, people. We waive the rules on this one. We lose our grip here and the consequences are too severe to even consider. The President has authorized total backup for you. What we have is a possible, and until we find otherwise, we go with that premise— possible nuclear strike on American soil. It can't be allowed to happen.

"Find those sons of bitches and put them down for good."

DON PENDLETON'S

STONY

AMERICA'S ULTRA-COVERT INTELLIGENCE AGENCY

MAN®

DAY OF
DECISION

A GOLD EAGLE BOOK FROM
W⊕RLDWIDE®

TORONTO • NEW YORK • LONDON
AMSTERDAM • PARIS • SYDNEY • HAMBURG
STOCKHOLM • ATHENS • TOKYO • MILAN
MADRID • WARSAW • BUDAPEST • AUCKLAND

First edition February 2004

ISBN 0-373-61953-7

DAY OF DECISION

Special thanks and acknowledgment to
Mike Linaker for his contribution to this work.

DAY OF
DECISION

PROLOGUE

Afghanistan, Near Border with Pakistan

Jamil Azul knew he would kill a man this day. He squatted in the dust at the head of the narrow trail, a battered Kalashnikov AK-47 cradled in his arms as he watched the approach to the meeting place. At his side a much-used rucksack held a canteen of water and a wedge of local goat's-milk cheese. He had arrived an hour ago, well ahead of the agreed-upon time. The first thing he did was to check out the surrounding slopes and natural places where a man with a rifle could lie in wait. Life was full of traps waiting to snap shut on the unsuspecting, and he hadn't lived as long as he had by being careless. Where money was concerned he trusted no one. The smuggler bringing in the merchandise would be expecting his payoff, and even the most innocent person could become treacherous when there was a large amount of cash involved. Azul had money with him, just for show if needed, because he had no intention of actually paying the smuggler—not with cash.

Men had died for far less. It was well-known that greed could blind the most honest individual. So Azul had made his preparations. The Kalashnikov was his insurance. He had to be seen to be carrying one. In this region the autorifle was the most natural item to be seen with. A man without a rifle would be regarded with suspicion. Beneath the folds of his robes Azul had a pistol tucked under his broad leather belt. It was a 9 mm SIG-Sauer P-226. He had carried the weapon for two years now, and it suited his purpose well. It was solid and powerful, delivering its load with accuracy, and could be depended on never to fail. There was also a keen-edged knife tucked inside his left boot in a concealed sheath.

Azul drew back the folds of his sleeve and checked his watch. Almost time. The smuggler was known to be punctual, despite the distance he had to cover. He had made this trip many times before, bringing in merchandise by pony train. In a way it was a pity this would be his last trip, and his final day on Earth. His death had been decided on thousands of miles from this desolate place, by a man far higher up the chain of command than either the smuggler or the man waiting to execute him. It had become necessary to sever all links with anyone involved in bringing together certain items, a precaution to prevent whispers starting concerning those items. The means of transporting them had avoided routing them through places where they might have been noticed. These days airports and docks were subjected to rigorous checks that might have uncovered the items. The old trade routes, with their unmarked trails and primitive means of transport, were still often overlooked by the authorities, especially in this desolate part of the country. Despite the tensions that still affected everyday life, the age-old smuggling trade carried on, now with an even stronger vigor because a percentage of the aid dropped by the Western powers fell into greedy hands and there was a good living to be made from re-sourcing the goods. The dusty back country allowed a certain measure of safety, but not one hundred percent. Even smugglers were tinged with curiosity. So once the goods were in Azul's hands, the smuggler would be dealt with.

A distant sound alerted the man. He listened, wanting to be certain he hadn't been mistaken. A smile edged his lips. His waiting was over. He laid the Kalashnikov on the ground at his feet and opened the rucksack, taking out the canteen and the wedge of cheese. He broke off a piece of the cheese and ate slowly, washing it down with water.

Now he could hear the sound of the approaching pack train, the clatter of hooves on the stony ground and the voice of the smuggler as he talked ceaselessly to his animals.

From the higher slopes a bitter wind began to blow, carrying the smell of winter with it. It swirled and eddied, breaking through the dry vegetation and lifting grains of dust that drifted like a pale mist. Azul felt the wind tug at his robes. He put away his food and recapped the canteen, placing both items back inside the rucksack. Reaching down, he picked up the Kalashnikov and made sure it was ready for use.

The smuggler appeared over the lip of the trail, muttering to himself as he shielded his face from the gritty wind. His head was bent toward his chest, turned slightly, so he failed to see the waiting man at first. It was only as he came fully into view that he stopped, the string of ponies jostling to a halt behind him. He squinted his eyes as protection against the drifting dust and stared at Azul.

"Have you been here long?"

"Some time."

"It's a long trail. A long way to come."

"So I understand."

"And lonely."

"I am sure it is."

The smuggler made a slight gesture.

"Talking to the animals loses its appeal very quickly."

Azul sensed something in the smuggler's tone.

"So I brought along my cousin for company."

A man appeared from the rear of the pack train. He was tall and broad, and a full beard covered the lower half of his face. His eyes were fixed on the buyer. He held an old American M-16 in his large hands, the muzzle pointing directly at Azul.

"If I was the sort to be offended, your cousin's lack of manners might cause bad feeling between us."

The smuggler glanced back over his shoulder, shaking his head in the direction of his "relative."

"I must apologize for his discourteous attitude. But in his defense he is only doing what I asked him. Protecting me."

Azul placed his own weapon aside, spreading his hands as he stood.

"In that case shall we proceed?"

"Please," the smuggler agreed rather too hastily.

He turned to the first pack animal, starting to loosen

straps so the buyer might inspect the goods. The pony shied away, stamping its hoofs against the hard ground.

"Child of misery," the smuggler yelled. "Be still or I will turn you into buzzard meat."

In the brief moment of confusion Azul moved to one side, the smuggler between him and the man's cousin.

"These beasts are..." the smuggler began, then became aware of a change in Azul's stance. He turned to look at the man and saw the SIG pistol Azul had drawn from beneath his robes.

Azul ignored him, leaning to one side, his gun hand lifting. As he cleared the smuggler's body and faced the bodyguard and his M-16, Azul already had the SIG on track. He pulled the trigger three times in swift succession. The weapon cracked sharply, the trio of 9 mm bullets striking the bodyguard in the chest, directly over the heart. The man fell back, hitting the rocky ground hard. His finger pulled back against the M-16's trigger, sending a short burst of fire into the air before the weapon dropped to the ground.

The smuggler turned about to look at Azul, uncertainty clouding his expression.

"I do not understand. Why?"

"It isn't necessary for you to understand," Azul said and pulled the trigger again.

Three shots and the smuggler went down in a huddle, curling up like a child in the womb. He jerked a little, pushing against the hard ground. Blood fingered out from beneath the body as Azul stepped back, moving quickly to take hold of the lead pony's rope. He held fast until the agitated animals had quieted. Still holding the rope Azul stood over the smuggler and fired a final shot into the man's skull. He did the same to the cousin, seeing the man's head bounce as the bullet cored into it. Satisfied, Azul tucked the SIG back under his belt. He retrieved his rifle and rucksack, then led the pack train around the bodies and farther up the trail. Once he felt safe he tethered the lead pony, then went down the line of six pack animals. He removed the merchandise from each, then took off the pack saddles. Finally he removed the rope harness and sent the ponies back down the trail.

He opened the packs and went through them until he found what he was looking for. Ignoring the food and medical supplies, he stood and held the sealed box in his hands. This was what he had been waiting for.

Placing the box in the rucksack, Azul slung it across his shoulders and adjusted the webbing until the load sat squarely. He picked up his Kalashnikov and started to walk, distancing himself from the area. He walked for the next two hours, stopping only to remove the canteen from the rucksack and take a small drink.

The wind blew around him, driving pale dust across his trail and wiping out his footprints. Azul drew his robes around his body, dragging the loose hood over his head to shield him from the gritty dust. The trail he followed, faint as it had been, was obscured by the wind-driven dust. Azul never once hesitated. He knew these rocky foothills as well as he knew his way around his apartment.

By midafternoon he had reached the rendezvous point. From a point beneath a cluster of rock he drew out a wrapped object. Removing the covering, he exposed a powerful transmitter unit. He expanded the satellite dish and positioned it. He switched on and used the digital settings to locate the signal. Using the compact handset he sent out his message, listening to the reply over the headset he had put on. Satisfied, he closed down the transmitter and sat in the shade of a large rock, patiently waiting for his pickup.

Paris, France

ABRIM MANSUR CROSSED the street and stepped inside the foyer of the apartment building. He stood for a moment, shaking the water off his leather coat. The door to the concierge's room opened and Madame Escallier stood there. When she recognized Mansur she smiled.

"*Bonjour, Monsieur Mansur.*"

Mansur nodded. "Paris, Madame. How delightful."

Her laugh was deep and throaty. She was a stoutly built woman in her late fifties, with the permanently flushed face of a consummate drinker.

Reaching under his coat, Mansur produced a bottle of moderately expensive red wine. He presented it to the woman with a slight bow.

"For you, Madame."

She took it with a coy smile, cradling it to her ample breasts.

"Thank you, Monsieur Mansur. You are too kind."

"It is my pleasure, Madame."

The wine was a ritual he observed a number of times each week. It kept the woman sweet, helping her endure the solitude of her position and served to maintain her silence. Madame Escallier was a woman of simple needs, and Mansur's attention had become something of an event for her.

"Wait one moment," she said and stepped back inside her office. When she returned she held a plain white envelope in her hand. "This came for you earlier."

Mansur took the envelope. "Perhaps this is what I have been waiting for."

"I hope it is good news."

"Merci, Madame."

Mansur climbed the stairs, aware that Madame Escallier was still at her door watching him. He reached the landing and turned, disappearing from her view. He climbed three more flights before he reached his floor. He walked along the passage until he reached the door to his apartment. Taking his key he let himself in, closing and bolting the door behind him.

The apartment was cool and shady. He crossed the room and opened the shutters, allowing the daylight to penetrate the gloom. From the window he could look out over the Paris rooftops. He stood there for a time, simply gazing across the dark, glistening buildings, realizing how much he liked this city of contrasts. Full of promise, yet sometimes a cold and unforgiving place. When he walked the crowded boulevards, another figure among the masses, he felt almost at home. Yet there were times he stood alone in the company of strangers. A man without a home. Dispossessed. Deprived of his birthright. Denied his place in the sun. Then he knew he didn't belong. He was without roots, wandering the streets, looking for something he knew he would never find.

He often stood and watched the river flowing by. The Seine drifted through the city, belonging yet separate. Paris and the Seine existed side by side each independent of the other. The city went about its business and the river moved toward the sea. Each lived its own life, briefly coming together, then moving on. The river flowed and joined with the sea, taking with it only the memory of its union, leaving the city as it found it. Mansur's time in Paris held the same meaning. He was here, and during his time the city embraced him. He allowed it to touch him, giving him momentary comfort. But he knew the day he moved on the city would fill the gap of his leaving and forget he had ever been there. Mansur turned away from the window, realizing he still held the envelope in his hand. He turned it over and stared at the handwritten name: Monsieur Mansur.

Mansur opened the envelope and eased back the flap. Inside was a single, folded sheet of paper. He took it out and unfolded the sheet. There was a brief message on the sheet: Contact me.

Mansur allowed himself a smile of satisfaction. It was happening. The day he had been planning for so long. There had been times when his spirit had momentarily allowed itself to weaken, when he believed his dream would never come to fruition. But faith always reasserted itself and Mansur pushed aside thoughts of defeat. During his isolation in Paris, planning and waiting, time had elapsed with agonizing slowness. He was, by choice, far removed from his compatriots. He had chosen this way himself. Knowing that he was more likely to be watched than any of the others, Mansur had placed himself in exile, traveling to Paris, a city he knew well. Despite this solitary existence, he remained in charge of the operation. He maintained contact by public telephone, always using his native language and never staying on the line longer than a minute or so. The secondary form of contact was via simple, hand-delivered messages such as the one he held now.

This message meant the operation had moved to the next stage. From now matters would progress at a faster pace, and Mansur needed to change locations. He would become much more involved. His time in Paris was coming to an end. He looked around the apartment. He would miss it. In its quiet solitude Mansur had found contentment. He had been able to sit in uninterrupted silence and contemplate the future beyond the operation. He never once considered failure. It wasn't an option. What they were doing was righteous. An act of justice. He saw no vengeance, no rage, no fanatical madness. The statement they were about to make had been a long time coming. Born of frustration. Created from years of being pushed into the shadows. Ignored and patronized. The victims of injustice and intolerance.

Islam stood alone, forced to watch as the world powers juggled with the balance of power and made the decisions regarding the world order. If they chose to punish, they did it with scant regard to the needs and desires of the recipients. The nation of Islam, misunderstood by a vast percentage of humanity, had been branded as the enfant terrible of the world. Its closeness to the word of its sacred book frightened those who didn't understand, nor wanted to.

Misjudged and sensational reporting branded the whole of Islam as a baying mob of potential murderers. The extremes of Islam were the only considerations. Only the worst excesses were ever shown.

Mansur could never understand why the rational face of Islam was never seen. The peace and calm of the Islamic character. He thought about this in the cool of the morning as he knelt in prayer and contemplation, his silent time of reflection with dawn rolling pale light over the rooftops of Paris. In the hush of a new day this was a fleeting time of rebirth. Thoughts and deeds came to him fresh and without corruption. For a sliver of time it was whole, clean, and in that frozen moment it hung as a fragile crystal of hope. Mansur tried to grasp that moment in his mind, only too aware how swiftly it would vanish, returning him to the reality of a world where intolerance and twisted thinking held sway.

America saw itself as the savior of the world, a force with the god-given right to dictate to other nations, under the guise of democracy, how they should live and how they should conduct their affairs. Looking beyond the surface gloss it became quickly apparent that what the U.S.A. really wanted was a world that ran according to America's desires.

The American dream had become the world's nightmare. A world power, having military strength of terrifying proportions behind it, America sent its envoys from Washington to cajole, threaten and bully those it needed to satisfy its own ends. Money and armament went to those it saw as allies. Sanctions and military diplomacy were used to isolate and suppress anyone not seen as healthy. Mansur had been to America. He had observed for himself how the country existed. Its citizens lived in a Disneyland culture of indulgence, many of them unaware of anything beyond their shores. As long as they were fed their junk food and entertained by the so-called media, they were happy. They saw little, nor understood anything beyond the television world in which they lived. A culturally deprived desert, the television channels pumped out daily doses of vapid, mind-numbing programs to a watching public incapable of absorbing anything containing reality.

A selfish, consumer-oriented nation, America was a vast machine that sucked in everything, digested it, then spat out the remains and cried for more. Despite the suffering thrust upon it by the terrorist attack on New York and the realization that it wasn't invulnerable, America had embarked on a course of retribution. There was now more unrest within the Islamic world than there had been before the strike on New York.

Mansur let his thoughts drift back to the very assembly of sympathizers who backed his plea for a response to the injustice done to Islam. How many months ago had that been? Three, four months, he realized. He was able to recall that final meeting with pinpoint clarity, the image in his mind as clear as if he were actually back there...

THE ATMOSPHERE in the assembly room had been one of expectation. The gathering waited in reverential silence as the leaders entered and mounted the platform, sitting in the seats provided. There was more waiting while the leaders concluded their deliberations, and then Mansur had stood, raising his arms for silence.

"Once again we have been ignored. Our voice has been silenced and the world pays lip service to the Americans and their friends the Russians. They will decide how the world should run, who has the weapons and the technology. Our needs and expectations are forgotten once again."

One of the seated leaders had leaned forward.

"Mansur, we are but a small voice."

"Then we must make our voices heard above everything," Mansur said. "Or spend our lives in the wilderness."

A murmur of agreement rippled through the assembly.

"Mansur makes his point well," the delegate named Hassad pointed out. It was the first time he had spoken since the meeting had commenced. "Listen to his words and he will show you the way."

All eyes were on Mansur now.

"The Americans talk around us," he began, "not to us. When it suits them they throw small concessions our way. Nothing large enough to cause them any loss. But mostly they decide what will be.

"They discuss the future of the world with the Russians. A nation that has lost its way and its power, and is becoming as degenerate as the rest. Even China has been asked to add its voice—but I believe this is nothing more than a sop because America needs to divert the Chinese away from Taiwan, its little puppet-on-a-string island they will use to threaten China.

"The Americans have their eyes on the world and what they can take from it. They have a hunger for the riches the world holds—oil to sustain their greedy economy, to satisfy the hunger of their obese population, for precious metals and raw materials. When the world wanted to reduce harmful emissions that are damaging the atmosphere and harming us all, the Americans reneged on their promises. All because it would not be in their interests. Their interests.

"The Americans look at the world and make the choices who should be in charge. Then they give them the means to subjugate their opponents. When do they ever look to us and give us those means? Never, my brothers, because we are the one nation they are unable to control. The nation of Islam. And because we refuse to kneel at their feet they shun us."

Hassad had glanced across at Mansur. He acknowledged the man as his superior. Mansur was blessed with an inner power that gave him great influence over the faithful. He told them what they needed to hear: that their destiny lay before them and they would need to make sacrifices in order to achieve it. His words were gentle, never delivered in hot anger, yet they reached out and held his audiences in rapt attention. There was a strange, often-frightening intensity surrounding Mansur, and it was this that gave him his hold over the masses.

"Is it agreed then? That we carry out our pledge?

That we show the Americans we must be listened to? We will not be ignored any longer?''

Arms had been raised, assent given in subdued responses. The whole assembly was aware of the great responsibility they were undertaking. There was no great joy, only a recognition that having been pushed to this point there was no going back—ever.

SINCE THAT MEETING, when they had endorsed the operation and had gone their separate ways, they had barely had contact with one another. Everything had been done through envoys, chosen people who carried messages, arranged the acquisition of materials and weapons. It had been a carefully organized operation, kept deliberately low key so as not to arouse any suspicions. The key members of Mansur's group had stayed out of the preparations as they would possibly be the ones under observation. This allowed the lesser known individuals to go about their work undetected, bringing together the segments that would eventually create the whole.

Mansur spent his period of exile in Paris. It was a city he enjoyed. Watchers wouldn't be surprised to see him there. He spoke excellent French, knew the city and blended well within the fabric of existence. Carefully leaked details concerning his search for an old friend were allowed to reach the ears of the watchers. Mansur built on the premise by visiting Islamic groups, individuals with no particular political leanings, and speaking to them only about the missing friend. He was never seen with his cohorts. Nor did he contact any of them. There was a telephone in his apartment, which he knew had been tapped shortly after he moved in. He never used it. Neither did he carry a cellular phone. He gave the French no reason to suspect him of any wrongdoing. His long-term history had shown him to be a moderate. A passivist in his words and actions. Mansur's cause was known as one of restraint. He had never once raised his voice against the West or made any threats. His very appearance and manner revealed him as a man of sophistication, of cultural gentleness. Abrim Mansur showed the face of Islam as the world wanted to see it. And for as long as it served his purpose he would go on with his masquerade.

He maintained his solitary existence. His days, when not pursuing his so-called search, consisted of long walks along the river, or through the city. He would visit the art galleries. Sometimes he would go to music recitals. He bought his own food and prepared and ate in the apartment. It amused him to think of the long, fruitless hours spent by the watchers. Their cameras would have nothing to record, nor would the tape machines waiting for calls over his telephone. Mansur was aware that his watchers would be checking out his mission. They would assess whether he was genuinely looking for someone or was simply biding his time. Whichever they chose to check would take time, and time was something Mansur needed. The arrangements for the operation were diverse. Certain matters would need to be undertaken with great care. The gathering of equipment would have to be done a little at a time, using delivery routes that wouldn't be suspected. The people they used to deliver the goods would have to be sacrificed for the sake of security. One of the problems associated with independent smugglers was their innate curiosity. They were blessed or cursed—depending on the point of view—with a need to know. If they suspected they were carrying something beyond the norm they would endeavor to find out what it was in case it gave them justification for a higher fee. It was nothing more than human nature, but in this instance that curiosity could cost a great deal if anything leaked out about the substance of the deliveries.

Mansur's days drifted into weeks. He waited safe in the knowledge that one day he would receive the brief message that would inform him the operation was near completion. Once he received that he would leave Paris and make his way to the next location, from where he would assume full control. The operation would then move into its next phase and the countdown would begin.

Islamabad, Pakistan

BY MIDNIGHT Jamil Azul was a long way from where the helicopter had picked him up. The moment the helicopter touched down, Azul climbed out and crossed to the car waiting for him. He was driven to where he had his apartment. The car dropped him off, then vanished into the darkness. Azul climbed the steps and let himself into his apartment. He disposed of the dusty robes, bathed, took time to drink chilled water from his refrigerator, spent time at his prayers, then retired and slept until dawn. Before he lay down he took the sealed box and slid it beneath his bed.

In the bright light of dawn he rose and showered.

He dressed in clean clothes and made a pot of rich, aromatic coffee. He sat on the veranda and waited for the telephone to ring. He was on his second cup when it did. He lifted the receiver.

"Good morning, brother. I trust you slept well after your long day?"

"I did."

"Are we able to conclude our business?"

"Yes."

"My car will pick you up in half an hour."

The car duly arrived thirty minutes later. Azul left the apartment and went downstairs, taking a zippered flight bag with him. In the rear of the car he settled in the seat and enjoyed the comfort of the air-conditioning unit.

The car drove through the city into the open country beyond. The journey lasted just under an hour, coming to an end when the car slowed and turned off the dusty road. It eased in through open gates that closed behind it, coming to a halt in courtyard surrounded by green vegetation and gently waving palms. Somewhere water trickled softly in the hushed surroundings. The buyer picked up his bag and climbed out. He crossed the courtyard as the doors to the house opened and the man he had come to see stepped out to meet him.

"Any problems?" the man asked.

Azul shook his head. "Not even during the flight from Afghanistan. We were not even challenged."

"A clear flight path had been arranged."

Azul smiled. "I understand."

"Good. Let us go in."

The buyer followed his host inside, followed him

through to a book-lined room. Closing the door, the host ushered his guest to a chair next to a large desk. The flight bag was placed on the desk and opened. The sealed package was removed.

"You realize now we have this that the project can go ahead?"

Azul nodded.

"It's been a long time coming."

Taking a slim bladed knife, the host cut the tape around the package, peeling back layer after layer of protective padding until the content of the package was exposed. The host picked up the two items, examining them carefully. They were almost identical in shape and size, looking something like TV remotes. They had been constructed from injection-molded, high-impact plastic, dull black in color. One had a short retractable aerial and a number of push buttons. The other had an aerial and a power switch only.

Seeing Azul's curiosity, the host showed him the items.

"This attaches to the device. With the power unit switched on it responds to instructions from the control device. This is the control. The buttons allow a code sequence to be set that will send the instructions telling the device to arm itself. At the same time the handler can also key in the detonation time sequence. He can choose anything from a minute up to an hour."

"I'm impressed."

The host placed the items back on the desk, then glanced at his watch.

"Mansur will be calling soon. Once he knows we have the items he will leave Paris."

Azul received the information with dismay. In all the time he had been dealing with the host he had never been told where the man named Mansur had been located. He had accepted it as part of the secure system designed to protect Mansur. Now, suddenly, he had been told where Mansur was, and he realized it was his death sentence. His mind whirled as he tried to take it in. Just as he had silenced the smuggler to prevent any leak of information, so, too, his host was about to do the same to him.

Azul stood and stepped back from the man, slipping his right hand under the flap of his jacket, reaching for the P-226 that was tucked into his trouser waistband. His fingers stroked the cool butt a second before the muzzle of a suppressed autopistol was pressed against his skull. The reduced sound of the single shot faded quickly. The dying Azul lost control of his limbs and dropped to the floor. He lay on his back, his life ebbing quickly, blood spreading from under his head in a widening pool.

The host—Khalil Hassad by name—had already turned back to the desk to pick up the items, which he wrapped in the original packing and replaced in the flight bag. He turned to the man who had shot Azul, the driver of the car, and indicated the body.

"Have him removed. Clean the floor. As soon as I have spoken to Mansur, we leave."

The driver nodded and left to get help with the body.

Hassad sat down, staring at the flight bag.

Now it could begin, he thought. After all the long

months of preparation and secrecy, they could go ahead.

The prospect both excited and terrified him. The project was far-reaching in its scope. The end result would be dramatic, bordering on cataclysmic. If it succeeded their voice would be heard around the world, and this time no one would be able to ignore it.

Hassad was startled by the ringing of the telephone on his desk. He reached out and picked up the receiver.

"Give me good news," Abrim Mansur said.

"Today there is only good news, my brother," Hassad replied. "The package has arrived."

Mansur gave a sigh of relief.

"You are leaving?"

"Within the hour. Nothing can stop us now."

CHAPTER ONE

Stony Man Farm, Virginia

Aaron Kurtzman pushed his wheelchair away from the cluttered desk, shrugging his aching shoulders. He surveyed the mass of papers spread across the desk's surface, glanced at the screen of his monitor and decided he needed a break. Glancing at his watch, he saw that he had been working nonstop for more than three hours.

Too long, he realized. The facts and figures were starting to merge into a meaningless blur. It was time to step back and relax for a while.

Kurtzman wheeled away from the desk and across the office he was using. It was actually the office that the late Yakov Katzenelenbogen had used and, like those of Hal Brognola and Barbara Price, was situated in the original farmhouse, rather than the new Annex. He liked it that way. The atmosphere in the old building was less hectic than Kurtzman's cybernetic wonderland, and it allowed him to sit and deliberate in peace and quiet when he needed to. He was still able to use the main data banks as the new cyberunit was hard-wired into the old Farm building. The project the computer expert was working on needed his full attention at times, and as the rest of the team was on duty at this time, he had made his way from the Annex to the quiet office.

He made his way out of the building and took a measured roll through the grounds. The fresh air drove the cotton wool from his mind. Kurtzman's wandering took him to where he could see the newly constructed wood-chipping mill, outwardly a new enterprise of the farm's owners. It was a genuine operation on the surface, but it had been built to camouflage the Annex extension that lay belowground. Beneath the surface and three feet of solid concrete was his electronic haven, connected to the Farm building by a thousand-foot underground tunnel, which even had an electric railcar to transport personnel back and forth.

Right now Kurtzman needed nothing more than fresh air and peace and quiet. For the time being trees and grass were his fix, away from monitor screens and telephones.

Despite his longing for a break it was hard for Kurtzman to disassociate himself from the Farm's real purpose. Here he was, in Virginia's Shenandoah Valley, a place of natural, rural beauty, rolling over the top of what was America's most covert organization. From this tranquil location were orchestrated the SOG's missions. Worldwide, Phoenix Force and Able Team spent their time facing up to some of the most insidious plots and schemes designed to interfere with freedom, peace, the rights of the many, however you wanted to label it. There was no denying that death and violence were an integral part of Stony Man's agenda. The people and organizations they went up against weren't known for their tolerance, or an acceptance of negotiation. They spoke via the gun. By the use of terror tactics and the threat of destruction. And resistance to all those threats was orchestrated from here, right under Kurtzman's wheelchair, in the air-conditioned, artificially lit operations center of the SOG.

Since the terrible events of September 11, even Stony Man had felt the extra burden of responsibility. The unexpected had become a grim reality, and the reverberations were felt all the way down the line. The shock of the attack had been added to by the sudden awareness that other things might happen, could happen, and it fell to all the U.S.'s security communities to remain on full alert 24/7. Along with every other agency, Stony Man took the added burden on board and retained a nonstop vigil, knowing well that attacks might come from within the country as well as from those planning their destructive schemes from thousands of miles away.

Which was why Kurtzman spent much of his time sifting through the mass of data that flowed into Stony Man day and night.

Kurtzman moved on, with no particular destination in mind. He was letting his thoughts sort themselves out, allowing the strands to fall into place. By the time he returned to his office more than an hour later, he knew what he needed to do.

He took a mug of coffee and wheeled himself behind the desk. The first thing he did was sort out the printed sheets of paper into a sequence that made some sense. They had all been printed off from screen images, so the whole of his information was in the data banks. He worked from the printed sheets, moving data around and inserting the details in time sequence. Once he had rearranged the information, highlighting key points, he discarded items he realized were nothing to do with what he was looking for. Kurtzman worked solidly for another two hours. He worked on screen now, moving chunks of data back and forth until he had it arranged sequentially.

He reached for the mug and raised it, then realized the coffee was cold. Kurtzman wheeled himself out of the office and returned with a fresh mug. He printed off a number of copies of his findings, made a couple of telephone calls and set up a meeting with Hal Brognola and Barbara Price.

Twenty minutes later Kurtzman sat facing them across the War Room's conference table. A copy of his data lay on the table in front of each of them. The computer expert waited patiently while they read through the information. Brognola finally pushed his copy aside and leaned back, looking across at Kurtzman.

"How do we read this?" Brognola asked. "A genuine threat, or what?"

"One thing I never see are terrorists playing games, Hal."

Brognola held up a hand in his defense.

"I didn't mean it that way, Aaron."

"Hal, take a breath," Kurtzman said. "I know exactly what you meant."

"Aaron, what do you make of all this?" Price asked, tapping the printout.

"Let's start with Mansur," Kurtzman said.

He activated one of the large, wall-mounted monitor screens. It flickered, then showed a head-and-shoulders shot of a lean-faced man with black hair and neat beard.

"Abrim Mansur. It's believed he's of Palestinian descent, but there are conflicting views on that. No one knows exactly where he originated. It's almost as if he walked out of the desert one day unannounced. We have him down as an Islamic fundamentalist. Mainly because it's the closest label we can pin on him. Strong in his views but always thought of as a thinker rather than a doer. He's been linked with a number of Islamic groups over the past few years, but as recently as a year ago he seems to have disassociated himself from all of them. Whether this is a calculated move on his part or a genuine separation because he's fallen out with their views, we don't know. What is accepted is his own brand of politics. He's got strong views on the U.S. Doesn't seem to like us very much. That comes over in the speeches he makes to his new organization, something he appears to be fronting. And intel that's come in suggests he has some wealthy and influential backers. Details on these backers are sketchy to say the least, but I'm looking into this right now. In the current situation it's getting harder to identify them. Most of them have withdrawn from the scene or have gone underground."

"What *are* his policies?" Brognola asked.

"Mansur isn't what we've come to expect from Islamic fundamentalists. He's low key. An intellectual more into issuing reasoned pleas for the Islamic world to be listened to. He makes it clear how he feels about the U.S. and her allies, but he talks softly and doesn't appear to be waving a big stick.''

"I sense a *but* in there somewhere," Brognola said.

"Aaron, didn't Mansur drop out of sight recently?" Price asked.

Kurtzman nodded. ''Well, he certainly dropped out of making speeches and hasn't been at a rally for the last three months. He'd drawn quite a following. Wherever he appeared to speak there were always big crowds. Mansur has a powerful presence. He holds his audience by simply talking to them. His followers seem to be drawn by his mystic persona. No rants. No outward shows of anger. He doesn't work his audiences into hysteria. The meetings are still taking place with stand-ins for Mansur. He was in Paris until a couple of weeks ago. Now he's vanished. During his exile in Paris, if you want to call it that, French intelligence reports say he simply lived the quiet life. The French had no quarrel with him. Likewise, any other Western government. The man has never done anything to cause offense. He was on his own in France. No contacts. No meetings. Mansur acted like a man marking time.''

"What about his second in command?" Price asked.

"Khalil Hassad?" Brognola said.

Kurtzman nodded and brought another face on screen.

"Hal, you never cease to impress me."

"I don't spend my free time watching reruns of *Baywatch Nights*."

Price made a face. "My God, Hal, I should hope not."

"Khalil Hassad," Kurtzman continued, "has been associated with Mansur for as long as we've known about him. He did a disappearing act about the same time as Mansur. He surfaced in Pakistan and from intel coming out of there, Hassad didn't seem to be doing a great deal, either."

"Where had Mansur been living?" Price asked.

"Rented a Paris apartment adjacent to the Gare du Nord. Spent a lot of time in it apparently. If he wasn't there he'd be out looking at the city. Lot's of walking. There was a story he went to France to look up an old friend from his youth. If that was true, he didn't find him. He was never seen with anyone. The only thing he did was go to music recitals. There was a café he frequented close to the apartment building, always alone. He made no physical contact with anyone, and made a few telephone calls from public boxes. There is a phone in the apartment, but it has never been used to make a call, nor has it received any since Mansur checked in."

"It's like he wanted people to know where he was because he was being watched," Brognola said. "But he didn't do anything to indicate he might be planning something."

"It draws the attention away from the rest of his organization," Kurtzman said. "Same with Hassad."

"So assuming they are planning something, what is it?" Price asked.

"And why should we be interested?" Brognola asked pointedly.

The question had been bound to arise. Kurtzman would never have gone to all the trouble of compiling the information and calling a meeting simply on the basis of its being interesting. He had seen something within all the data that had alerted him to a possible threat against the U.S.

"Bear with me on this, Hal, Barb," Kurtzman said. "It may take some explaining before you get the logic behind it."

"Take your time," the big Fed told him. "We've got it to spare right now."

"Accept what I'm going to tell you is all fragmented information. It's come in from a number of sources. Agencies in the Pakistan and Afghanistan regions. A snippet here. Another there. Sound bites courtesy of Echelon. Filed reports from Mossad. When I started to pick up on this, it made little sense until I started to collate it."

Kurtzman opened his file and ran through the data he had collected.

"First we have the deaths of two contraband smugglers on the Afghan-Pakistan border. Nothing too significant there. Both shot with 9 mm bullets. Fatally hit. But they were then both shot again. Single tap to the head. Clean shots to targets already dying. Not the usual mark of local bandits. Also, the pack train the smuggler had brought in was found running loose. Someone had removed the packs and harness. The contraband was found at the side of the trail. Apart from having been opened and gone through, none of the contraband goods seemed to have been taken. Contraband in this instance means food and medical supplies identified as being from the air drops by the U.S. and allies over Afghanistan. In the current situation out there, who leaves behind that kind of contraband?''

Kurtzman allowed the details to sink in.

''Why hijack a pack train and leave the goods untouched?'' Price asked.

''Because whoever did it found what he wanted and took it?'' Brognola suggested.

Kurtzman nodded. ''My guess is the pack train was being used as cover to bring in a special item. Something the end user didn't want advertised.''

Brognola flipped through the pages of notes.

''Next up we have a body being found in a ditch outside Islamabad. Is there a connection?''

''The dead man was a buyer named Jamil Azul. He dealt in contraband goods and was well-known in the border region. He'd been shot in the head at close range. No signs of any resistance marks on his body, so it was assumed the shooting wasn't expected by the victim.

''The reports I read concerning Azul told me that *he* always put a final shot into the head of any person he killed. It was his personal signature. He had a reputation of being a man you wanted to keep as a friend.''

''So Azul claims his package after killing the smugglers, then turns up in Islamabad with a bullet in his head?'' Brognola observed. ''Why?''

''Azul was seen arriving at a house in Islamabad.

He went inside but never came out. His body was found two days later.''

''Do we know who lived in this house?'' Price asked.

Kurtzman turned back to the wall monitor where the image of Khalil Hassad was still showing.

''The house had been used by Hassad during his time in Islamabad. When the authorities moved in, Hassad had gone. The house was empty. Some traces of blood were found and checked. It was the same type as Azul's.''

''Have you found any other connections?'' Brognola asked.

''Abrim Mansur left Paris the day Hassad vacated the house in Islamabad. Hassad took a flight to the UK,'' Kurtzman said. ''I checked, and the British are aware of his presence in the UK. Now Hassad hasn't done anything to affect a ban on his visitation rights to the UK, so all the authorities can do is keep an eye on him. There is a suspicion, and that is all at the moment, that Mansur's organization has a paymaster based in London. Supposedly this guy collects donations, hands out cash when it's needed. But no one has been able to pin this man down, or even find any hints where the money is. British security is looking at the problem. Hassad showed up in London approximately two weeks ago. We've only just started to collate these fragments of information.''

''You noted movement of Mansur's followers, various groups coming together in the UK, more in North Africa. All pretty low key. Details of them meeting up then moving on again soon after. Splitting into smaller groups. Not staying in one place too long.''

"Makes it hard for the security details to build up any cohesive pattern,'' Price pointed out.

"Exactly,'' Kurtzman said. "I just get the feeling something is in the wind. Right now I don't have a clue as to what, but I've got this feeling.'' Kurtzman produced a single sheet of paper and passed it to Brognola. "This was my most recent find.''

Brognola read the text, then raised his eyes to meet Kurtzman's earnest gaze.

"You sure about this?''

Kurtzman nodded. "I double checked.''

The big Fed pushed the paper across to Price, who read it through.

"Someone has been making a lot of cell-phone calls.''

"Haven't they. Gabril Yasim is a known follower of Mansur. In essence he's a coordinator, a person who makes things happen.''

"Just what is he making happen this time?'' Price asked. "Calls to Russia, the UK and the Middle East.''

"I wouldn't want to get his bill for the last month,'' Brognola said.

"Mansur has never concealed his opposition to the U.S.,'' Kurtzman said. "His speeches always nail us as the shadow behind all the ills that have befallen Islam. We create situations that escalate into incidents. Our commercial interests are linked with the military. Mansur has convinced his followers that the U.S. and her allies orchestrate scenarios that pinpoint Islam and isolate it from major decisions.''

"Are we *that* bad?" Price asked. "Or is it just Mansur's personal opinion?"

"He sees us as wielding so much power around the world no one dares to move against us. Not just because of our military power. His mandate points out how much commercial influence we have on global policy, multinational conglomerates, heavy financial operations that tie countries to the U.S. He makes a strong case, especially when he's delivering it to disenfranchised people like himself. They feel isolated, pushed into the wings, never allowed much say in decision-making that can, by way of natural occurrences, affect them."

"I thought you said he was no rabble rouser?" Brognola said.

Kurtzman smiled. "There are more ways than one to get your message across. Mansur chooses to use the softly-softly approach. He goes for the mind rather than the heart. Plants the suggestions ever so calmly, then lets that germ of an idea get to work. His audience goes away on a low, but his words are planted inside their heads and they consider them later. He doesn't go for the quick fix, the impassioned response that has an individual strap a bomb to his chest and walk into a crowded café. That gets a result, but it's a gut reaction done in the heat of anger. Mansur doesn't work like that. From what I've read about him, watched on videos of his speeches, he isn't the kind of man who would be content with blowing up a bus. If Mansur decides to make a statement, it'll be planned and designed for maximum effect. Something devastating. Something that will have long-term consequences."

Price tapped a finger on the table, gazing at Hassad's image.

The face of the man staring back at her, rounded and heavy cheeked, gave her an uneasy feeling. Price examined it closely. What was it that unsettled her? Perhaps the wide-eyed expression? The taut set of the mouth?

"What could be so important that it necessitates the deaths of three people?" she asked. "Got to be more than a package of drugs, or a cache of illicit diamonds."

"I agree," Kurtzman said. "But until we can pin down something solid we're running on fresh air."

"We could make some checks of our own," Brognola said, "and see what pans out. If it shows we have nothing to worry about, all we've lost is a little time. But in the present climate, with everything that's going on, we can't be too complacent."

"Hal, I said at the start that this is just conjecture based on isolated scraps of information," Kurtzman said.

"Hey, no modesty, Aaron," Barbara Price said. "You don't sound the alarm without good reason. I agree with Hal. It's worth a look."

"I want you to bring in the rest of the team, Aaron," Brognola stated. "Let them take what you've found and expand on it."

"Fine by me," Kurtzman said.

Yorkshire Dales, England

DAVID MCCARTER'S EXPRESSION warned Mei Anna that the telephone call had presented him with a problem and, whatever the implications, one of the effects would be an interruption of their time together. She watched him make his way back to their table. He sat without a word, reaching for the bottle of wine and filling his glass. He drank half before meeting her gaze.

"Tell me," she said. "I need to know what's happened before I order a main course. I mean, will I have time to eat it?"

A scowl began to form, then McCarter's humor won through and he laughed.

"We've got all the time we need," he told her.

The woman picked up the menu and she began to scan the various dishes on offer. After a moment she peered over the top of the menu. McCarter was drinking more wine, his gaze straying away from their table as his mind worked over whatever had been discussed during the ten-minute telephone call.

Anna began to feel that the time she had been spending with McCarter was about to end. She wasn't surprised. Their relationship, moving on each time they met, was based around McCarter's responsibilities to the team of specialists he commanded. He was on permanent standby, always in the position where he might be called away at any moment, day or night. Her background was similar. As the leader of an antigovernment unit resisting the machinations of the mainland Chinese, she had worked under the same restrictions. However, since her recent wounding during a confrontation, Anna had been undergoing a period of recuperation that was taking longer than initially anticipated. She had been carrying the bullet lodged in her body for some time, having undergone emergency medical aid while on the run. The crude surgery used to remove the bullet had barely been enough to keep her alive, and by the time it had been discovered her body had been weakened to the extent that she became desperately ill. Stony Man had arranged for her to be admitted to a clinic in England, and Anna had begun the long journey to recovery.

McCarter's latest period of R&R had seen him in England, spending every moment he could with Anna. She was still recovering, but was strong enough for short breaks away from the clinic. They had spent a couple of days touring the Yorkshire Dales. It had been a good time for both of them, despite the knowledge that it could be interrupted at any moment.

That eventuality had been at the back of McCarter's mind. He was only too aware that things could change very quickly, and his misgivings had proved correct with the telephone call from Stony Man.

His discussion with Aaron Kurtzman had been to the point, leaving the Briton more than a little confused, and with a touch of irritation. He had kept his feelings concealed. McCarter, like the rest of Phoenix Force, was a consummate professional. No matter what he might have personally felt about requests from Stony Man, he responded positively. As Kurtzman had gone through his dissection of the data he had been collecting, explaining his feelings, McCarter had listened in respectful silence, only jumping in when he had a need to clarify something. His admiration for Kurtzman's skill was already strong, and it was growing even more. Aaron Kurtzman was nobody's fool when it came to analyzing incoming data from his cyberworld. His insight was invaluable. He had a tireless curiosity coupled to an active mind. He probed and sifted and juggled facts, searched databases and intelligence reports at an alarming rate, seeing things that others passed over. Kurtzman never accepted anything at face value. If there was something that stood out, Kurtzman would spot it, dissect it and expose what lay beneath.

Despite his mild irritation McCarter knew he would follow up Kurtzman's theory. If there was something to find, McCarter would lock on to it and track it to the source.

"David?"

McCarter drew himself back to reality as Anna's gentle voice pushed through. He glanced across the table at her.

"You decided what you want?" he asked.

She smiled at him, a mischievous sparkle in her eyes.

"Not everything I want is on the menu," she said, reaching out a slim hand to touch his. "But I suppose I'll have to be satisfied with what's available."

McCarter returned her gaze, beginning to regret he'd taken Kurtzman's call.

"Hey, you don't have to go right now, do you?"

McCarter shook his head. "Look, why don't we skip the starters and go straight for the main course?"

Anna feigned surprise. "You can read my mind as well. What else don't I know about you?"

"I'll tell you over coffee," McCarter promised.

London

THE COLLAR of McCarter's all-weather coat was turned up against the rain. He wore a tweed cap and had his hands pushed deep into his coat pockets. Since taking Mei Anna back to the clinic at the end of their short break, he had driven back to London, regretting every mile that distanced him from the beautiful Chinese woman. He had enjoyed every moment with her. The cherry on the top of the cake had been the unexpected and lingering kiss she had given him before she had walked back inside the clinic. Not a word had been spoken between them in the aftermath. It hadn't been necessary. The touch of her lips had said it all. McCarter had driven away with a grin on his face that would have been the envy of every schoolboy whose adolescent fantasy had just come true.

His current situation did nothing to make him feel better. London, overcrowded and noisy, battered his eardrums. He had fought his way through heavy traffic, the journey to his destination in the city seeming to take longer than his run down from Yorkshire. At least up there the country roads were quieter, less thronged with traffic, and the people had a sense of pace and time that had long since deserted the capital city.

McCarter studied the house, which stood on a residential street where every building was the same—brick-built with curving bay windows. Many of them had been carved up into small apartments; others were in various stages of renovation, with metal skips positioned outside to collect the building debris. Being London, every available foot of curb space was occupied by parked cars and panel trucks. McCarter had driven down the street on his arrival and had found no empty spaces, so he'd had to drive down two more connecting streets before he found a place to park. He had locked his rental vehicle and hoped he would find it still in one piece when he returned.

He had walked by the house, on the opposite side of the street, then returned, pausing briefly in the scant shelter of one of the trees to make observations before moving farther along. McCarter wasn't fully sure what he was doing. Kurtzman had furnished him with the address and the few facts he had on the possible occupants.

The information had come via links with the British intelligence establishment. The U.S. and England were cooperating on a day-to-day basis, their networks feeding each other details gathered from any number of sources, and one of those sources had traced a group of Iranians to the address in London. A security team was organizing a close watch on the group, which had done nothing except take up residence in the house. Checks on their credentials had them down as a group of Iranian businessmen in the country to negotiate a deal with a British engineering company. Until proof of anything illegal taking place could be established, the Iranians couldn't be touched.

But there had been suggestions that the Iranian group had something other than business contracts on their minds, especially when Kurtzman had identified one of the group as a man named Fayed, known as an Iranian agent. Kurtzman had a long memory when it came to putting names to faces.

Kurtzman's connection between Fayed and Hassad had come about when he recalled a scrap of a telephone conversation picked by the Echelon listening system. Hassad's name had been one of the flagged key words, along with Mansur. The scrap of conversation, in French, had been between Fayed and an unknown listener. Fayed had been making a sketchy report and had brought both Hassad's name and London into the conversation. Nothing more. Simply the two words, but Echelon's electronic ear had plucked them out of the mass of incoming data, had identified and collated them, placing them on the ever-growing list that was fed into the intelligence data banks. Kurtzman, during his initial focus on detail gathering, had drawn the information out of the wealth of sound bites and placed them in his computer file. Once he had sifted and filtered his data, Kurtzman had made his own conclusions. As with much intelligence gathering, final decisions often had to be made based on extremely sketchy detail. Educated guesses went hand in hand with hard facts. The sharp proof provided by a photograph was just as conclusive as a judgment gathered and decided on by a keen intellect. Inspired deliberations sometimes paid off with highly successful results.

Kurtzman had offered his conclusions to Brognola, who in turn had instructed him to pass along his orders for McCarter to follow up and check it out. Hassad was in England for reasons of his own. Stony Man linked his visit to the abrupt change in the status of Abrim Mansur and the occurrences in Afghanistan-Pakistan.

All of which placed the Briton on a cold, dark, rain-swept street in London. McCarter made his initial observation of the house, then moved on.

CHAPTER TWO

Nerpichya Naval Base, Russian Northern Fleet

Heavy dark clouds hovered over the dark waters of Nerpichya. It was cold, with a scattering of snow mingled with the fine rain sweeping in across the water, and the temperature low enough to keep all but those on duty in their quarters. Snow layered the slopes of the low hills on the far side of the stretch of water. There were a number of massive Typhoon-class nuclear submarines moored alongside the jetties that pushed out into the water. Weighing in at more than 26,000 tons, the Typhoon was capable of carrying twenty, SS-N-24/26 nuclear missiles. It could also deploy torpedoes. The Typhoon-class submarines had once been the pride of the Russian fleet. Now the massive vessels were under threat of being decommissioned, and only one of the subs was in readiness for a voyage.

A heavy-load truck was parked alongside the submarine, the canvas cover over the body frame flapping in the keen wind. The truck was dwarfed by the huge bulk of the vessel. The crew from the truck was loading supplies on board the boat, going about their task with little enthusiasm. The only bonus to the work was when they were actually inside the sub, able to enjoy the warmth provided by the heating system. Unfortunately the supply chief kept them moving, his barking tones echoing around the companionways if he thought they weren't delivering the goods fast enough.

There was a mood existing within the work crew that the supply chief had noticed quickly. They said little, which was unusual. Work crews were normally a noisy group. They were extremely vocal, ribbing one another as they worked, always ready to give as good as they got. This crew was the quietest the chief had ever come across. It was almost as if they had something on their minds that was keeping them silent. He might have taken his thoughts further if the day hadn't been so cold. The chief wanted the assignment to be over so he could get back to his quarters and the warmth of the stove that was kept burning day and night. His duty was over for the next couple of days. He intended to stay inside with a bottle of vodka and make the most of his free time. The chief's mind was on his intended free time, so he let his observation of the work crew go.

Surprisingly the loading was achieved within the time allowed. The chief signed off the supplies. His job was done after that. He walked down the gangplank, his manifests tucked under his arm, and made his way along the dock. The work crew were left to sort themselves out. All they had to do was climb back in their truck and drive away.

That happened, but not before a number of well-armed men clad in black combat clothing emerged from the supply truck where they had been waiting during the unloading. The stacked supplies had concealed their presence and as the load had been reduced the group had remained at the front of the truck body, where a pile of rolled canvas helped to hide them. Not that there was much need. No one paid much attention to the supply truck, and no one was on the dock now that the supply chief had left.

The late afternoon was shadowed by the heavy clouds still sitting low in the sky. The armed group took the opportunity to board the submarine in the final moments of the work crew taking their leave. They went up the gangplank smoothly and quickly, shielded by the work party as they walked down the gangplank. The transition was done with such ease no one at the other end of the dock would have noticed, even if they had been paying attention. As soon as the last armed man had stepped inside the submarine, the gangplank was removed and the hatch in the sub's hull swung shut.

The supply truck rolled along the dock, passing the checkpoint, and turned along the exit road and away from the naval base.

TWELVE MEN WERE in the boarding party, and each was fully armed with an AK-74 and a 9 mm automatic pistol. Knives were strapped to their legs. Each man had a state-of-the-art transceiver clipped to the front of his tunic, and they all wore headsets and microphone communicators. Two of the party carried backpacks that contained a primed set of compound explosives. The packs could be detonated by the simple expedient of the wearer pulling a detonation wire.

The boarding party split into two groups once they were inside and the bulkhead hatch had been secured.

Seven men made their way toward the engine room and the missile room. The submarine had only a skeleton crew on duty, and they were taken completely by surprise by the armed boarders.

The remainder of the boarders made their way to the control room of the sub where they confronted the commander and his operations crew. They positioned themselves so they could cover all points of entry. There was little the crew could have done, and they had the sense not to resist. Within the confines of the control room there was little else they could have done.

The sub commander, Captain Petre Rashenski, held his hands clear of his body as he was confronted by one of the boarders.

"Well?"

"Are you ready to leave?" the boarder asked.

"Almost."

"Then carry on with your preparations. When you are ready we go."

"Where?"

"All in good time, Captain Rashenski."

"You know me?"

"You would be surprised how much I know. When you make contact and tell them you are ready to leave say nothing else. Don't try to be smart and give them any hints we are on board. I understand communication protocols. Believe me. Do anything stupid, and I will have you killed on the spot. If necessary I will command this vessel myself.''

RASHENSKI FELT he had to believe the man. There was something in the tone of his voice that convinced Rashenski he was telling the truth.

''This submarine is due to leave for the navy yard at Safonovo. We are going there to have refit work carried out. Our missiles are not armed and there are no launch codes on board, so what do you want?''

''Perhaps I am just a submarine fanatic who wants one for his collection,'' the boarder said, smiling.

Someone laughed. It was one of the boarder's men.

Rashenski held back his anger at the flippant attitude of the man. He turned his attention back to the leader.

''What do I call you?''

''You can call me Varic if it will make conversation easier.''

''So tell me, Varic, who are you? What is this all about?''

Varic hesitated. He glanced around the control room, eyeing the equipment, then turned back to Rashenski.

''First let us get this submarine out of here. I will feel safer once we are in deep water. Then I will give you your new course. Work now, Captain. Questions later.'' Varic indicated one of his men. He was one of the two carrying the explosive backpacks. ''We are serious about this, Captain. This man and one other are quite prepared to detonate the packs they carry. If you do anything to jeopardize our mission I will order them to set those devices off. They are packed with high explosive. Set off in here they will create enough of an explosion to cripple this sub and kill everyone in the vicinity. If we are deep enough at the time, the blast might even fracture the hull. Do I have to say any more?"

Rashenski shook his head.

Varic glanced at his man.

"Stay with the captain. Listen to what he says. Do not allow him to make contact with the shore unless I am at his side. Understand?"

The man nodded and moved to stand beside Rashenski, the muzzle of his AK trained on the sub commander.

Varic checked out the other half of his team. They were standing at opposite sides of the control room, their backs to the steel bulkheads, weapons covering the crew. He nodded in satisfaction. His people would carry out their tasks fully. They knew what was at stake, the intentions of their mission, and each was as committed as Varic himself.

He activated his transceiver and contacted the other team members. He listened and heard that they had taken control of the reactor room and had the skeleton crew under their command. As Varic had explained to Rashenski, there would be no toleration of any defiance, nor would there be any second chances. Anyone who made the wrong kind of move would be killed on the spot as an example to the others.

Varic relaxed a little. It had been estimated that they would have at least twelve hours before suspicions were aroused. By then the sub would be out in the deep, bitter waters of the Barents Sea, on the bottom and running on standby power. It would be difficult for the navy to find them. Typhoon-class subs were large, but they were designed for stealth operations, and it was a well-known fact that the Russian navy was woefully short of sophisticated equipment, especially the kind needed to locate a submarine that didn't want to be found. He had their course already worked out. Once it was locked into the sub's auto-navigation system, the computer would take over and guide the vessel to the laid-down position. On reaching the position they would submerge and remain on standby until the rendezvous with the ship bringing in the expert who would return the sub to its offensive capability.

Varic studied the control-room layout. It was exactly as he remembered from his previous time on board one of the Typhoon-class subs. That particular one had now been in dock for almost eight months. If something wasn't done, it would slowly rot away. The submarine had become a victim of the destabilizing program that would reduce the Russian nuclear capability significantly. Before that happened to this particular vessel, Varic and his team would utilize the strike force contained within the submarine to reinforce the statement soon to be made by Abrim Mansur and his group.

Varic's train of thought was interrupted by a disturbance just beyond the control room. Raised voices mingled with the thud of blows. The commotion went on for a minute before it settled down and two of Varic's men manhandled a groaning figure into the control room. The sub crewman's face was bloody and battered, one cheek laid open almost to the bone.

"What's going on?" Varic demanded.

The leading figure, armed and with a bruise forming on one cheek, held up an automatic pistol. He waved at the groaning man, being held under the SMG of the second man.

"We have a hero," he said. "This idiot still thinks the revolution is going on."

Varic turned to Rashenski. "Always one who has to prove something. Understand, Rashenski, this is what happens when my orders are ignored. Pay attention. We are serious. The next one who steps out of line will be killed. No second chances."

Rashenski made no reply. He knew Varic meant what he said. The man wouldn't hesitate if it came to killing someone. Not after what he had already done. It made no difference how Rashenski felt personally. He had to think of his loyal crew members. Their lives were at stake here.

"Do we understand each other?" Varic said.

Rashenski nodded. He indicated the injured crewman. "Let me take care of him."

Varic nodded. He gestured to one of his men. "Go with them, Kerim. Keep an eye open, too."

"There won't be any more trouble," Rashenski said. "You have my word."

He supported the injured crewman and led him from the control room. As they moved along the passage, Rashenski freed a first-aid box from the bulkhead and took it with him. The armed man followed close behind as Rashenski led the way to one of the officers'

cabins and sat the crewman on the edge of the bunk.
He ran water in the small steel sink.

"Berin, this may hurt," he said to his crewman.

Berin made an attempt to smile. "My own fault, sir.
They were heading for the missile room. I tried to stop
them. It was a foolish thing to do."

"With good intentions," Rashenski said. "Haven't
I always told you to use your initiative?"

"Yes, but always with consideration for the consequences."

"You two should be in bed together," the man
named Kerim said.

Rashenski ignored him. He soaked a towel with
warm water and wiped away the blood from Berin's
face. He examined the open gash in the man's cheek.

"I can't do much for this cut. It's deep. I'll put a
bandage over it."

Berin nodded. His face paled as Rashenski pressed
the flap of skin back in place, then held a sterile pad
over it. He taped the pad into place, took a plastic
container from the first-aid box and opened it, tipping
white tablets into his hand. He filled a small tumbler
with water from the sink tap and made Berin wash the
tablets down.

"Painkillers. They might help," he said to Berin.

"Captain, I'm sorry for—"

"Just stay here and rest," Rashenski said. "I'll look
in on you later. See if the bleeding has stopped."

"Yes, Captain."

Berin lay back on the cot.

"We can go back to the control room now," Rashenski said.

Kerim only smiled at him, gesturing with the SMG.

"If it was up to me that little shit would be dead now."

Rashenski stared at him. "Then it's a good job you are not in charge."

When they reached the control room Varic caught Rashenski's attention.

"Your people report that we are ready to set sail," he said. "Rashenski, bear in mind what I said. Just do what's needed to get us out of here. No more."

Rashenski picked up the radiophone and contacted the base communications center. He requested the assistance of the tugs in moving the submarine away from the berth. They had been standing by and moved in. With Varic at his side Rashenski went up to the conning tower and instructed the tugs from his exposed position. Huddled in his thick parka, Rashenski stared across the widening gap between his submarine and the dockside.

So close to safety he thought. But there wasn't a thing he could do to alter the situation. Varic and his armed crew held the upper hand, and unless their orders were obeyed to the letter the only expectation for Rashenski and his men was death.

The tiny tugs moved back and forth, their padded prows nosing the huge submarine away from the dock, out into the channel. In contact with the tug leader, Rashenski followed their commands and instructed his engine crew to give him maneuvering speed. Power from the pressurized water reactors turned the submarine's powerful screws and the brooding hulk of the massive vessel slid silently into deeper water.

With the maneuver over, the tugs began to retreat, moving back to the dockside. Rashenski stared across the misty water, watching the base fade from sight in the thickening snow, and as Varic ordered him back inside he wondered if he would ever see Nerpicheya again.

The hatch clanged shut, the locking mechanism pulling it tight against the sealing rings. Varic gestured with his weapon, following Rashenski down to the control room. Rashenski removed his parka and stowed it away, turning to Varic.

"And now?"

"For the moment you keep to your course. I'll let you know when it's time to change." He smiled. "And don't waste time asking where we're going. It isn't going to make any difference to you one way or another."

Rashenski went through the motions of command, knowing that he was no longer in charge of the submarine. He spoke only when he needed to pass on orders, remaining silent for the rest of the time. His emotions were in a turmoil. He felt both anger and helplessness. The taking of his vessel left him bitter. He tried to understand the motives of Varic and his team. What did they want with his submarine? Nothing pleasant, he was sure. The Typhoon-class was a weapon of destruction. It had been created for a single purpose: to wage war. Designed for deep-water, unobtrusive operations, the submarine's role was to deliver destruction in the shape of its nuclear-tipped missiles. Yet without them it was nothing more than a silent behemoth, a huge metal tube that could move and hide in the depths of the ocean. And without the firing and arming codes, that was exactly what the submarine would remain.

The more he thought about it the more concerned Rashenski became. No one would go to all the trouble of stealing a submarine like his without a reason. He studied Varic as the man moved about the control room. Varic knew submarines. His manner and the way he constantly checked control and readout panels revealed a deep knowledge of the workings. He had to be a naval man, Rashenski thought. Perhaps an ex-naval man. Not that it made much difference.

"Nerpicheya is on line, sir," the communications station informed him. "They require confirmation of our position and course."

Rashenski responded automatically.

"Inform them we are on course for Safonovo and are encountering no problems," he ordered.

Varic nodded. "You see how easy it is, Captain. Continue like this and we will have no problems."

Rashenski remained silent. He had nothing to say to Varic. Engaging the man in pointless conversation wasn't about to alter things. His efforts would be of more use if he devoted them to commanding the sub and attempting to devise some way of reversing the situation. He had no idea how to do that at the present moment. Time might present him with an opportunity, though he admitted even that was a slender possibility. Given that Varic's team was in total command, removing them all without putting his crew in extra danger and retaking the sub seemed an unlikely prospect.

Even so he had to explore the idea.

CHAPTER THREE

New York

He walked home as he always did, from the taxi garage to his apartment. It was routine and had been for the past four years, ever since he got the job driving a taxi around New York. He had lived in the city for ten years, having a number of jobs, until he joined the taxi company and settled into regular employment. True, the hours were long, but Nadir Muhan didn't complain. The work was steady, he enjoyed it and it brought in a regular wage. He needed the money for his family. He had a wife and two young children. America had given him his chance and he had taken it. In the early years it had been hard, the work he undertook not pleasant, but he didn't complain. Muhan put in long hours, happy to work the overtime because it all went toward the savings he and his wife were making. She had work in those early years, her clerical skills keeping her in employment until their first child came along. After that Nadir became the sole provider. Slowly they improved their living conditions and were able to gather around them the material things that made life more comfortable. They weren't greedy or too ambitious, keeping a steady grip on their finances, and eventually they made the move to a better apartment. Life became rich as far as Nadir was concerned.

Until he received the news from a cousin in the Middle East that there was to be another terrorist strike against New York. The words left a chill in Nadir's heart. Surely this couldn't happen. Not again. The city was still recovering from the last terrible attack, which had destroyed one of its great symbols and left thousands dead. Recovery *was* happening. The population had picked themselves up, and New York, as ever, remained the power it had always been. The worldwide reaction to the destruction had also been overwhelming. In the weeks and months following September 11, a great coalition had been formed to fight back against world terrorism, and that association had forged many new alliances.

No one had ever denied the possibility of more attacks. Many changes had taken place in attitudes and practical terms. The nation as a whole had been put on its guard. If the news Muhan had received was true, then everything New York had done to put the past behind it might come to nothing.

His cousin had warned him of a strike that would leave the earlier attack looking like a minor incident. This time the results would be on a scale no one could envisage. His cousin's final words of advice had been for Muhan to take his family and get away from New York, to move to another part of America, hundreds of miles from the city. There was no mistaking the sincerity in the caller's voice. His final words revealed to Muhan that he wasn't a part of the group, but working undercover to prevent what was happening. The caller hung up, leaving Nadir staring at the silent phone in his hand. He might have stood there longer if one of the other drivers hadn't come to the phone and asked to use it. Muhan passed the phone over and walked away, his mind trying to come to terms with the information he had just received.

Leaving the garage, he had walked out into the fresh morning air. The city was starting to fill with people on their way to work. Muhan walked with little purpose. The city surrounded him, but he saw nothing. On any other day he would have enjoyed the walk home. The twenty-minute journey refreshed him, drawing him into a new day with its sounds and color. Now it was a backdrop to his confusion. It might have been nothing more than a painted canvas.

How much later he never remembered, but he came out of his daze and found himself sitting on a bench, gazing out at the passing traffic.

What did he do? How did he react to the news he had just received?

Taking his family and leaving seemed to be the wise thing to do.

But where to go?

How far?

And what about his own friends? There were the people he worked with. Neighbors. And his wife's family. The more he thought about it the longer the list became until it seemed he was taking in the whole of New York. His reasoning wasn't so far from the truth. He *was* a New Yorker. This was his city and the people in it were his extended family. New York had a habit of drawing in those who lived there, absorbing them into the very fabric of the place. It had always been one of New York's attractions.

Muhan drew breath. He left the bench and located a pay phone. He called home to let his wife know he was on his way. She had started to worry because he was late. He was never late. He assured her he would be home soon, that she need not worry.

With that done he moved on. He found a coffee shop and ordered himself a large black coffee. He took it to a table and sat down by the window.

He thought back to the telephone call and the chilling words he had heard. His cousin, despite his precarious position working undercover, still retained enough loyalty to warn Muhan what was to come. He had taken a calculated risk with his fellow dissidents and the possibility that by warning Muhan he would set in motion a reactionary process. Warning Muhan didn't rule out the chance that his cousin might alert the U.S. authorities to the proposed attack. Muhan considered this and took the process to the next step. Even if he did warn the authorities, he had no idea how they might react. He had read newspaper reports about supposed strikes against the U.S. since the previous atrocity. In a number of cases they were simply hoaxes. Others had been investigated and found to be nothing more than mistaken reports. He did wonder if there had been any that turned out to be genuine and had been foiled by the authorities. There was so much that went on behind the scenes that was never allowed to reach the eyes and ears of the public. Might his warning be treated as a hoax? As nothing more than someone trying to alarm the public? Because of his ethnic background Muhan might find himself being drawn in as a suspect himself. He was innocent of anything, but he could see how, in the present climate his protestations could be ignored. What if he ended up behind bars? Job lost. Home lost. How would his wife and children fare if they lost him?

He drank his coffee, something he usually enjoyed. This day it tasted bitter in his mouth. Nadir pushed to his feet and left the coffee shop, his steps taking him toward home. He had no idea what to do. As he neared his apartment building, he made one decision—to tell his wife about the call. Yasmin was an intelligent young woman. He had always admired her coolness in difficult situations. He knew he could count on her making a logical response.

He climbed the stairs to the apartment and unlocked the door. His son and daughter ran to greet him and he embraced them both tightly, holding them close. He felt their warmth, the smell of freshly bathed young bodies, and he could have wept. But he didn't want to alarm them, so he held back the tears.

"Nadir, where have you been?"

He looked up at his wife. Slender, her black hair cascading almost to her waist, she stood in the kitchen door, holding a plate in her hand. She wore a gray sweatshirt that bore the New York Yankees logo and a pair of dark slacks. As usual in the apartment she was barefoot. She was an extremely beautiful young woman, and Muhan often wondered how he had been so lucky to have found her.

He felt the chill of fear inside him when he recalled his cousin's words.

"Sorry," he mumbled, not wanting to say anything in front of the children.

Yasmin sensed his unease. She called the children and took them to their room, setting up a game for them to play. When she returned, her husband was standing staring out of the window, deep in troubled thought.

"Come on, Nadir, tell me. And don't pretend nothing is wrong. Is it trouble at work?"

He shook his head, turning to look at her, searching her lovely face, looking into her deep, dark eyes.

Trying to hide the tremble in his voice he told her, word for word, about the telephone call from his cousin. Yasmin listened in silence, her eyes widening as Nadir finished speaking.

"We should tell the authorities. This is too much for us to handle on our own."

He knew she was right. Despite the impulse to take his wife and children and just run, Muhan felt the tug of responsibility. It wouldn't be right for him to desert the city that had taken him in when he arrived in America. He thought of his children in danger, yet he could also see the thousands of children who lived within the city. How could he sacrifice them to save his own?

"You're right," he said. "But who do we contact?"

Maggie Stilwell was a friend of a friend of Yasmin's. She knew an FBI agent who worked in the New York field office.

There was a tremor in Stilwell's voice when she

contacted her friend and passed along the information she had received via Yasmin. Her agent friend, well versed in the complexities of such information, took down the details and logged it into his computer. He advised that Muhan and his family stay put until someone from the Bureau contacted them to take the matter further. When he put down the phone, the agent reread the information, considering how to deal with it. One of the problems of the present situation was the deluge of such information. The agent wasn't trivializing the data, he was assessing where to place it on the long list of information bites that came into the field office every day. He fed the data into the FBI's main database, where it would be assimilated and given a priority designation by someone higher up the chain. Then he printed out a copy and took it through to the agent in charge of the field office.

Stony Man Farm, Virginia

THE DATA THAT WAS SENT from New York to the FBI database was picked up just over an hour later by the Stony Man search program. Since Kurtzman's brainstorming session with Brognola and Price, the cyberteam had been running sweeps of all incoming and outgoing data that might relate to the Israeli's theory.

That in itself put a lot of pressure on Kurtzman's setup. He had the best in electronic search and analysis programs. His computers were the latest and best money could buy, but none of that meant very much without the keen eyes and brains of the people who were operating that equipment. Computers were capable of searching out and stacking long scrolls of data. They could collate and store all kinds of information, but in the end it was people who found the needle in the electronic haystack.

"Look at this," Akira Tokaido said. He pushed data from his monitor across to Kurtzman's.

"What am I looking at?"

. "The report we picked up from Carmen's FBI trawl. A guy in New York reporting a possible strike against the city. He claims to have taken a call from a distant cousin somewhere in the Middle East."

"With you so far."

"I did a workout using the data we have. The guy, Nadir Muhan, is clean. So is his wife and her family. Nadir said he received this call from his relative and believes the guy is working undercover with some hostile group."

"The Bureau will have assigned the matter a case number and stacked it up against all the others they have," Carmen Delahunt explained, "which means they might not get round to looking at it for a while."

"Nadir's relative is named Waris Mahoud," Tokaido said, and waited for Kurtzman's reaction.

"That's the name of one of the security operatives we had listed when we hacked into the Iranian network," Kurtzman replied, "and it came up with some others in that CIA file Hunt located."

Huntington Wethers swung his chair around.

"The CIA has been maintaining a low-profile liaison with the Iranians ever since September 11. They haven't come right out and said it, but they're walking on eggshells over there. The attack left them jittery, so they've been doing some cooperative work with U.S. agencies.''

"Are we saying this Mahoud is on the inside of Mansur's group?" Tokaido asked.

"Could be," Kurtzman said.

"Maybe he realized the game was over and wanted to give his relative a chance to get out of the city," Delahunt suggested.

"Muhan took the call at a pay phone at his place of work. I ran a trace on incoming calls, and there was one from an international network," Tokaido said. "If we can pick up on it, so can others."

Kurtzman nodded. "Mahoud's call could be traced through to Nadir's workplace. Wouldn't take too much to run down the names and addresses of people who work there."

"Leaves this guy, Muhan, and his family a little exposed," Delahunt stated. "Taking it to the extreme, what if Mahoud's people decide he might have passed on information that might compromise their operation?"

"Muhan's family is right in the firing line." Kurtzman reached for the phone. "Let's bring Barb and Hal in on this. Could be we need Able on standby."

New York

ABLE TEAM WAS in New York early afternoon of the same day. Blancanales was driving a rented Chevy 4×4, painted black and brand-new. The odometer showed it had done 250 miles. It looked and smelled new inside, the soft leather seats exuding richness. The powerful engine ran smooth and silent.

In the rear Schwarz had a city map spread across the seat.

"We should only be a block away," he informed his partners.

"That include Chicago and Philly city limits?" Blancanales asked.

"There's nothing wrong with my map reading."

"Yeah, but you read it like a crossword without the clues," Lyons pointed out.

"Take the next left," Schwarz said, ignoring the comments.

Blancanales checked the street sign. "Well he got that part right."

"Nadir's building should be midway along. On the left." Schwarz leaned forward and pointed out the large apartment building.

Blancanales hauled the Chevy to stop and they checked out the building.

"Third floor, apartment 306," Lyons recited from memory. "Let's go take a look."

He paused to check his holstered Colt Python, then pushed open his door and stepped out. The others followed, Blancanales locking down the Chevy. They entered the lobby and located the stairs rather than the elevators. Lyons in particular had an aversion to them when he was working. The confines of an elevator could easily become a death trap in the event of a combat situation. Small matters to the untrained mind, but to the professional a potential hazard.

They reached the third floor without incident and

sauntered down the hallway until they reached apartment 306.

"Door's open," Lyons said. He unleathered the Colt Python and flattened against the wall on the left of the door. Schwarz took the right side, leaving Blancanales with the unenviable task of pushing the door fully open.

The apartment lay silent and deserted. There was no response, no click of weapons being cocked. The only sound they could hear came from somewhere in the apartment, a soft, dripping noise. Lyons led the way in, sweeping left and right, with Schwarz hard on his heels. Blancanales held his position in the corridor, covering his partners from just outside the door.

Lyons and Schwarz checked the living room thoroughly. It wasn't large but someone had spent a great deal of time decorating it. The furnishings were solid, of good quality. It was clean and airy and empty.

"Something's going on here," Schwarz said. "Looks fine but it isn't."

Lyons nodded. He pointed to the leather armchair in the living room. It had been pushed out of place, the rug under it wrinkled into folds by the drag of the legs. They glanced across the room, Schwarz spotting a small clay pot tipped on its side, the flowering plant flat against the smooth wood floor, soil fanning out toward the kitchen door. When they stepped through, the first thing they saw was the bottle of red wine that had been knocked over on the kitchen table. The wine was still trickling from the mouth of the bottle. It had formed a large red stain on the white tablecloth and had soaked its way to the edge. Wine was dripping steadily from the cloth and hitting the hardwood floor. It was the sound they had heard when they had first entered the apartment.

"Can't have been here too long ago," Schwarz said.

They turned and went back to where Blancanales was waiting.

"There must be a back way out," Lyons said.

"That way," Blancanales stated, a mental image of the building plan directing him. "There's a parking lot out back, with an access down a rear stairway."

"Give me the keys," Schwarz said. "I'll bring the car around."

Blancanales tossed him the keys and Schwarz headed back the way they had come in.

Blancanales led the way to the rear exit, Lyons on his heels, and they hit the door on the run. The stairway was narrow, angling to the left at each floor. The exit door swung open as Blancanales pushed the bar. It opened on an expanse of concrete, boxed off into painted parking slots for the residents. A chain-link fence bordered the parking lot, with a sliding metal gate for allowing exit and entrance. The gate was open, a dirty gray panel truck blocking it. The rear doors were open and two men were struggling with a third, manhandling him into the truck. The third man was resisting them and seemed to be winning out until one of his abductors hit him across the side of the head with the barrel of the large autopistol in his hand. The captive slumped to his knees, still resisting, but weakened by the blow.

"End it now," Lyons yelled, bringing his Colt Python

on line. He braced himself in a shooter's stance, the big Magnum revolver in a double-handed grip.

The man who had struck the captive spun, his eyes wide with rage.

"Fuck you!" he yelled, bringing his autopistol over his left arm and pulling the trigger.

He had to have thought that a shot would deter Lyons. Far from it. The Able Team leader stood his ground, his Colt Python already set on its target. He triggered a single round, the big magnum slug catching the shooter in the left shoulder and blowing out a large chunk of flesh, bone and tissue. The impact of the hit knocked the shooter away from his captive, slamming him against the panel truck. He lost all coordination, due to the shock trauma that engulfed his body, and went down hard.

Blancanales had moved in a wide semicircle, bringing him in line with the second abductor. Clad in washed-out jeans and a suede jacket, the guy had watched his partner go down, seen the bloody mess that Lyons's slug had made of the man's shoulder and made a dash for the truck's passenger door. He might have made it if he hadn't taken time out to fire off a couple of shots in Blancanales's direction.

Concrete chips spattered against Blancanales's trousers. He brought up his Beretta and put two 9 mm rounds in the guy's left leg. The slugs cored through the back of his knee, exploding out through the cap at the front, taking bone and muscle fragments with it. The man screamed wildly, stumbling and falling, clutching at his shattered limb. He screamed even more as pain flared when his fingers sank into the bloody mush of shredded skin and bone, pressuring torn nerve endings.

The truck's engine roared as the driver hit the gas pedal. The vehicle jumped forward, then stalled as Schwarz brought the black 4×4 along the alley and blocked his way. The driver booted open his door and scrambled out, pulling a sawed-off shotgun with him. Blancanales exited the 4×4 and was on him before he could bring the weapon into play. The Able Team commando hit the truck door, slamming the driver back against the frame with force enough to shatter the window and buckle the door. The man's left arm was crushed against the body frame, the shotgun dropping from his hand. As the door sprang back, exposing the dazed driver, Blancanales hit him with a roundhouse punch that caught him across the jaw, taking out two teeth and ripping the inside of his cheek. The driver went down on his knees, spitting blood and shards of broken teeth.

"You want to tell me what the hell is going on?" Blancanales asked, rubbing the reddened knuckles of his right hand.

Lyons didn't answer until he had searched all three perps, collected their weapons and IDs. He tossed the weapons into the rear of the truck and started to go through the items he had collected.

"Take a guess," he said. "I'm tired of being shot at every time we ask someone to just up and quit what they're doing."

Schwarz was kneeling beside the man the snatch team had been trying to force into the truck. The blow to his skull had opened a five-inch gash. It was bleeding profusely, but it wasn't life threatening. The man was already sitting up.

"Tell me this isn't happening," he said.

"It happened. Are you Nadir Muhan?"

"Yes," the man said cautiously.

"In that case we're the cavalry," Schwarz said, "and we need to get you to a hospital. That head needs treating."

Muhan rested his elbows on his knees, his head hanging, blood dripping onto the concrete.

"This cannot happen again," he said, his words soft, as if he were talking to himself.

In the distance the sound of approaching sirens reached their ears. New York's finest was on its way.

"What about your family?" Lyons asked. "There was no one in the apartment."

"They are safe, well on their way to California to stay with friends."

Lyons took out his cell phone and speed dialed Stony Man Farm. He spoke rapidly to Barbara Price and was still on the line when a pair of NYPD cruisers swung into view. As they came to a stop, armed, uniformed police officers left the vehicles, covering the scene with their handguns.

Blancanales and Schwarz stepped forward, holding up their ID wallets showing the Justice Department badges they carried.

"What's going on?" a burly sergeant demanded.

"We need medical units here," Blancanales said. "Call it in, please, then we can explain."

The sergeant looked over the scene, his experienced

eye taking in the wounded perps, and the professional manner exhibited by Able Team.

"Somebody call it in," he yelled.

"Hey, Sarge, that's Rick Jenelli," one of the patrolmen said, indicating the man with the knee wound.

The sergeant took a closer look at the wounded man, and Blancanales was sure he saw a faint smile edge the cop's mouth.

"You guy's shoot that piece of shit?" he asked.

Schwarz nodded.

"You can't be that bad then," the sergeant said. "We've been after that walking disaster for a long time."

He crossed to take Schwarz's hand.

"Name's Lassiter. What happened here?"

Lyons completed his call and joined them.

"Guy on the ground with the head wound is our witness. We came to pick him up and found those three had snatched him. We got lucky and reached them before they were able to take off."

Lassiter pointed to one of his men. "Get the first-aid pack out the car, Vince. See what you can do for this guy."

"I hear you know one of these lowlifes," Lyons said.

Lassiter indicated the man identified as Jenelli. "Yeah. Rick Jenelli. Runner and distributor for one of the local drug organizations. Never been able to get much on him. Always has a high-priced lawyer up his sleeve. Walks away free and clear every time we bag him. He's got away with every crime in the book up to now, including aggravated assault."

"His luck just ran out," Blancanales said.

"Couldn't happen to a nicer piece of trash," Lassiter affirmed. He looked in Muhan's direction and then back at Jenelli. "So what's the connection? Your guy anything to do with the drug trade?"

Lyons shook his head. "Goes a lot further than that."

Lassiter waited. He got no more. "Jesus, I guess the door just closed on me, huh?"

"What can I say? Don't take it personal, Sarge, but there's nothing else I can tell you."

"Hey, why should I get downhearted? You guys just took down three lowlifes we've been after for a long time. As far as I'm concerned, you did me a big favor. What happens to the three stooges, anyway?"

"They might have information we need, so get them seen to, and then make sure no one can get in to see them. You'll get all the backup you need, so you can have a ball telling any lawyers to take a hike."

Lassiter was grinning now. "This is getting better and better. Hey, I owe you guys a drink. And I mean that."

"One day we'll collect," Schwarz said.

"By the way I'm Hanks and these are Redford and Newman," Lyons said.

Lassiter thought about the names, then nodded. "Okay, I get it. You guys are working undercover?"

Lyons nodded. "Something like that."

"That makes me Schwarzenegger then," Lassiter said. "Why not? It works for you guys."

AN HOUR LATER Blancanales was driving Nadir Muhan to an SOG safehouse in New York's Upper West Side that Brognola had speedily organized. Muhan had been treated at a local emergency hospital, his head wound treated and sutured. He was sitting beside Blancanales in the 4×4, staring out through the windshield and not saying a great deal. The Able Team commando left him to his quiet contemplation of recent events. There would be ample time to question the man once they were in the safehouse. Muhan had assured Blancanales that he was physically fine except for a headache, which, considering the blow he had received, wasn't surprising.

Blancanales had questions he wanted answered. The main one centered around the involvement of the drug dealers. He was trying to figure out how they were connected to Muhan. He tossed the numbers around in his head, not coming to anything resembling an answer until they were nearing the safehouse. As he turned onto the quiet residential street a faint flicker of awareness blossomed. He held it in his consciousness as he parked the vehicle and stepped out. Blancanales moved to the passenger door and opened it for Muhan. Securing the car, he led Muhan up the short rise of stone steps to the front door. It was opened before the Able Team commando even knocked. A blacksuit from Stony Man Farm stepped aside to allow Blancanales and Muhan to walk inside.

"We secure?" Blancanales asked.

The man nodded. "Team's in place," he said. "I got four more people in position."

Blancanales guided Muhan through to the living room.

"Take a seat. I'll be with you after I make a call. You need anything?"

Muhan shook his head. He crossed to sit in a leather armchair, leaning his head back.

"Stay with him," Blancanales asked the security man.

Leaving them, Blancanales made his way to a smaller room where a communication setup had been installed. He picked up a phone and put a secure call through to Stony Man.

"I need to talk to Aaron," he said when he got through.

"I THINK YOU HAVE the connection, Pol," Kurtzman agreed after Blancanales had outlined his thoughts.

"It was the only thing that made any sense. We know there are drug deals going down with suppliers from Afghanistan. I figured, okay, maybe there was a request for some of our homeboys to handle Muhan for Mansur's group. They were on the ground here, close enough to act fast. They know the turf and the guy who asked for the favor had no need to tell the truth about why. All he wanted was Muhan and his family taken away and silenced."

"I'll do some background checks," Kurtzman said. "See if I can find a link between your dealers and Mansur. Pol, what's the situation with Able right now?"

"Carl and Gadgets have taken a ride with a local cop. He's going to show them where this drug gang has its HQ. You know Ironman. He can't sit around long and wait for things to happen.''

"I know," Kurtzman said. "In this case I don't think we have much time to follow the rule book. Carl's impetuous nature should come in handy on this one."

"Talk to you later," Blancanales said. "I want to find out if Muhan can tell us anything more."

THE SQUAD CAR PULLED to a stop beneath a shadowed underpass. Sergeant Lassiter leaned forward to indicate the large, semiderelict industrial building along the street. A few cars were parked at the curb.

"According to our latest information, this is where the dealers hang out. I can't tell you much more about it because the sheet only came in yesterday. We would have got around to it eventually, but these days we have our hands full with more urgent matters."

"So this is where Jenelli and his buddies would have gotten their orders?" Lyons said.

"The chief scumbag is a guy named Tarrant. Douglas Tarrant. Big guy. Always dresses like he just stepped out of a catalog. He has pale blond hair and always wears it in a ponytail. This is where he does his business. He lives somewhere out in the Hamptons. He does deals with the Colombians, the Asian runners and the suppliers from Afghan. But like I said about those jerks you creamed, there are always high-price lawyers in the background, just waiting to be called on if their clients get caught."

Carl Lyons unleathered his Colt Python and made certain it was fully loaded before he reholstered it.

"That was my backup, Sarge," he said. "It might not have a diploma in law, but it gets results."

Lassiter had to smile. "I like you, pal. You talk like a street cop."

"I'll let you in on a secret," Lyons said. "I used to be one."

"I knew it. You guys need any help on this?"

"I'd be grateful if you watched our tails when we go in." Lyons said.

"You got it."

Lassiter pulled an Ithaca pump-action shotgun from the rack between the front seats and checked the loads. He jacked the slide and put a round into the breech.

"Let's do it," Lyons said.

They exited the patrol car and took a walk along the empty street.

"They have any spotters on the prowl?" Lyons asked.

"They have at other locations. Always one at the door."

As they closed in on the entrance to the building, a broad, powerfully built man stepped out to meet them. He wore an expensive gray suit, had one ear full of gold rings and eyed the three visitors with unconcealed amusement.

"Sergeant Lassiter, you giving guided tours now? Who are your buddies, Bill and Ted?"

"You didn't tell us this guy was a comic," Lyons said.

"Oh, Henry? He's not a comic. He's just too dumb to understand when he's in deep shit," Lassiter said, moving ahead of Lyons and Schwarz. He brought up the Ithaca, which he had kept in line with his right leg. He swept it up and hit Henry across the side of the head. The blow dropped the big man to his knees, blood welling from the gash in his flesh. Lassiter took out his handcuffs and locked one shackle around Henry's left wrist. He dragged the dazed man inside the building, snapping the free end of the cuffs to the heavy door handle. Bending over the man, Lassiter frisked him, pulling a heavy autopistol from under his jacket. A further search produced a switchblade.

Henry struggled vainly to free himself, cursing violently.

"Let me out of this, Lassiter. You're making a big mistake here. This ain't funny anymore."

Lassiter placed the muzzle of the Ithaca hard up against Henry's throat.

"Move or make another fucking sound, Henry, and I'll show you funny."

"I'll take the rear," Schwarz said.

Lyons nodded, pulling his Colt Python.

"Go ahead," Lassiter said. "I'll keep this way clear. Don't worry. Nobody gets in or out unless it's one of you two."

CARL LYONS MOVED through the shadowed lobby of the building. The place looked as if it hadn't been cleaned in years. Dust covered the floor, and lines of footprints directed him to a wide staircase leading to the upper floors. He started up, the Colt Python leading the way. When he reached the first landing, he picked up the sound of music coming from somewhere along the corridor that stretched away from him. He followed the scuff marks on the floor, which led him to an opening that brought him to a narrower flight of stairs. Lyons paused at the foot, hearing the music increase in volume. He began to climb the stairs, watching the top where it opened up into what turned out to be a wide, spacious room with windows on the far wall letting in ample light. The illumination showed Lyons just what he had expected to see.

The drug operation was in full swing. Long trestle tables held large bags of drugs that could be broken down into smaller packs for street distribution. There were scales and stacks of small plastic bags, all the paraphernalia that went with drug preparation, and nothing Lyons hadn't seen a hundred times before. Yet it still angered him. He recalled the results of the drugs, the suffering and misery it caused. It was pain and death for the users, money in the bank for the distributors.

The room appeared to be deserted. Lyons moved off the final step, his gaze focused on the far end of the room. He caught a moving shape coming up on his right and instinctively dropped to a crouch as something was swung at him. He heard his attacker's grunt of effort, then reacted, dropping on his butt and sweeping the guy's legs from under him. The attacker hit the wooden floor with a heavy crash. The sound of a shot rattled around the room as the downed man's finger jerked against the trigger of the weapon he was holding. The bullet burned its way out through the roof. Lyons was already halfway to his feet. He heard the guy on the floor trying to suck air into his lungs, saw the M-16 in his hands and swung a booted foot into the guy's head. The solid impact snapped the guy's head back, blood flying from his crushed lips. The back of his skull whacked against the floor and he lay still.

Lyons snatched up the M-16, jamming his Colt Python back in its holster. He checked the rifle and confirmed that the magazine was full.

That was when he heard the thunder of heavy boots on the wooden stairs. He glanced around him, seeking a way out. There was none. The windows he had noticed had bars over them, and the only way out was down the stairs he had climbed to reach the room.

The Able Team leader racked the rifle, making sure it was on semiautomatic, and moved to the side of the room away from the head of the stairs.

The first gunman to reach the top loosed off a burst from his SMG. Bullets ripped slivers of wood from the wall facing the stairs. A second burst achieved little more than adding to the damage done by the initial blast. There was a pause, then Lyons picked up the sound of muttered words a second before a dark-clad figure lunged over the top step, taking a low dive that took him in a roll across the floor. He hauled himself upright, the muzzle of his SMG arcing back and forth as he sought his target. Behind him his partners moved up the stairs to back him.

Lyons triggered his assault rifle, firing a semiauto burst that hit the attacker in the chest. The force pushed him back against the wall, surprise etched across his face as the effect of the shot gripped him. He turned sideways, facing the stairs, and looked directly at his partners as their headlong rush exposed them to Lyons's fire.

A triburst took the next man in the side of the head, snapping it around and blowing a ragged hole in his skull. He flopped back, getting in the way of the next man up, who pushed him aside as he leaned across the top step, triggering his SMG into the room.

Lyons had already moved, lunging to the far wall, away from the stairwell. He lined up his rifle and fired. The burst tore into the floorboards at the head of the stairs. Wood splinters blew up into the face of the man with the SMG, who gave a startled yell as the slivers gouged into his flesh. One of the slivers pierced his right eye and the shooter dropped his weapon, clasping his hands to his bloody face.

Caught on the narrow stairwell the other men became aware of their vulnerability. They turned to drop back down the stairs, their wounded partner panicking blindly, losing his balance and crashing into them.

Lyons gave a wild yell, moving to the head of the stairs, firing as he went. His autoburst caught the attackers partway down the stairs, his bullets drilling into them, blood spurting as they cored into living flesh. The attack turned into a bloody rout, with Lyons forcing the pace, leaving the kill team at the bottom of the stairs either dead or dying.

He kicked aside any weapons he found, keeping an eye on the team.

"Son of a bitch," one of the wounded said.

"What do you expect?" Lyons asked. "Did I get it wrong? I mean, were you coming up those stairs to offer me a box of brownies, or what?"

The man took his hand from his blood sodden side and stared at it.

"Bastard, you fuckin' shot us to pieces."

"Yeah. That's what bullets do, pal. You come looking to kill me I get temperamental."

The sound of someone running caught Lyons's attention and he turned.

"It's me. Lassiter," the cop called out.

He came to a stop, checking out the results of Lyons's blitz.

"Holy shit, what did they do to upset you?"

"Lassiter, you have some lousy friends."

The NYPD cop grinned. "You're not wrong there, pal. I'd better call in for help."

"You see any others?"

Lassiter shook his head. "No. But I thought I heard someone moving around in back of the building. Could be they were heading for the basement garage."

Lyons backed off until he was safe enough away to be able to take out his cell phone. He hit the speed-dial number and made contact with Schwarz.

"Where are you?"

"Basement. This place is a dump."

"Well, keep on your toes. Could be you have company. Maybe some of Tarrant's crew making a break."

Lassiter picked up on Lyons's message to Schwarz.

"I'll follow it through and back him if the shit hits the fan."

Lyons nodded. The NYPD cop turned and moved toward the rear of the building, leaving the Able Team leader with his own agenda.

THE BASEMENT GARAGE held a number of cars. Some looked as if they might actually be able to move, while others were in various states of disassembly. Parts of the underground garage were littered with piles of wooden crates and assorted debris. Water dripped from the low concrete ceiling. Pools of light alternated with areas of shadowy gloom where tube lights had stopped working.

Somewhere on the far side of the basement Schwarz heard a door slam, then picked up the rap of hard-soled shoes on the concrete. He heard someone speak.

His cell phone rang then, and Schwarz acknowledged Lyons's short warning message. As Schwarz put away his cell phone he heard the low, throaty rumble of a souped-up engine. He glanced back over his shoulder and saw the car the moment it started to move. Tires smoked against the concrete as the dark-colored vehicle accelerated with alarming speed, and Schwarz realized its line of travel was bringing it directly at him. He glanced around, looking for possible cover if the need arose. He saw he was standing alongside one of the parked cars and realized he had few choices. The oncoming car would be on him in seconds. He couldn't outrun it, or even move away from the vehicle he was standing by. Schwarz did the only thing left open to him. He turned, hauling himself up onto the hood of the parked car, a battered Ford. The roar of the souped-up engine filled his ears. He felt it come into contact with the side of the Ford, rocking the vehicle. The right fender brushed his leg as he pulled himself across the hood. Even though it was only a sweeping impact, the force threw Schwarz across the hood, pain numbing his lower right leg. He fell clear on the far side, slamming into a stack of wooden crates, and dropped to the concrete.

He heard tires squeal on the oily concrete. The onrushing car came to a sudden stop as it collided with one of the thick, concrete support pillars. Glass shattered. The engine howled, then ran to a stop. Doors opened and shoes clattered on the concrete, voices shouting to one another. Footsteps approached his position.

Schwarz stayed low, reaching under his jacket for the holstered Beretta and flicking off the safety. Peering under the chassis of the Ford, he saw legs, counted three pairs. Saw them separate. They were moving in for the kill.

He heard a bolt being snapped back.

Schwarz didn't wait. He lowered his gaze to take in the movement of the closest pair of legs as the owner stepped around the front of the Ford. Bracing his left hand against the concrete, Schwarz pushed himself upward, the muzzle of the Beretta tracking in, so that the moment the man's upper body showed, he was already a target.

The image imprinted itself on Schwarz's mind. A long topcoat. An angry, bearded face, and a 9 mm Uzi SMG clutched in gloved hands. The man turned his head from side to side, checking the position of his partners before moving on. He was looking to the left when the Beretta cracked loudly in the confines of the garage. Two shots, driving the 9 mm slugs into the target's skull just forward of his right ear. The short range added to the impact of the bullets as they cored in and up, exiting through the top of the skull. The target's thick dark hair was pushed away by the resulting eruption of shattered skull fragments. The target fell out of sight for a moment, then Schwarz saw a single upturned foot, moving in erratic spasms.

Raised voices reached Schwarz as the other two skirted the Ford. He was under no illusions as to their intentions. He twisted and peered beneath the Ford. The pair had separated, one making for the rear of the car, the other the front.

Schwarz assessed the position of the two. The man at the rear would present the harder target, his body blocked by the bulk of the Ford's bodywork. The guy at the front would be in a more exposed position, so he was the one to deal with first. This time Schwarz didn't wait for the gunner to show himself. He flattened against the concrete, pushing the Beretta forward. As he spotted his target's boots and ankles, the Beretta cracked three times in rapid succession. The 9 mm slugs tore into the exposed ankles, shattering bone, and the gunner let out a howl of pain, losing his balance. He slumped against the hood of the Ford, pain erupting as the weight of his body pressed down on his crippled limbs.

The Able Team commando hauled himself upright, grabbing one of the door handles. As he turned his body, he saw the blurred outline of the third man pushing his way across the rear of the Ford. Leveling the Beretta, Schwarz fired, triggering a trio of close-spaced shots that punched through the rear window of the Ford. Glass exploded, showering the moving gunner in the wake of Schwarz's 9 mm slugs. One caught him in the left shoulder, spinning him off stride. He tried to regain his balance, but Schwarz had made it to his feet and as the guy's head showed above the Ford's roofline Schwarz fired. The gunman's head snapped around under the impact, spraying a wide arc of blood through the air. He toppled backward, his body rigid, and hit the concrete with a hard thump.

A strangled cry of agony came from the man Schwarz had shot through the ankles. The guy was struggling to move, but all he managed was to put more pressure on his damaged limbs. Wounded as he was the man might become a source of information, Schwarz figured, and headed toward him. Even though the man had been wounded he still had the use of his hands. Schwarz kept that in mind as he skirted the Ford, his pistol tracking ahead.

The crackle of gunfire echoed in the Able Team commando's ears as the wounded man opened fire. Bullets peppered the Ford, glass blowing out from windows. Schwarz dropped to the concrete, muttering darkly at his mistake in leaving the target alive. Wounding wasn't always the wisest option. Even a hit target could still fire back. And a wounded man might consider he had little to lose, taking reckless chances that sometimes could pay off.

The gunfire slackened. Schwarz heard the last tinny rattle as shell casings bounced off the concrete. He held himself still, listening, and picked up his opponent's harsh breathing. Then he heard the slithering sound of someone dragging himself across the concrete. Schwarz checked his Beretta, gripped it two-fisted, and launched himself off the ground, rounding the front end of the Ford.

Leaning out, Schwarz caught a glimpse of a bloody trail where his wounded man had hauled himself across the floor. He felt the Ford sway as a solid weight pushed against the far side, then the wounded guy's head and shoulder showed above the hood as he pushed up on his knees, dropping the muzzle his 9 mm Uzi across it.

"You die," the man said, his finger jerking against the Uzi's trigger.

Not today, Schwarz thought, powering himself across the front of the Ford. He cleared the shooter's side of the car, heard the man yell as his intended target cleared himself from the fire zone. Before the guy could acquire his target, Schwarz angled his upper body, Beretta extended, and shot the guy through the chest and throat. The target was slammed back, dark flecks of clothing and bloody debris erupting from his body. He bounced off the side of the Ford, his body taking on a stiff attitude in response to the numbing impact of the 9 mm volley. He hit the concrete on his back, spitting blood and expletives. Schwarz didn't wait this time. He pushed to his feet and approached the squirming, bloody figure, kicking the Uzi out of the guy's reach. Schwarz dropped the exhausted magazine and snapped in a fresh one, feeling the Beretta's slide kick back as the first bullet slid into the breech. He held the cocked weapon on the dying man, making no more concessions.

"Newman? You okay?"

It was Lassiter. The New York cop appeared, shotgun at the ready. He scanned the area, taking in the downed men, and Schwarz.

"I'm fine, Sarge," Schwarz said.

Lassiter moved from body to body, checking them out.

"Who the hell are these guys?" he asked, glancing back at Schwarz. "One thing for sure, they ain't any of Tarrant's. Look like out of towners to me. You any idea who they are?"

Schwarz shook his head. "One way or another we'll find out."

THIRTY MINUTES LATER the area was ringed by NYPD cruisers and ambulances. The supposed deserted area around the building became besieged by a curious crowd of onlookers. It didn't take long before Lassiter's superiors showed up, dark cars sweeping into the area, and grim-faced suits started to make their presence felt.

Before this happened Lyons contacted Brognola. The big Fed, warned, set the wheels in motion.

"You catch any flak, just put them through to me," he said. "This could be a lot more important than some local drug problem right now. So don't take any shit, Carl."

There was a pause. Lyons didn't say a word. In the end Brognola cleared his throat.

"Damn silly of me to say that. I forgot for a moment. You don't take shit from anyone."

"One of my better qualities, Hal," Lyons said.

"Yeah. So wipe that smirk off your face."

"How did you know, Hal?"

"That's one of *my* qualities, Carl. I see things."

LASSITER BECKONED to Lyons. When the Able Team leader reached him the cop held out a plastic bag that contained a number of items. Lyons took the bag and pushed it into one of the spacious pockets of his leather jacket.

"These are the personal effects I took from those three in the basement. And Douglas Tarrant. He was one of those you tangled with in there. Took a couple of your shots in his leg. Not fatal wounds I'm afraid," Lassiter said. "He was searched like all the others and his stuff is in the bag. I figured it might be of some help."

"Lassiter, you're a man after my own heart."

The cop shrugged. "What the hell. You guys just took down a bunch we've been trying to stop for a long time."

"Hey, how is your chief going to take this?"

Lassiter, staring over Lyons's left shoulder, rubbed his chin.

"You can tell me. He's coming up behind you right now." Then he added quickly, "Captain Rick Toscanni. Has his sights set on being commissioner."

Lyons turned slowly, putting on his best smile, and held out a hand as the well dressed Toscanni strode up to him with a heavy scowl on his face.

"Captain Toscanni, nice to meet you at last. I'm Agent Hanks. Justice Department out of Washington. I've been hearing good things about you in the capital. Hell of a team you have down here. It'll all go in my report, and as me and my people are working this assignment undercover, the credit for taking down Tarrant's organization will be credited to your department.''

Lyons would give anything to have been able to see Lassiter's expression. Toscanni took a mental step back, his mouth partway open as he had been about to speak prior to Lyons's unexpected praise. To his credit he recovered quickly, gripping Lyons's hand firmly. His shoulders went back and he quickly clicked onto a positive response.

''We pride ourselves on doing a good job. But it's always a pleasure to assist any outside agency. Is it possible for you to give me any details on your assignment?''

''Sorry, Captain, but my orders are quite explicit. I'm sure a man of your caliber will understand the need for caution. All I can say is this does concern something far above drug dealing. What I would appreciate is Tarrent's people being kept away from lawyers and the media. We don't want them talking to anyone. No leaks about them being taken into custody. We're running on a short fuse, Captain.''

Toscanni nodded.

''I'm sure we can keep these people out of the limelight for you, Agent Hanks.''

''I also need that building locked up tight. Some of my people are going to need to check it out. Once we're done, you can go ahead and take over for your drug bust. From what I saw there was one hell of a load of stuff in there.''

Out the corner of his eye Lyons spotted Schwarz beckoning.

"Would you excuse me for a moment, Captain."

He joined Schwarz.

"Pol just called. The guy, Muhan, couldn't add anything to what he'd already told. He and his family will be looked after until this is over. The guy's really scared. We need to go and pick up Pol. Hal wants us back at the Farm. It looks like things are moving faster than we expected. Aaron picked up some intel from the Iranian security net. Reading between the lines it looks like their undercover man, Mahoud, got picked up by some of Mansur's supporters in the Afghan badlands. And before you ask, it looks like Phoenix has drawn the short straw. As soon as David gets back from London they could be shipping out."

CHAPTER FOUR

London, England

Fayed glanced up when he heard the door of the apartment open. He recognized Badir and relaxed, reaching for the cup of coffee he had just poured.

"Well?" he asked. "Have you located him?"

Badir helped himself to coffee. He stood at one of the windows, looking out across the London skyline, which was heavy with dark clouds.

"He has moved from the apartment he was in last week. The landlord doesn't know where he is now."

"That is a great help," Fayed snapped. "So what next?"

"I spoke at length with the landlord. He did mention that he is expecting someone to call tonight to see if there had been any mail for Hassad. We know the time and place, so if we have someone there the pickup man can be followed."

"Can we trust this English landlord?"

Badir shrugged. "Like anyone he is greedy for money. I paid him and promised the same again if he helps."

"Enough to keep him honest?"

"Unless a better offer comes along."

"Let the others know as soon as they come back. Badir, I want this bastard. We can't afford to let him slip through our fingers again."

"I understand," Badir said. "It's difficult in this city. It's so big and there are too many places he can hide from us."

"I don't care how big London is. We find him or we don't go home. Remember our necks are on the line as our American *friends* would say."

Badir sat down, drumming his fingers on the arm of his chair.

"What is it?" Fayed asked.

"I have a feeling we are not the only ones looking for Hassad."

"Have you been followed?"

Badir shook his head. "No, not followed. Perhaps watched."

"By whom? Some of Hassad's people?"

"No."

"Who then? The police? British intelligence?"

"Could be."

"If they know he's in the country, they'll be observing him. We'll need to be cautious. The British are capable at this. And never more than now."

"If they decide to arrest him, we'll lose our chance."

"Then we have to get to him first."

"We should put all of our people on the street. This pickup man is our only link to Hassad. Lose him, and we may as well go home."

It was Fayed's turn to smile.

"If we don't deal with Hassad, going home will be an unpleasant experience."

Badir finished his coffee. He stood up, angry at Fayed.

"I did not need to be reminded of that. It's bad enough having to come to this miserable country without being told I may not be able to go home. Who are those people who can point a finger and decree *we* are to be punished? Let them come here. Let them do what we have to do before they condemn us."

He turned and left the apartment, his body taut with anger. In his wake Fayed sank back in his seat, sighing wearily. He understood Badir's resentment and sympathized with him. It was difficult for all of them. Their masters placed a great responsibility on their shoulders without understanding the extremes the team faced, or even showing any tolerance of failure. It was only the loyalty and the strong faith of the team that kept them going.

He stood and crossed to the window, looking out on the same vista Badir had. Hard, cold rain was now falling from the gray sky, making the tiles on the house roofs glisten. The street below, tree lined and narrow, was clogged with traffic. Fayed yearned for his native land. He thought of the sun-bright, dusty landscape, the cool interiors of the white houses and the smell of spices coming from the kitchen. In his mind he saw the rich colors of woven blankets, the soft caress of fresh cotton. He could hear the gentle trickle of water from the fountains and the melodic rhythm of music coming from the radio. He wondered what his wife would be doing right now, and in the same moment asked himself whether he would ever see her again. His reflection stared back at him, lean and dark. He felt uncomfortable in the ill fitting clothes he was wearing. They were thick and heavy compared to the cool, light garments he wore at home. The indifferent, damp climate of England had forced him to wear such clothes to keep out the cold.

As he made to move from the window, his attention was drawn to a figure moving along the sidewalk on the opposite side of the street, a tall man, clad in an all-weather coat and one of the flat caps the British liked to wear. The man paused under the trees for brief time before moving on.

Fayed watched the man disappear from sight. Had he been studying the house, or merely taking shelter from the rain? Fayed admitted to being anxious. The situation he and his team were in generated such thoughts. He stepped away from the window after peering out for a time, his eyes searching every shadow, studying every house he could see, the gardens that fronted them. If he wasn't careful he was going to start seeing things that weren't there. It was how the mind played tricks, convincing the watcher that a shadow was actually a man. And that man was watching the watcher. It could turn a man crazy, make him imagine things that didn't exist. It forced him into making reckless moves.

Fayed turned and crossed the room. He opened a drawer and took out his autopistol, checking the clip and cocking the weapon. He set the safety, placing the pistol in the holster he wore on his left hip.

Whatever happened next was in the hands of God.

Succeed or fail, Fayed and his men would find out with the passing of time. He just wished the waiting time could be over. Once they were fully operational it would be easier. Carrying out their mission was far better than standing around simply doing nothing.

The telephone rang at that moment and Fayed moved to answer it. He recognized the voice on the other end of the line instantly, and with relief.

''Go ahead,'' was all that was said.

The line went dead. Fayed replaced the receiver, a nervous smile edging his lips. His mouth was suddenly dry, and he felt the slight churning in his stomach that always followed the order to make an assignment live. There was always concern. When the assignment was in limbo, the operatives waiting for the signal that would turn them loose, they worried about what they would do if the signal didn't come. And then, when that signal had been given, the concern was of a material kind. Then it was about who would live and who would die. No assignment was without its risks. Bullets or knives had no regard for a man's politics. They killed the evil and the just.

For some reason he moved to the window again, looking left and right. There was no sign of the man he had seen just a short time ago. Fayed shook his head. He was starting to see problems where none existed. Think of the assignment, he told himself. Get it done so they could all go home. It was as simple as that. Which he knew was a lie. Nothing in life was that simple.

Nothing.

Fayed looked around the room until he spotted the

cell phone. He picked it up and pressed the speed-dial number that would connect him with Badir. There was a long pause before Badir answered. It was in Fayed's mind to ask him why he had taken so long, but he let it go, not wanting to antagonize the man further.

"We can go," Fayed stated. "Find the others quickly and come back to the apartment. Leave two men with one of the cars to watch out for the pickup."

"We'll be back soon."

"Make certain whoever you leave has his cell phone. We may only get one chance to spot this pickup man. If he shows and is identified, the team must follow him and guide us to him. They cannot afford to lose him."

Fayed put down his phone and prepared to move. His loaded pistol went into the holster on his belt. He pulled on his topcoat and went to the window. Rain still fell, pebbling against the glass. The street glistened. Fayed suddenly felt thirsty, his throat dry. He turned and crossed the apartment, opening the fridge and taking out a bottle of water. He removed the top and took a long drink. He could feel his hand trembling. When he put the bottle away he held both his hands before him, seeing the gentle tremor.

He clenched his fists tightly, took a breath, then uncurled his fingers again. A nervous smile edged his lips. His hands were steady now. This happened more often than it had ever done before. The commencement of any assignment had this effect on him. Fayed kept his concerns about his state of mind to himself, aware that if his superiors ever found out he would be immediately withdrawn from active service. They had exacting, high standards, with little sentimentality where their operatives were concerned. Once an operative outlived his usefulness his days were over. If he was lucky, he might be offered an administration position. If not he would simply find himself cast out, no longer an asset. Fayed tried to envision that. It would mean he could be with his family and not chasing around the world, placing himself in danger on every assignment. Yet there was another part of him that craved the excitement, the danger, even the violent conclusions. It added to his life, gave it purpose. An edge, and more so in a world that had become an infinitely more dangerous place since the events of September 11. That day had pushed the entire world into a new era. No one, no country, was as impregnable as it previously imagined itself to be. America, the one place believed to be untouchable, had been penetrated by acts of sheer madness. The death and destruction, wasteful in the extreme, had served only as a catalyst, generating a monumental response from the U.S.A. The effect of the strike against America had sent out ripples that had engulfed the world. And there was no going back.

The madness of the terrorist threat, that there would be a reprisal for every strike America made, only heightened the precarious balance. If vengeful responses from terrorist cells were to be believed, and Fayed had little difficulty in doing so, then the results could reach out and harm them all. Nuclear strikes. Biological warfare. These were the machines of total insanity. They each produced effects that were capable of running wild, ignoring borders and territorial restrictions. Radiation could be carried by winds, as could the deadly biological strains. They weren't affected by political or religious constraints and would destroy Christian and Muslim alike. It was a condition Fayed's own country refused to accept, and it was why he and his team were here in London, on a search-and-destroy mission, with Khalil Hassad as their target.

The choice was simple in the extreme. If Abrim Mansur was developing some atrocity scenario, which in essence would even outclass the September 11 attack, then something had to be done to disrupt that coming nightmare. The information provided by the undercover agent had indicated Mansur's determination to create such an event. It was in Iran's interest as much as anyone's to put a stop to the plot. As they uncovered information, it had become Fayed's responsibility to take his team into the field and to do what they could to turn that information into decisive action.

That had brought them to London, on Hassad's trail. Although they had seemed to have come to a dead end, the possibility of resurrecting the initiative now appeared probable. However tenuous that possibility might seem, Fayed and his team had to move on it. The consequences of not acting were too worrying to ignore.

As it turned out, Fayed didn't have long to wait. His cell phone rang just thirty minutes later. He answered it and received the signal that the pickup man had arrived at the hotel. The informant inside had

pointed the man out to Fayed's waiting men and they
had begun to follow him the moment he left.

Badir and the other two members of the team had
already rejoined Fayed in the apartment. They had left
the moment the call was received. They had a car
parked in the small yard at the back of the house.
Badir drove, with Fayed beside him. The others sat in
the rear. Fayed had the cell phone connection still
open and received instructions from the pair tailing the
pickup man.

Because of the hour and the bad weather the streets
weren't busy. Badir drove steadily, aware of the speed
limits, and also because he was not overly familiar
with London. They were all concentrating on the task
at hand, eyes fixed on the road ahead.

None of them noticed the car that picked them up
the moment they left the rear of the house.

DAVID MCCARTER STAYED well behind the Iranians'
car. He had located the yard at the rear of the house
and had been watching when Badir and the other two
had returned. He saw them leave the house again less
than thirty minutes later, accompanied by Fayed. They
all climbed into a Toyota sedan, pulled out of the yard
and turned down the street. McCarter started his own
car and settled back to tail them. The Briton felt better
now something was actually happening. He had no
idea at that moment just what, but the hurried way the
four men had left the house suggested they were on
some kind of urgent business.

He followed them across London, his knowledge of
the city telling him they were heading for the East

End. After a twenty-minute ride, the Toyota made a left and cruised along a narrow, badly lit street between industrial buildings. A number of them had For Sale signs displayed above the entrances. The Toyota came to a stop, and its lights were extinguished. McCarter pulled his car into the parking lot of a deserted building and shut down. He sat in the dark and watched as Fayed and his team stepped out of the Toyota, coat collars turned up against the rain.

Two men eased out of the shadows and joined them. They all stood discussing something and then split into two groups of three. One trio went down the side of the building while Fayed and the others approached the front.

McCarter waited until they had all moved out of sight before climbing out of his own vehicle. He moved to the front of the building, pausing as he heard the sound of someone moving along the side of the building. He was about to move off again when he saw something that held his attention.

A number of black-clad figures came out of nowhere, briefly illuminated by a security light on an adjacent building. He counted at least six of them. They moved quickly, without pause, and the capable way they did raised a memory in McCarter's mind. A brief recall of his past. He remained where he was for a few seconds, considering his next move, and moments later that decision was made for him when the crackle of autofire broke the near silence. He heard glass shatter, voices shouting briefly, then more gunfire. A man screamed, once, briefly, and then McCarter heard the familiar dull thump of stun grenades going off. He headed down the side of the building, pulling his Browning Hi-Power from under his coat.

Something told him he wasn't going to like what he found inside the building.

CHAPTER FIVE

Halfway along the length of the building McCarter spotted a partially open door. He eased up to it, peering inside, and saw the interior was in shadow. A distant light cast sufficient illumination for him to see his way. The Briton slipped inside, crouching just on the other side, his back to the cold brick wall. He listened as faint noises reached his ears—the murmur of voices, faint scuffing sounds as men moved around in near silence. He could smell smoke, the tang of recent gunfire. The low sound of a man groaning in pain reached his ears. McCarter felt the cold slap of rain against the back of his neck. It was coming in through the door to his left and was enough to make him move. He had confirmed that the passage he was in was empty. He stood and crept forward, his eyes searching the way ahead, his Browning at the ready.

McCarter hated this kind of situation. Creeping around in virtual darkness, not knowing what the hell had just gone down. He had no idea who was inside the building. The only thing he knew for certain was that he had heard a firefight, short and ferocious as most of them were, and someone had gotten hurt. There might even be fatalities.

Just ahead, dry hinges creaked softly as someone pushed against a door. McCarter turned in the direction of the noise, the Browning's muzzle ahead of him, tracking through the shadows. He saw a figure in black slip out through the open door, moving ahead on light feet. Not a sound from this one. At the back of his mind lurked a suspicion of the man's identity, but he needed to be absolutely certain before anything else happened.

The Briton followed the black-clad figure. At the end of the passage the man slipped through another door, with McCarter close behind. The room ahead was in deep shadow. McCarter saw his man just ahead. He was motionless, breathing held to a minimum as he scanned the room. The more he observed the man the more certain the Phoenix Force leader was about his identity.

His back to a wall, McCarter waited while his man continued to check out the room. The tall Briton held his Browning close to his chest, both hands around the grips, watching the black figure complete his circuit and move back toward the door.

He let the guy come on. The dark figure was close to the wall himself now, still checking out the room, as if he weren't fully certain it was empty. McCarter allowed himself a thin smirk of pleasure, because he was reaching his conclusion as to the guy's identity.

A whisper of sound as material brushed the wall. It came from his left, close by, and McCarter brought around the muzzle of the Browning, peering into the shadows. He caught the merest suggestion of movement as the black-clad figure shifted position. It was enough for McCarter. He lowered himself a few inches, leaning forward, and established the bulky shape of the figure dressed in black. Even as he committed himself, the Briton made out the shape of an auto weapon. Then he was going for the figure, pushing the weapon aside as he caught hold of the shoulder, pulling him away from the wall and spinning him. As the man banged against the wall, McCarter jabbed the muzzle of the Browning into the side of his neck.

"Leave it, chum," he said, curling his fingers around the autoweapon and recognizing it as a Heckler & Koch MP-5. "You're not fast enough to outsmart a bullet."

McCarter felt the man relax, a silent surrender of his stance, indicating he wasn't about to make any futile gesture.

Urgent whispers of sound reached McCarter's ears, metallic words coming via a headset the man was wearing. McCarter had heard those hushed cadences himself on many occasions. He knew now that he had been correct in his assumption. He knew whom he was up against.

I know it's true, but I don't bloody believe it, the Briton thought.

He tapped the Browning against the side of his captive's face.

"You blokes based at Hereford by any chance?"

The man under his gun cleared his throat. "What?"

"Don't bugger about, mate, I've clocked you. SAS and don't deny it. But what the hell you're doing here I haven't a clue."

"Now look…"

McCarter sighed with frustration.

"Just call your people in, sonny," McCarter said. "I'm not the bloody enemy."

The SAS man hesitated. He wasn't trusting his captor so easily.

"Who have you got on your team?" McCarter asked. He reeled off a list of names until he felt the SAS man stiffen slightly. He grinned. Reaching up with his free hand, he took the headset off his captive and held it in place while he spoke into the small mike.

"You listening, Vic? Come on. None of your silly games. Let's knock off this bloody pantomime."

There was a hesitation before a familiar voice came through the headset.

"Mac? That you?"

"It's me, you silly sod, now show yourselves because I'm getting tired of hanging on to this bloke of yours."

Someone chuckled briefly.

"Stand down, team. Mac, you can let go of him now."

McCarter eased off, shaking his head as he leaned back against the wall. He could hear voices somewhere in the vicinity. Moments later a door was opened and light flooded the room. A quartet of black-clad, armed figures crowded inside the room. The one on the lead peeled off his headgear, revealing a face McCarter knew well.

"I knew this had to happen one day," Vic Cappell said.

McCarter put away his Browning and reached out to take Cappell's outstretched hand.

"Hate to have disappointed you," he said.

The rest of the team, including the man McCarter had caught, took off their headgear. They all looked very young to McCarter.

"Mind explaining, boss?" one of them asked.

Cappell ran a hand through his short hair. He was a broad, rugged man with an easygoing expression on his face.

"David McCarter. He's one of us. Used to be in the regiment."

"Had me worried back there," McCarter said. " I wasn't sure who it was running around in the dark."

"What the hell are you doing in on this assignment, Mac?" Cappell asked.

"Long story with complications."

Cappell nodded. "Nothing changes as far as you're concerned. Okay, team stand down. Someone call it in. We need a clean-up squad in here. Tell you, Mac, it's like a bloody slaughterhouse back there, and we hardly fired a shot. Jacko, get the guys together. Soon as we head back to base. You lot go ahead. I'll follow on with this loose cannon here."

"Sir, what about the surviving casualty?" one of the SAS troopers asked.

"Take him with you. Have the medical team alerted."

McCarter touched Cappell's arm. "Casualty?"

"We found him when we arrived. He'd been shot a couple of times. Had one of my boys treat him as best he could."

"He been identified?"

Cappell slung his MP-5.

"Very much so," he said. "We know him as Fayed. Iranian. Security service."

"What about the others?"

"It's a bloody mess. We have seven dead. Five of them are Fayed's people. The others are Khalil Hassad and a man we know as Razak. We learned recently that Razak was a money man for Abrim Mansur's organization. He raised cash, made deals. He ran a small investment company here in London, but it now looks like most of the money went to Mansur. It only came to light because of government clampdowns on cash suspected of being collected for terrorist organizations. A computer trawl through some suspect trading threw Razak's name in the hat and once our people started digging they hit paydirt, so to speak. We were sent in to snatch Hassad and Razak. Problem was, the moment we arrived all hell broke loose. Fayed's bunch went at Hassad and Razak, but they weren't about to quit. When we came on them they were shooting at each other. It was all over in no time. Fayed is the only survivor."

"Hassad was here to talk money with his paymaster?"

"That's only part of it, David. You'd better come with me and have a look at something we found."

Cappell led the way through the building. It was a maze of corridors and damp, empty rooms. They eventually reached a steel door that opened onto a steep flight of steps that led to the basement. The air had a stale odor to it, wafted up at them by air currents coming from deep under the foundation. At the bottom of the steps Cappell guided McCarter through the first section of the basement. Low ceilings brushed the tops of their heads. The floor under their feet held large pools of water.

They came to another steel door. McCarter noticed that this one, like the first, was fairly new. Cappell swung it open and led him into a room. He flicked a switch on the wall and the room was lit up by a couple of powerful fluorescent lights. The room was twenty feet square, and housed a couple of desks, one holding a computer. Both had papers scattered across their tops, while some had been knocked to the floor. On one of the desks stood two large cases. Cappell crossed to the desk and opened the cases. They were full of money. McCarter moved closer and saw stacks of U.S. hundred-dollar bills in one case. The other case held a similarly large amount of UK banknotes. He picked a bundle out and thumbed through it.

"A lot of money there, pal," he said.

"Too much for my simple brain to absorb," Cappell answered. "Shall we take one and do a runner?"

McCarter grinned. "Don't tempt me." He took a second look at the money. "Vic, this is more than just pocket money for a local cell. Mansur didn't set this up to buy groceries for the bloody weekend. These blokes were on the verge of something really big."

"This to do with why you're here?"

"Not a thousand light-years away. Listen, did you turn up anything else?"

Cappell walked around to the front of the computer and pointed at the monitor. It showed an e-mail, partly written. Someone had left it in a hurry.

"Either Razak or Hassad. One must have warned

the other that they had company and they went out to face them,'' Cappell said. ''The way we found the bodies suggests that. Hassad and Razak must have been able to come up on Fayed and his team before they were spotted. They must have simply opened up and cut down Fayed's people before any of them could respond. Majority of Fayed's people took it in the back. Somewhere along the line his team responded and took out Razak and Hassad.''

''Where did you come in?''

''At the tail end. By the time we located the fire zone it was almost over. We tossed in stun grenades and fired warning shots. By the time we moved in it was over. I spread my team around to check if there were any other hostiles in the building. This was all we found before you showed your ugly mug.''

McCarter wandered around the room, picking up papers and examining them.

''Vic, I need to take all this stuff with us. I can't understand a bloody thing that's written here. We need it translated. Fast.''

''What about the e-mail?''

''That's the easy bit. I'll send it to my people. They can work out what it says.''

McCarter bent over the keyboard and tapped in the address that would send the unfinished e-mail to Stony Man. He put in a line of his own at the bottom of the text message, asking for a translation, then hit the pointer over the send button and posted the message. The machine acknowledged that the message had been sent. McCarter switched the computer off, took out all the connections and picked up the CPU.

"Hard drive?"

McCarter nodded. "Never know what we might find tucked away somewhere," he said.

Cappell had placed all the documents he could find into one of the attaché cases, snapping the lid shut.

"Let's get out of here," he said.

SAS Safehouse, Near Canary Wharf, London

"This is just a temporary set up," Cappell explained.

"Rent must be terrific," McCarter said. "Hope they don't take it out of your pay."

He was standing beside Cappell, looking out across the river, a large mug of hot, sweet tea in his hand.

"All arranged courtesy of the MoD."

"What it is to have friends."

"Talking about friends," Cappell said. "Where the hell have you been lately?"

"Vic, don't ask 'cause I can't tell you." McCarter took a swallow of tea and moved back across the room. He slumped into a low, leather armchair and leaned back.

Cappell took a seat across from McCarter. He still wore his blacksuit but had removed all the external trappings. Around them the room—in reality an expansive, open-plan office—was filled with electronic gear. Computers and peripherals. Monitors were alive with data and infrared scans. State-of-the-art communication gear sat on other desks. The area they were in had a number of armchairs scattered around a low coffee table that held a collection of well-thumbed magazines covering subjects from weapons to pin ups.

McCarter and Cappell were the only people in the room.

"Okay, I won't embarrass either of us by asking again, David. The message I got when I was on the phone to my CO more or less said the same thing. Looks like you've got clout, mate. My instructions are to cooperate but stay behind the barrier."

"Bloody hell, Vic, don't you go snotty on me. That's the last thing I need. It's just the way my bosses work. We run a tight ship. Simple as that. No different than the SAS. Only we don't go around writing bloody books about our exploits," he added with a grin.

Cappell snorted. "Don't tell me," he said. "'Bleedin' prima-donnas. And I was always told it was women who couldn't keep their mouths shut."

"From what I've been hearing, you blokes have been keeping busy lately."

"Hardly had time to shave the last few months," Cappell said. "But that's what they told us when we joined."

"Been anywhere interesting?" McCarter asked.

"Depends on your definition of interesting. Came back from operations just a couple of weeks back. We were rotated out, got shipped to London and this assignment."

"All your boys come back with you?"

"Yeah. We were lucky. Two of my team took hits but they're okay."

McCarter sank more of his tea. "Can I make *my* call now?"

Cappell stood and took McCarter across to one of the satellite radio communication sets.

"All yours. Take your time, mate. I'll go and find out about Fayed."

McCarter sat at the desk and keyed in the Stony Man code. He picked up the handset and waited as the signal was bounced around the satellite decoders.

"Bloody hell, did you screw up my vacation time, pal," he said when Brognola's voice finally came through.

"Crap happens," Brognola replied. "You okay with your old SAS buddies?"

"They made me a mug of tea so I guess things must be kosher. Hal, what the hell is going on? You know who we have being treated for a bullet wound here in London?"

"Iranian security operative named Fayed? Am I right?"

"Okay. Listen, has that e-mail told you anything?"

"We're still waiting for the translation."

"I have a package I'll be bringing back with me. Something for our cybergang to play around with. Plus some paperwork."

"I have an Air Force plane on permanent standby at an RAF base outside London. Ready for you as soon as you've finished something over there."

"And what's that?"

"Fayed."

"What about him?"

"You need to go talk to the man. The Iranians are involved in this. We need to know."

"Mansur?"

"Yeah. And it seems they had an undercover man

in Mansur's group. He called a relative in New York telling him to get the hell out because something was going to happen. No specifics, but it doesn't take too much figuring it's going to be big.''

"Can't this bloke get more info out?''

"Be difficult under the circumstances, David.''

McCarter sensed the undertone to Brognola's words.

"I'm listening.''

"Seems the guy had to get out because his cover had been blown. It became a bigger problem when he went on the run in Afghanistan and some of Mansur's local supporters picked him up.''

"Bloody great. The one person who might tip us what Mansur is up to.''

"So talk to Fayed. Find out what you can about Mansur and the Iranian undercover man. It might help when Phoenix goes looking for him.''

"That's it?''

"For now. Phoenix is on standby.

"We active?''

"All the way. David, we'll talk later. Promise.''

"Promises? You're the bloke who promised me a vacation without strings.''

Brognola laughed. "I get you every time, sucker.''

"Bloody Yanks.''

"Tight assed Brits.''

McCarter had a broad grin across his face as he put the handset down. He finished his tea and went to find Cappell and ask for a ride to the clinic where Fayed was being treated.

FAYED GLANCED UP as McCarter entered the room and pulled a chair up to the bed. The two men eyed each other for a moment before Fayed spoke.

"I recognize you. I saw you from the window watching the house. Am I right?"

McCarter nodded.

"You were looking for us? To stop us?"

"Hoping you might lead us to Hassad, which you did."

"Fate delayed your arrival so you lived."

"How's the shoulder?"

"It hurts but at least I am alive."

"Bad luck about your team. I'm sorry."

"Are you? They were only Muslim fanatics."

McCarter stiffened. He sat upright in the chair.

"Don't believe everything you read in the media. The idiots who write that sort of thing are out to sell newspapers so the cheap shots are the easiest way."

Fayed sighed, letting his head flop back on the pillow.

"Is Hassad dead?"

"Yes."

"Then at least my people did not die for nothing. We achieved something. But it has taken the lives of my team to reach that conclusion."

"Why was Hassad here in England? He didn't come for the scenery. Neither did you. Why were you after him?"

"Should I tell you? Can I trust you?"

"Fayed, what the hell was I doing? The same as you. Trying to get my hands on Hassad. We were both after the same thing."

"Your reason?"

"Intelligence had Hassad linked to Abrim Mansur. The collected information pointed to the pair of them being involved in some kind of operation that threatened the U.S. My people are looking into that possibility."

McCarter paused, studying Fayed's expression. He knew he was on the right track. Fayed had the same information.

"Am I right?"

Fayed nodded.

"We had one of our people in Mansur's organization. He had started to feed back information. Nothing definite. All isolated until we began to put the data in order."

"And then they started to point to a larger picture?"

"Yes. We couldn't understand what it meant. When we did and reported our findings to our analysts we realized Mansur's intention."

"An attack against the U.S.?"

"Exactly. Something on a vast scale. Far worse than anything before."

"Such as?" McCarter said, though he had his own ideas what it might be.

Fayed shrugged. "We only have basic information. It was the last thing our man sent us. He did suggest there might be a nuclear agenda behind Mansur's planned operation. He was unable to be any more specific.

"But you went after Mansur and Hassad."

This time Fayed smiled. He could understand the way McCarter's mind was working.

"Why should a Muslim organization pursue their

own? A simple answer. Self-preservation. We have our madmen too. Can you imagine what the Americans would do if another large-scale strike was aimed at New York? Or anywhere in the United States? There would be massive retaliation. Maybe this time the end result might be different. Maybe this time the U.S. would launch missiles. Even nuclear ones. Can you imagine the aftermath? In this we would all suffer. I have family. The same as many others in my country. As in the U.S. and here in Britain. Let us be practical. Nuclear detonations would affect us all. Heat blast. Fallout. Radiation that will linger for years. What kind of a world would the survivors inherit? The Americans have the power to destroy us all. Mansur has no concerns over what his strike might bring down on us. We had to do something to stop this man.''

''Tell me about Mansur. What's his grievance? His profile suggests he's a moderate, a man who uses words rather than action. Why would he choose to do something like this? It's a complete step back from his normal self.''

''Abrim Mansur is a man without roots. Everything he believes in has been taken away from him. He is a relatively young man who was born into a country at war. His true place of birth we believe was Palestine. The problem is even that is hard to verify, since he spent much of his early life on the move. We know nothing about his family background. He has lived his life in the shadow of war. His world was one of poverty and desperation. Much of his life was spent as a refugee, pushed back and forth by different regimes, never able to settle and build a stable life until his midtwenties. Then he managed to establish himself and go to school where he picked up politics and religion. We have learned that he absorbed his teachings at an alarming rate. He impressed his teachers and they took him and made him study under many scholars. His ambition took him into the highest ranks very quickly. By the time he was thirty Mansur was already gathering a devoted following. His moderate stance drew many to him. He gathered sponsors, began to receive money and assistance from many quarters within the Islamic world. He sees Islam being isolated from world affairs, never given a true voice. We are always pushed to the side when decisions are made. The world makes those decisions for us, takes sides against us. There are times when we are given small concessions to appease our feelings, but in general we are second-rate citizens. The American reaction to the Trade Center attack would have been the final insult. They bombed Afghanistan, and Mansur sees that as nothing more than an excuse to destroy Islam.''

''What was the U.S. supposed to do? Just ignore what happened? Lie down and take it?''

''Whatever the intention of the September 11 attack, it backfired,'' Fayed said. ''The strike could not have been ignored. The Americans made their decision and took it.''

''Is this how you see things?'' McCarter asked.

''If we lived in a perfect world, my friend, we would not be having this conversation. In truth we are separated by fundamental matters. Politics. Religion. The distribution of wealth and raw materials. Those who have desire only to retain it. The poorer nations watch this and want their share. It is human nature to covet what your neighbor has. Is this true or not?''

"I can't argue that point. But how does detonating a nuclear device over New York achieve anything?''

"Mansur is a good man who has reached the end of his patience. He must be aware that change for the better will not come in his lifetime. So he has decided to make a change himself by inflicting the suffering of the Third World upon America. He has a statement to make, a point to emphasize. And he chooses the world's largest, richest nation as his example. Not out of rage. Not out of anger, or even a deep-seated hatred of the U.S. Mansur will make his strike because he has to show the world Islam can no longer be ignored, that we have the power to make ourselves seen and heard. In his mind this is an act that will place Islam on the world stage like no other has ever done.''

"Doesn't he see the end result will tear the bloody world apart? If the Americans take this strike, they'll hit back. Does anyone expect them to suffer a second onslaught and not react again? And this time it'll be with every damn thing they've got. Has Mansur considered this? He could die just as the millions in New York, and the same goes for his own people.''

"Don't you see?'' Fayed said. "Mansur has gone beyond that kind of rationalization. A man in his state of mind—disenfranchised, stateless, with no place to go. He only has gestures left, something that will transform the suffering he carries inside him into a tangible thing. He has nothing else to leave the world, so he gives the world his emptiness.''

McCarter pushed his chair back and crossed to stare

out of the rain-streaked window. He looked at the dark outline of the city, seeing the lights reflected on the street below. Cars slid by silently, leaving silver trails behind as water sprayed up from their tires. He saw the same scene duplicated in a hundred cities around the world. People going about their business and pleasure, unaware of what Abrim Mansur had planned. His mind projected itself across the Atlantic to the enduring city on the Hudson. New York, the beacon of America, rebuilding itself in the wake of the worst terrorist atrocity ever visited on a nation. McCarter had been to New York and had seen for himself the stubborn vitality of that city. The Big Apple was regaining its image as a vibrant, pulsating place that refused to knuckle under. Something inside McCarter refused to even consider the possibility of the city being totally destroyed.

There was no way he would sit back and let that happen again. Not while Stony Man had the will and the ability to stop it.

"Fayed," he said, turning back to face the man in the bed, "we have to get your people and mine together. We need to talk. Your information and ours. Whatever we have. And I mean now."

"I understand. Pass me that telephone and I will talk to my superiors."

"I don't care where they are, or what they're doing. Make them understand we don't have time for any shit about protocols, or need to bloody know. If we get this wrong we could all go down the pan."

Fayed tapped in a long number, waiting as his call was connected. When someone answered he began to speak in his own language. He seemed to be having difficulty getting through to the person he wanted. His tone altered as his patience wore thin. He caught McCarter's eye, shaking his head in frustration.

"Is this how it is with your people?"

"It happens," the Briton said.

Fayed returned to his telephone conversation. After a pause his tone altered and he began to speak in a less strident manner. His conversation was long and eventually Fayed raised his eyes and managed a thin smile. He carried on his conversation for a while longer and then put the receiver down. He looked very tired, his face glistening with perspiration.

"That sounded like hard work," McCarter said.

"Let us hope it is worth it."

"I have a name for you, Fayed. Tell me if I'm correct. Waris Mahoud. Is he your man in Mansur's organization?"

The expression on Fayed's face told McCarter he had hit the spot.

"How did you get that name?"

"Mahoud has a relative living in New York. He called him from somewhere in the Middle East to warn him to get out of the city because of what Mansur is planning. My people were informed and went to speak to him. They arrived just in time to stop a kidnap attempt. Turned out the kidnappers worked for the drug organization in the U.S. who import heroin that initially comes in from the Middle East. They also clashed with three people who turned out to belong to Mansur's group. They must have visited New York to ask for local help to get to Mahoud's relative."

''Whoever said the world was a large place?''
Fayed sank back on his pillow. ''The chain grows
longer. One link to another. We know that heroin production has helped to fund Mansur's group.''

''And the son of a bitch will kill the drug pushers
in New York if he sets off his bloody device. Nice
guy.''

''Mansur would not see that as a problem for his
conscience. His way is pure in his mind. Sacrifice of
even his own people becomes necessary if he is to
succeed.''

''I won't pretend I understand how this guy thinks,
Fayed. Religion isn't one of my life supports. Life is
tricky enough without shouldering something I can't
see or hear. If that makes me a bad person, then I'll
live with it. Every man to his own. No disrespect to
you, or your beliefs, but isn't Mansur twisting religious logic there to feed his own ego?''

Fayed considered McCarter's words.

''Mansur exists for his religion. For him it *is* his
life. In itself that is not a crime. There are millions of
his fellow Muslims who believe as strongly, but the
difference is they read the words from another—how
do you say—*angle?* They use their religion to help
them through their daily struggles. They turn to it in
times of difficulty and it allows them to reflect on what
has happened. It gives them inner peace. Strength in
times of adversity. Yet they carry on with their lives
wanting little more than to maintain what they have.

''Mansur has taken that step beyond. He sees our
material world as offering nothing but denial to his
people. The simplicity of a lonely farmer struggling to

exist, working hard all day for little, but content because he is comforted by his beliefs. Mansur is blind to such faith. He looks through a dark glass and sees a world that is denying his people their right. All he can see is the division between the West and Islam. The rich and the poor. Oppressed and oppressor. And America is the target that stands above all else. A rich, powerful nation that displays its wealth for all to see. And there have been times when America has acted without consideration for the long-term results. An alliance here. Money and weapons placed in the hands of a state currently in favor. In looking back I am sure America regrets some of the places and people it once thought of as friendly and to whom it gave so casually. Those who were ignored do not forget. Mansur does not forget.''

"Fayed, you should be a bloody politician,'' McCarter said. ''Your man, Mahoud, we need to talk to him. If he's been inside Mansur's organization he could know a great deal about this upcoming plan of Mansur's.''

"Yes. But here is where we have our first problem. We have learned that Mahoud had to break cover and leave. His last communication to our people was that he feared for his life. He was going to try to get back home. Unfortunately there was no time to make any arrangements.''

"We had the same information. That he's on the run in Afghanistan.''

"Exactly,'' Fayed said. ''And we have no idea where at this moment.''

McCarter had a feeling Phoenix Force would be going online for a rescue mission. If Waris Mahoud had escaped from Mansur's group, the possible knowledge he carried inside his head could give Stony Man one hell of a boost when it came to seeking out the people behind the threatened strike against New York.

"Tonight at least has deprived Mansur of three of his top people," Fayed said. "Their removal will be felt by his organization."

McCarter turned to stare at the Iranian. "Three? Fayed, there were only two. Hassad and the guy he met. Razak."

"No, there was a third man. His name is Jafir. He is one of Mansur's followers. He had a briefcase with him, chained to his left wrist. When we clashed with them, he shot two of my men. Then I was hit. I thought you had them all."

McCarter shook his head. "I was told two men."

He pulled out his cell phone and called Cappell's number. The moment it was answered McCarter spoke.

"Seems we missed one man involved in the shooting party," he said. "Fayed says there was a third bloke with Hassad and Razak. Name of Jafir. He had a briefcase manacled to his left wrist. Known to be an associate of Mansur."

"Soon as you're done there have my driver bring you back. In the meantime we'll run a trace on this Jafir. See if the memory banks throw anything up on him."

"Anything special about this Jafir?" McCarter asked Fayed once he was off the phone.

The Iranian considered for a moment. "We know

he worked in the media and had positions in television production companies. The last company he worked for was based in Germany. That's all I know.''

McCarter crossed to Fayed's bed and held out his hand. The Iranian stared at it for a moment, then took it.

''Find these people,'' he said. ''For all of us. If these people carry out their plans we all suffer.''

SAS Safehouse, Near Canary Wharf

''JAFIR IS SOME KIND of media player,'' McCarter said.

Vic Cappell glanced up as McCarter entered the room. The SAS man was seated at one of the computer stations. He gave McCarter a long look.

''Always one step ahead.'' He grinned.

McCarter leaned across Cappell's shoulder and peered at the monitor screen, reading the text.

''So why does Mansur need a television producer on his team?''

Cappell leaned back, tapping his fingers along the edge of the keyboard.

''Mass communication can be a handy tool for terrorist groups. Helps get their message to a large audience.''

Cappell tapped at the keyboard and brought up an image of the man named Jafir.

''This is a couple of months old, but this is Mr. Jafir.''

McCarter memorized the image for future reference. He crossed the room and dropped into a chair, watching the rain stream down the large windows.

"I'm bloody interested in that briefcase Jafir is carrying round with him, Vic. You have anything on Jafir's contacts in London? People he knows? Places he might hang out?"

"Special Branch picked up on a woman he became friendly with some months ago. She runs a small beauty salon off the Edgeware Road and has an apartment over the shop. That's about it."

McCarter stood. "Worth a look don't you think, Vic, my old mate. You want to drive?"

CAPPELL PARKED across the street from the parade of shops. It was still raining, the wet black surface of the road reflecting the lights coming from the streetlights and the windows of the shops. Only two of them were open for business—a small private cab company and a brightly lit convenience store. A small group of teenagers was clustered around the entrance of the store and a gaudily painted car was parked at the curb, heavy rock music pounding from powerful speakers inside the vehicle.

The beauty salon was situated midway along the line of shops. Its front window showed subdued light coming from inside the unit. The lights were nothing more than illumination for security purposes.

McCarter scanned the two wide windows that fronted the apartment above the salon. No lights showed there.

"Service road runs along the rear," Cappell said. "Each unit has its own rear entrance and parking area."

McCarter took out his Browning and checked it before slipping back into its holster.

"You'll want me to stay here and watch the front I suppose?" Cappell said.

"At least you'll be able to keep dry," McCarter said as he opened his door and climbed out.

Cappell's cell phone rang. He answered it and listened, signaling for McCarter to wait.

"Our contact in Special Branch came through. The woman who owns the salon is away on holiday. She's somewhere in the Greek Islands getting a tan. So the apartment should be empty. How's that for up to the minute information?"

"Bloody great. But I'm still getting wet out here."

"Don't catch cold, mate," Cappell said.

McCarter turned up his coat collar and snugged the cap down on his head. He shoved both hands deep into his pockets and waited for a London Transport double-deck bus to roll by before he crossed the street. As he passed the convenience store a teenaged girl looked him up and down.

"Hey, you looking for business?" she called in a mock sexy tone. When McCarter ignored her she sniffed loudly. "Dirty old bugger."

"Not so much of the old, love," McCarter said.

One of the boys turned to scowl at McCarter. "You lookin' for trouble, or somethin'?"

"Go back to your old lady, son, she's probably tougher than you," McCarter advised. "Don't even think about rattling yours balls at me."

He turned away and walked down to the end of the line of shops, turning the corner and making his way to the service area at the rear. The salon was six units down. There was a wheeled trash container pushed under the framework of metal stairs that led to the rear entrance to the apartment. McCarter took out the Browning and kept it in his right hand, inside the large pocket of his coat as he made his way up the stairs to the top. He paused to check the door. Someone had forced it open. The wood frame around the latch was splintered. The exposed wood under the paint was clean and fresh. Whoever had broken in had done it recently.

McCarter pulled the Browning from his pocket and used his left hand to ease the door open, hoping that the hinges weren't going to start squeaking. The door opened without a sound. He slipped inside and closed the door behind him, pausing for a moment, listening hard to pick up any sound. At first the only thing he did hear was the rain dripping from his own clothing. As his eyes adjusted to the gloom, McCarter made out the shape of a small kitchen. He felt warmth off to his left, which came from the nearby stove. McCarter passed his left hand over the gas rings and felt heat still radiating from one of them.

He could make out the shape of an open door on the opposite side of the kitchen. Treading lightly McCarter moved forward. He paused at the threshold and peered into the main living area of the apartment. There was enough light coming through the windows to allow for movement in the room. The first thing McCarter became aware of was the aroma of coffee. He scanned the room again, saw nothing, heard nothing, until he sensed movement to his right.

It was followed by an intake of breath as someone tensed prior to making a hard move. McCarter bent his knees, lowering his head and heard the soft rustle of clothing and the whoosh of sound as an object was swung at him. The weapon missed him by a fraction of an inch and thudded against the doorframe. McCarter swiveled and lunged at the attacker. His right shoulder drove into an exposed body, knocking the attacker back.

Using his forward momentum, the Briton struck again, using the Browning to strike at his shadowy attacker. The hard metal came into contact with yielding flesh, followed by a grunt of pain and a man's voice cursing in a language McCarter failed to understand. Not that it bothered him. He didn't really give a damn about his attacker's nationality, just that the bastard had tried to crush his skull. Even that thought was dismissed as the Briton was put on the defensive again as his opponent made another, frantic, ill-timed second strike. This time the weapon he was using impacted against McCarter's right shoulder, with enough force to jar the Browning from his hand. The pistol thudded to the carpeted floor, bouncing out of his reach.

As McCarter stepped back, he made out the dark outline of his attacker. The man clutched some heavy clublike object in both hands, and he began to sweep it back and forth as he advanced on his adversary. McCarter backed up, managing to stay just out of range, but he was aware that eventually he would find himself in a corner, with nowhere to go. If his opponent managed to step in close and land a solid blow,

McCarter would end up in deep trouble. The Phoenix Force commando knew he had to make a fast response to the situation. He did it in the same breath, dropping to the floor and knocking his attacker off this feet with a powerful leg sweep. The man went down hard, thudding to the floor on his back with force enough to drive the air from his lungs. Rolling over, McCarter gained his feet and towered over his attacker. The guy made another attempt to strike out with his club, this time one-handed. McCarter launched a kick that cracked against the man's wrist. The club flew from his grip as the guy cried out in pain. McCarter bent and caught hold of the guy's coat, hauling him to his feet. He swung the man around and bounced him off the wall, waiting until the guy was laid wide open, then swung a bunched right that broke the man's nose and laid him out on the floor, moaning.

McCarter moved to the door he had come through and located the light switch. He flicked it on and flooded the room with light. The first thing he did was cross to pick up his Browning. He saw that the knuckles of his right hand were split and bleeding from hitting the man on the floor.

"Serves you right for doing it," he muttered to himself.

He fished his cell phone out of his pocket and dialed Cappell's number. When his SAS friend answered, McCarter gave him the all clear.

"Around the back. Door's open at the top of the stairs. Don't take too long because I'm liable to hit this sneaky bugger again if I'm left alone with him."

"Just contain your enthusiasm, Mac, I'm on my way."

McCarter glanced around the floor. He spotted the "club" his attacker had used. It was a hand-carved figure about two feet long, cut from dark hardwood.

"Glad he didn't clout me with that," McCarter said to no one in particular.

Taking a full look around the neat, well-furnished room McCarter saw a leather briefcase with a set of handcuffs attached to the handle, resting on a low table. Beside it was an automatic pistol, a mug and a coffeepot.

Turning his attention to the man on the floor, McCarter watched him roll on his side, one hand cupped over his shattered nose. Blood was streaming between his fingers. It had already spilled down the front of his light tan topcoat and more had dripped onto the carpet.

"Made a mess of that carpet, chum," McCarter observed. "Glad I won't be here when your girlfriend gets back. She's going to be truly pissed off when she sees that and the broken door. Hope she's the understanding sort."

The man, whom McCarter had recognized as Jafir from the image on Cappell's computer, sat upright. There was a bloody gash over his left eye from where the Briton's pistol had struck him. Tears of pain streamed from his eyes, but even they failed to conceal the rage that was consuming him. Jafir spit viciously, shaking his head. Blood sprayed from his crushed nose. He stared at his bloody hand, wiping it down the front of his coat.

"Who are you?" he asked. "What do you want with me?"

"Stop playing innocent, Jafir," McCarter said. "I've already seen what you and your late friends got up to earlier this evening."

"No. I have been here all day."

"Chummy, you are a liar," Vic Cappell said as he stepped through the kitchen door. "We have a live witness who identified you at the scene of a fatal firefight this evening. Hassad and Razak were your accomplices. Since they're both dead, it's all down to you."

Jafir struggled to his feet, supporting himself against the wall, his eyes suddenly busy as they flicked back and forth. He was seeking a way out. McCarter saw him glance at the pistol lying on the table and he could almost read the thoughts racing through the man's mind.

"Go ahead," McCarter said. "Try for it, Jafir, and I'll blow off your kneecaps. While I think about it, face the wall, hands over your head. Now! Check him for weapons, Vic."

Cappell ran practiced hands over Jafir's body, searching the man thoroughly. He emptied the captive's pockets, tossing what he found on the table alongside the briefcase. Apart from a slender switchblade knife he found only personal belongings, including a cell phone he passed to McCarter.

"We can check this later," McCarter said.

He stood over the table, checking out the items Cappell had recovered from Jafir's pockets. He saw a couple of keys on a metal ring and picked them up. On impulse he tried one of the keys in the handcuffs and nodded to himself when it opened them. He freed the cuffs from the handle of the briefcase and held them up for Cappell to see. McCarter threw the handcuffs to the SAS man.

"Hands behind your back," Cappell ordered, showing the handcuffs to Jafir.

Jafir's reaction at the sight of the handcuffs was instantaneous. He gave a wild scream of frustration, swinging around and striking out at Cappell. One glancing blow caught the SAS man in the throat, making him gag as he found himself struggling to breath. Jafir body slammed him, shoving Cappell away, then hurled himself at McCarter. Jafir ignored the Browning pistol in McCarter's hand. He lowered his shoulders and caught the Briton head on. The Phoenix Force leader was propelled backward, his legs catching the edge of the table. He went down on it, Jafir crashing down with him. They rolled off the table and onto the floor, each attempting to gain control.

McCarter grunted as Jafir slammed an elbow into his side. The man hauled himself to his knees, one hand pressing down on the Briton's chest as he drew back his other to aim a blow at his face.

Sod this, McCarter thought, and brought both arms up, crossed at the wrists. He absorbed the impact as Jafir slammed his fist down. The Briton's free hand caught hold of Jafir's wrist and turned it hard, pulling the man off balance. McCarter kept on turning his adversary's wrist. He felt bone crack. Jafir sucked in his breath. He tried to drag himself free, but McCarter's response was to head butt him full in the face with all the force he could muster. Jafir's already shattered nose crunched under the impact. He suddenly became a deadweight, flopping down across McCarter, blood gushing in steady streams from his damaged face. McCarter shoved him aside, rolling the unconscious man to the floor. The Briton climbed to his feet and crossed to Cappell. The SAS man had sagged against the wall, massaging his swollen throat. He stared at McCarter, unable to speak as the Briton took the handcuffs from him. Returning to Jafir, McCarter cuffed his left wrist, then dragged him across the floor and locked the free end of the handcuffs to the solid wall heating radiator.

McCarter went through to the kitchen and found a glass. He filled it with cold water and took it back to Cappell.

"Try this, mate," he said.

Cappel took a swallow, letting the water ease down his throat.

"Thanks," he croaked.

"At least it's going to shut you up for a while," McCarter said.

Cappell raised the glass. "Up yours."

"That's a good sign."

The briefcase was on the floor, knocked there during the struggle. McCarter picked it up and placed it back on the table. He used the second key on the ring and unlocked the briefcase. Opening the case, McCarter found it contained a number of CD disks and half a dozen videotapes. They were professional quality, made to a much higher standard than the kind bought by the home user. Each of the tapes was numbered, as were the CDs. There was nothing else in the briefcase.

"He didn't want to give these up," McCarter said. "Must have something bloody important on them for him to make such a hard fight."

"Maybe he collects porno movies," Cappell suggested. "Even he has to have a hobby."

"They might not be blue movies, but I'll bet whatever is on them is bloody sick," McCarter said.

He glanced at the semiconscious Jafir, then back at the briefcase.

"It's been bloody great seeing you again, Vic, but I'm going to have to move on."

"You never could sit still for long, Mac. What do you need?"

"A ride back to your base to pick up that stuff we collected. Then a ride to the RAF base to get my flight home." McCarter jerked his head in Jafir's direction. "I want him put on ice for the duration. No contact with anyone. He vanishes until the word comes down what to do with him. Total isolation. Whatever else happens, don't let him get away, Vic."

"Mac, would I do that? Go on, tell me whenever have I let you down?"

"What year do I start with?" McCarter said.

CHAPTER SIX

Flight 291

Hanni Amir watched the runway slide by as the Boeing 747 picked up speed. He felt the power of the huge engines rise, felt himself pushed back in his seat as the aircraft left the runway and began its rapid ascent from Athens International Airport. Amir closed his eyes, beginning a prayer that wouldn't end until the 747 leveled off at cruising altitude. No amount of devotion or faith ever released him from the dread of takeoff. Simply put—Amir hated that part of flying.

He felt a presence close by and opened his eyes. The flight attendant was standing beside his seat, smiling down at him.

"Are you all right, sir?" she asked. Her accent was British, subdued, gentle, polite without being intrusive. She was young, blond and very attractive.

Amir returned her smile. "I'm fine, thank you."

"Would you like something to drink?"

"Water would be nice."

She turned away. Amir watched her go.

Soon, he thought, you won't be smiling.

He glanced at his watch, calculating the time and

distance the plane needed to make before he moved. He felt a slight sensation of tension rise within him. It was a mix of excitement and agitation. He knew what lay ahead, what depended on the success of the operation, and how important his part was in the affair.

The attendant brought his water. It was chilled and helped to refresh his dry throat. Amir glanced out the seat window. The day was clear and bright. Thick white cloud lay beneath the 747 as it winged its way across Greece. This particular flight's final destination was supposed to be JFK International, with a brief stopover at Heathrow. Amir knew different. Flight 291 was due to make a diversion, and if everything went according to the timetable, Abrim Mansur's plan would move to stage two.

Amir glanced at his watch. In ten minutes he would leave his seat and the hijacking of Flight 291 would begin.

AMIR SAW that it was time. He rose from his seat and made his way down the aisle and entered the rear toilet cubicle. He locked the door. On his knees he slid his hand behind the toilet unit, locating the handguns fixed there by adhesive tape. He took them out, checking that they were both fully loaded. He dropped one of the pistols into his jacket pocket, along with a spare magazine. The other gun went into his waistband, the second spare magazine going into his other pocket. Amir reached up and freed the air duct cover. He removed the small pack of explosives, examining it. Satisfied, he placed it inside his jacket, then turned to look at himself in the mirror above the hand basin. He was sweating slightly. Amir took some paper towel and dabbed at his face. He straightened, took a deep breath before uttering a short, heartfelt prayer.

Turning about, he unlocked the door and stepped out of the washroom. He made his way to the galley where the flight attendants were based. Only one was there. It was the British woman who had spoken to him earlier. She glanced up when Amir appeared.

"Can I help you, sir?"

"Very much," Amir said.

He took the pistol from his belt and aimed it at her. The woman stared at the weapon, then looked at Amir.

"No," she said quietly. "Please, no. Not again."

"Do as I say and there will be no reason for anyone to get hurt," Amir said. "If you do not, I am quite willing to set off this device and destroy this aircraft." He took out the explosive pack and showed it to her. Using his thumb, he pressed the button that activated the device. A red indicator light came on, winking steadily. "All I have to do now is press this second button and we will all die."

The woman was transfixed by the winking light.

"What is your name?" Amir asked. He had to repeat the question before the girl looked back at him.

"Susan Morris."

"Susan, I want you to pick up that telephone and speak to the captain. Explain what is happening. Tell him I am serious. Then tell him that I want him to simply change course and fly the plane where I tell him to go. We are not going to crash into any buildings. This is not what I want. When he alters course, he will see we are going to fly over water. Tell him not to do anything that could make me press this button. No contacting the authorities. If I see any military aircraft following us, I will detonate this bomb. Make him understand that the plane will remain safe unless he does something stupid. Now do it, Susan. If you do not, I will shoot the first person I next see."

SUSAN MORRIS SURPRISED herself by remaining calm and coherent as she contacted the captain and explained what she had been told. For his part, the captain accepted her word concerning Amir's attitude. He listened until she had finished, then asked to speak to Amir.

"Sir, this is Captain Percy Dexter speaking. I want to cooperate as much as possible. My concern is for my passengers, so I will try to accommodate you. You say you don't intend using this aircraft to destroy anything. Can I trust you on that?"

"Captain Dexter, my intention is to simply borrow your aircraft for a time and use it and your passengers in an exchange. If we can work together, there should be no need for any of us to get hurt. You have my word on that."

"You understand my difficulty, sir. And I hope you realize the position of the United States government with regard to any hijacking requests?"

"I understand that, too, Captain Dexter. However, my part in this is simply to bring this aircraft safely to its new destination. You may then discuss these matters with my superior and your government."

"How do I know you have the means to carry out your threat if I refuse to cooperate? For all I know the weapons you have may be fake. Anyone can create the illusion of a bomb showing a flashing red light, if you see what I mean.''

''The answer to that question is easily resolved, Captain Dexter. All you have to do is force me to prove it. Let me assure you that I am willing to die for my cause. If that means killing all the passengers on board, then that is how it will have to be. How about you, Captain Dexter? Do you wish to be responsible for the deaths of over two hundred of your fellow Americans? To keep them alive all you have to do is to follow my instructions.''

One of the other attendants stepped into the galley area. She saw the gun in Amir's hand and opened her mouth to scream. Amir turned the weapon on her.

''Do not scream. Not a sound. Tell her, Susan.''

''He's serious, Kay,'' Susan said. ''Do as he tells you and he promises we won't be harmed.''

''Lie down on the floor, Kay,'' Amir said. ''Facedown. Quickly. Good. Now put your hands behind you and keep them there. You see, it was not difficult.''

''What's going on?'' the captain demanded.

Amir explained.

''Captain, we need to alter course now.''

Amir recited the course change he had learned. He waited for Dexter's acknowledgment.

''New course entered,'' Dexter said.

Amir felt the 747 tilt slightly. He peered through one of the galley windows and watched the wing dip as the aircraft began its turn.

''Thank you, Captain Dexter. You will hold this

course until I tell you otherwise. Maintain cruising altitude of 35,000 feet and speed at 530 miles per hour."

Amir handed the telephone back to Susan Morris and she hung up.

"What do we tell the passengers if they notice we've changed course?" she asked.

"I will leave that to you and your capable crew," Amir said. "I suggest you refrain from telling them the truth." He placed the explosive package on the shelf close to his hand and took out his second pistol. "Understand, Susan. I would regret any need to use these if I was confronted by someone in a heroic mood. No threats will be needed if you do not tell the passengers what is happening. You can tell Kay to get up now. Bring the other attendants here one by one so they can be told."

"All right," Susan said.

As she turned to go, helping the other woman up off the floor, Amir said, "Remember what I said, Susan. No stupid heroics."

Somalia

JEFFREY HARDIN WIPED SWEAT from his face again. He was finding it hard not to sweat. The problem was that it was not all from the heat. On the floor at his feet were wads of paper towel, dark with sweat stains. Hardin's clothes were wet, clinging to his lean body. His thinning dark hair clung to his head, curling against his ears from the sweat that layered his scalp.

This was one of the moments he wished he had never agreed to the contract with Sadiqi. He hadn't been told he would have to spend weeks stuck out in this shitty desert, with nothing but hot winds and sand flies for company. He just wanted the damn thing to be over. But the money had been the lure. So much he had been unable to resist. The acquisition of money had always been Hardin's downfall. He obsessed over it, had no control over his desire for it. All his adult life he had been afflicted with a desire for great wealth and the things it could bring him. He was a clever man. Being able to design and create all manner of tactical nuclear devices had meant his talents were sought after by any number of government and non-government agencies. Working for governments placed great restrictions on his personal liberty, so Hardin chose the commercial avenues, where he was freer to move around and gained financially, too, because nongovernment agencies had a tendency to pay better. To insure total loyalty they paid well. Hardin had satisfied a number of contracts over the past couple of years, stepping away from his contract with exceptionally high paychecks. All tax-free. Hardin knew that what he did would be considered illegal by the regular government agencies, but he had no illusions about their credentials. They all had their own agendas to work to, and he wasn't so naive as to be fooled by their moral high-stand of his kind of enterprise. Governments made a lot of noise about rogue states and renegade scientists but conveniently forgot about their own back-door dealings in armaments—the kind of operations that were done in the shadows and erased from memory when it suited the agencies.

Hardin was a free agent. He asked for nothing from·

anyone and expected the same courtesy for his actions. Business was business, and no one lived forever.

He stood and crossed the room to the water bottle that stood on a small table. He filled a glass and drank. The water was barely cold. He swallowed noisily. His throat was sore and a little swollen. He rubbed at it, coughing to try to relieve the feeling. It failed to help.

Pulling open the door, Hardin stepped outside. The heat enveloped him, the impact almost physical. He glanced around the area. He wouldn't be sorry to leave the place.

He heard someone approaching. It was Sadiqi. The man was small and lean, his dark hair brushed back from his forehead. He had a hungry look in his eyes that gave him a permanently serious expression. He wore light tan colored shirt and pants, and he looked cool and relaxed.

"You will be able to leave soon," he said to Hardin, sensing the man's discomfort.

"I can't say I won't be relieved. Got to say, Sadiqi, this is a miserable place to be stuck in. I can't understand why anyone would want to fight over a chunk of sorry real estate like this. No offense meant."

"You have no understanding of our ways, Hardin," Sadiqi said. "Desert or forest does not matter. This is our place and we will always fight to keep it. It is our blood and our flesh. It is holy land our people have preserved for thousands of years. We should give it up? Allow ourselves to be sent away because others wish to take it from us?"

"In a hundred years who'll give a damn?"

"We will. Always." Sadiqi bent to scoop up a handful of gritty dust. "When I die I will become dust. Life will carry on and from the dust others will be born and so it will go on." He peered at Hardin. "Have you no faith?"

"I keep it in my wallet and my bank account."

A call attracted Sadiqi's attention. One of his people was crossing to where he waited. He spoke quickly to Sadiqi. The moment Sadiqi had the message he beckoned to Hardin.

"Time for you to make ready, Hardin. The plane will be here soon."

"Good. That means I can get out of this damn place once I'm finished. Right?"

"Of course, my friend. As soon as you have concluded your end of the bargain."

Hardin nodded and made his way across the dusty ground toward one of the buildings standing some way off from the collection of tents.

He pushed open the door and stepped inside. It was cooler inside the building. A small air-conditioning unit, powered via a diesel generator on the outside of the rear wall, purred smoothly. The cool air felt good to Hardin as he made his way across to the workbench and climbed onto the stool. He ran his eyes over the squat, metallic device sitting on the bench. He was pleased with his work on the device, a powerful nuclear bomb that would generate a ten-kiloton blast. His bomb was a particularly dirty weapon and would leave lingering radiation in the blast area for a long time. Hardin had designed the whole thing, even down to the compact, hand-operated control device that would be used to set off the bomb.

The components for the bomb had been obtained through a number of sources, each piece being brought in individually. It had been necessary to do it in such a way because of the extra vigilance of security and enforcement agencies. But there were ways around even the most stringent barriers. It had taken time and cost a great deal, though that part had been of no concern to Hardin's principles. Money was no more than a means to an end, and they had a variety of sources providing income. From contraband smuggling to the distribution of heroin. Sadiqi called them means to an end. As far as he was concerned, his organization would use any means available to fund their fight.

Hardin had no interest in their cause. He was simply working on a contract-for-hire deal. Sadiqi wanted a product that Hardin could create. He provided the raw materials and components to Hardin's requests, and Hardin put the thing together. Once he had done that and set up the device, his work was done. He would take his money and move on. If Sadiqi and his opponents wanted to blow each other to pieces, that was their concern. As long as they let Hardin leave the battle zone, they could go ahead and do what they wanted. From what he had seen of the desert wasteland it wouldn't make much difference if they did nuke it.

Leaning over the nuclear device, Hardin began the final stage. He had to set and activate the power pack, then key in the code that would lock it into the hand-control device. Once he had completed that phase, the weapon would actually be armed and ready to be detonated. Hardin worked steadily for the next hour, stopping only twice to wipe his sweating face and take a sip of water from the bottle standing on the bench. When he finally sat back, smiling in satisfaction at his handiwork, the device was ready. A small red light winked on the power pack fixed to the outer casing of the bomb. Within the pack a response chip sat waiting for the signal it would receive from the handheld control device. They were electronically linked now. Hardin had keyed in the number code that invisibly joined them. He picked up the control device and flicked the switch that activated it. A signal light came on. Hardin felt a chill of excitement course through him as he realized what he was holding in his hand.

He had the power to detonate the bomb right there and then. All he had to do was tap in a simple four number sequence and the bomb would arm itself. Following that there was a timing sequence to implant. The digital readout was registered in minutes—one to sixty. With the time tapped in there was a final key to press. This set the time sequence in motion. There was no abort button. Once the final activation was set the bomb couldn't be shut down. This was a no return device. Full commitment.

Hardin could feel his fingers tingling with an impulse to tap in the numbers. It was a moment of madness that was both glorious and scary. Like holding a loaded gun to his head and teasing the trigger. Wondering just what it would be like to actually make the final move. It was only when Hardin felt sweat running down his face and stinging his eyes that he let go. His body sagged on the stool and he laid the control device on the bench, pushing it away from him.

He exhaled and wondered just what he had been thinking in those delirious moments. It had been the power in his hand. The realization that he, Hardin, had the ability to set off the nuclear device by simply tapping in a few numbers.

He leaned forward and clicked off the bomb's power pack, watching the red light fade. He did the same with the control device. Hardin felt chilled. It was the cool air reacting with the sweat on his body. The feeling brought him back to reality with a jerk. He stepped down off the stool and crossed the hut. Opening the door he stood in the opening, letting the exterior heat wash over him. More than ever he wanted to leave this desolate place, simply take his money and run. He looked up at the empty sky, wishing the plane would come. He wanted to be on it and gone.

THIRTY MINUTES LATER Hardin was packed and ready. He sat in his room, the door open, still watching the skies. He had shown Sadiqi the completed bomb and had gone through the priming sequence. Sadiqi had chosen the four number activation sequence, and Hardin had entered it for him. All Sadiqi had to do was switch on the power and the bomb would be ready, waiting to be activated by the time sequence and final button press. Hardin had handed over the control device with genuine relief. He had left Sadiqi and crossed to his tent, packing his few belongings.

Sadiqi reappeared, carrying an attaché case. Hardin's money. He placed the case on the floor in front of the scientist.

"Count it if you want," he said as Hardin opened the case and gazed at the thick layers of notes.

Hardin took out a wad of hundred-dollar bills and flicked through it. Every wad within the case contained the same denomination notes.

"I trust you," he said.

Sadiqi only smiled, turning away as his ears picked up a distant sound.

"It is here," he said. He moved away from Hardin, stepping outside. "And on time."

Hardin had followed him outside. Now standing alongside Sadiqi, scanning the sun-bright sky, it took him a while before he spotted the dark shape. He continued to watch and saw the shape increase in size. It took a minute or so before he realized he was looking at a full-sized airliner. It looked like a 747. As it loomed large and swept by, he realized it *was*.

He turned to Sadiqi.

"Very impressive up close," Sadiqi remarked.

"What the hell is this?" Hardin asked.

"The aircraft we have been waiting for."

"No, no, this is not what we've been waiting for. You told me a plane was coming to lift me out of here. A small plane. Not a fucking jumbo jet. Where the hell is that going to take me?"

"Nowhere," Sadiqi said. "This has nothing to do with you. This is *my* plane. The one that will deliver *your* bomb."

Hardin looked from Sadiqi to the 747, then back to Sadiqi. A sickly feeling began to grow in his stomach. A sense of foreboding as he started to turn things over in his mind.

"You told me that bomb was to do with a local war. You wanted something that could be delivered in the trunk of a car."

Sadiqi was watching the 747 as it turned on its landing approach. "Oh, that," he said. "I lied, Hardin. You're an American, so you will understand what lies are. Your country has been doing that to us for years."

"Jesus Christ," Hardin said. "Where is that bomb going?"

"I suppose it is safe to tell you now. The bomb is going to be delivered to New York."

"You son of a bitch," Hardin yelled. "What the hell are you doing?"

Sadiqi moved to one side, out of Hardin's line of vision. Hardin turned to find him, then felt the cold muzzle of an autopistol as it was pressed against the side of his head. For a fleeting moment he recalled his brief fantasy about wondering what it would be like to hold a gun against his head and press the trigger. That moment vanished when Sadiqi did pull the trigger.

Hardin found his answer, and it was like nothing he could have imagined.

Sadiqi put away the pistol. He didn't even bother to look at the dead man sprawled in the dust. He beckoned to a couple of his people.

"Take that away and bury it," he said, then picked up the attaché case of money and made his way to the former control tower. He climbed to the control room and stepped inside. There were three of his men in the room. One sat at a radio, in contact with the 747's pilot.

"You should be able to see the runway now. It has been cleared for landing. The length is a little under what you would prefer, but I have no doubt you will make a satisfactory landing. Do exactly as you have been instructed and land. If not, the plane will be subject to a bomb blast that will cripple it and you will crash. The choice is yours, Captain."

Sadiqi tapped the man on the shoulder.

"Will he do it?"

The radio operator shrugged.

"It's up to him."

Sadiqi sighed. He was becoming impatient. It was vital that the next part of the operation go ahead without too much delay. There was a great deal to do.

He went outside to where one of his men was studying the 747 through powerful glasses.

"Well?" Sadiqi asked.

"He's coming in. Yes. He's put down his landing gear and flaps."

"Good. Let's get everyone ready. I want that aircraft surrounded and made secure."

THE 747 MADE its landing on the first run. The wheels threw up great clouds of choking dust as the airliner touched the runway. The surface was less than perfect due to neglect and the pilot had to hold the aircraft steady. Because of his skill he kept the 747 on line, braking smoothly and compensating for the undulating surface. He brought the aircraft to a stop with feet to spare.

"I wouldn't want to see that done a second time," one of Sadiqi's companions remarked.

Sadiqi made no comment. His throat was dry from watching the great airplane make its landing. When he felt able he turned and waved to the waiting trucks. They pulled away and followed the 747 as it turned at the end of the runway. Sadiqi watched them pull in line with the aircraft, then went across to his waiting military-style jeep and climbed in. He nodded to his driver and they moved off.

By the time he reached the aircraft the engines were already shut down and the swirling dust was drifting away. The jeep circled the 747, coming to a stop where Sadiqi could stand and look up at it.

One of the trucks had an aluminum access platform roped down on the rear. Willing hands manhandled the structure from the truck and pushed it into place in line with the hatch that swung open. The moment it was in place armed men from the other truck climbed up into the 747. As the last of them vanished inside, Hanni Amir appeared in the door and came down the steps to greet Sadiqi. They embraced for a few seconds, then Sadiqi stepped back.

"Here is your plane," Amir said.

"I never doubted it," Sadiqi replied. "I knew you would do it."

"The worst moment was when we were landing. For one moment I thought we were going to go off the runway."

"The pilot is very good," Sadiqi said. "We must look after him. After all, we need him to carry on the flight to New York, don't we?"

"His name is Percy Dexter. When I first spoke to him, he was certain I wanted him to crash the plane into something. But I told him all we wanted was to use his plane and passengers in a negotiation.''

"Did he believe you?''

Amir shrugged. "The fact he is still alive and on the ground should help convince him.''

"The passengers?''

"There was a little panic at first. Now they seem to have accepted their fate.''

"We need to keep them calm.'' Sadiqi beckoned one of his men. "Go on board and talk to the passengers. Allow them to use the facilities. Have the cabin crew pass out food and drink. Then bring Captain Dexter to me.''

The man left, making his way toward the 747.

"What about the bomb?'' Amir asked.

"It is waiting to be placed on board.''

"Sadiqi, are we going to succeed?''

"God willing,'' Sadiqi murmured. "Nothing is certain.''

"But it *must* succeed,'' Amir insisted. "Too much has been put into this to fail. Mansur says—''

"I understand Mansur and I understand his need for this to happen. If fate allows, we *will* succeed.''

"Take us back to the tower,'' Sadiqi told his driver.

When they arrived Sadiqi turned to Amir. The man appeared agitated, restless.

"Hanni, go and rest. You have been under a great deal of pressure. Now it's my turn. Go. Go now. That is an order.''

Amir nodded and made his way toward the tent Sadiqi pointed out to him. Sadiqi made his way back up to the control tower.

CAPTAIN PERCY DEXTER had been flying for all of his adult life. He had spent five years in the U.S. Air Force, one of his tours of duty in the Gulf War. Since then he had moved into commercial flying. The last six years had seen him at the controls of airliners. The job suited him. Dexter was a relaxed, easygoing man. The stress of the job had never bothered him. After bombing runs in the Gulf, commercial flying held no fears for him. The shock of the Trade Center attack had knocked them all back for a while, and even Dexter's cool shell had been cracked. In the aftermath there had been a great deal of speculation. People were scared to fly and the reverberations of the murderous strike had affected the whole country. But there had come the point where America had dug in its heels and had shown its strength to the world. Life went on, albeit intrinsically changed. People were more cautious. They took a step back, reassessed their lives and perhaps trusted less. But they carried on, because there was no other option. Slowly, life picked up its pace, and in Dexter's sphere, air flights began again, though under stricter control.

The flight from Athens to New York was nothing out of the ordinary. Until a hijacker revealed himself and made it clear to Dexter that he had the means to destroy the 747 if the pilot refused his demands. The hijacker had told Dexter his intention was not to destroy the plane. All the hijacker wanted was for him to change to a course heading he would provide and to fly and land the plane at a spot he would be informed about later. After talking to his flight attendant, Susan Morris, who was being held by the hijacker, and listening to the hijacker, Dexter accepted the compromise because there wasn't a damn thing he could do to reverse the situation. He did exactly what Hanni Amir told him.

With the plane on the ground Dexter and his flight crew sat it out. They hadn't been told what was going to happen. After a long forty minutes, armed men came inside the plane and asked Dexter to join them. The pilot was removed from the aircraft and ordered into a jeep. He was driven away from the 747 to what had to have been the control tower during the airstrip's working life. There were some vehicles in sight and a group of armed men patrolled the area.

Dexter was taken out of the jeep and pushed inside the tower. He went up the stairs to the control room. He noticed a satellite dish on an aluminum pole fixed to the exterior wall. He had also spotted a radar scanner turned on its base on the roof of the tower on his way across the airfield. His armed escort opened the control room door and pushed him inside.

The control room was occupied by three men, one a soft-eyed man dressed in khaki pants and shirt who seemed to be in charge.

"Please sit down, Captain Dexter," Sadiqi said to the American pilot. He waited until Dexter was seated. "I will not insult you by apologizing for our actions. But I will tell you we have no intention of causing any more inconvenience than we have to."

"Why are we here?"

"A number of our people are being held by the Americans at the military base at Guantanamo under suspicion of what you call terrorist activity. We want them released, put on a plane and flown to a destination we will specify. Once that has been done and we are assured they are safe you will be released and allowed to continue with your flight to New York. We have a fuel tanker outside and your plane will be refueled before you leave.''

"You know as well as I do that the U.S. does not negotiate with any hijackers, terrorists, or whatever you call yourselves. The government will refuse your demands. You understand that as well as I do.''

"Perhaps. But things are different now. We have nothing to do with the events of September 11, but every Islamic organization is being targeted now. Our people were not involved in any aggression against the U.S.A. We want them free. So we offer a bargain. Your people for mine. Very simple. Very clear. And I want you, Captain Dexter, to talk to your government and convince them that we are serious. Make the trade or suffer the consequences.''

"Now *that* sounds like a threat.''

Sadiqi spread his hands.

"Life determines our actions, Captain. How we see ourselves and how others see us, our personal needs make hypocrites of us all. I told you we do not wish to see your passengers inconvenienced any longer than necessary. That is true in the sense that as long as negotiations continue no harm will come to them. If your government refuses to cooperate, however, and the situation is not resolved, I will not hesitate to order the deaths of everyone on that plane.''

Percy Dexter studied Sadiqi. He had no doubt on his mind that the man meant every word he uttered. If he had learned one thing during his life, and especially when he wore the uniform of the U.S. Air Force, it was read his enemy. And he read Sadiqi clearly. The man was deadly serious. He didn't rant and rave. He had shown no desire to become violent with Dexter, or to make any injudicious threats. He simply told it as it was, which made his pronouncement concerning Dexter's passengers all the more chilling. Within the couple of minutes he had been in Sadiqi's presence, Hal Dexter knew he was looking at the face of death, and it scared the hell out of him.

"What do you want me to tell them?" he asked.

Stony Man

"LISTEN TO THIS," Carmen Delahunt said. "We picked it up during one of our scans of incoming."

She clicked the replay button and the cyberteam listened to Percy Dexter's conversation with a member of the State Department. The content of the discussion was simply stated. Dexter was the pilot of an American 747—Flight 291—that had been hijacked by a Middle East organization. Dexter had made no mention of where the plane was, most probably under instruction from his captors. The group holding the 747 and its passengers wanted the release of imprisoned members of their organization being held at Guantanamo. If their demands weren't met by a fixed time, they would destroy the plane and all the passengers.

Kurtzman listened to the relay. He tapped in a number on his phone and caught Hal Brognola in his office.

"Hal, listen to this. Carmen, patch this through to Hal's office."

Kurtzman waited while Brognola listened to the message.

"What do you think? A connection with our current mission, or just a coincidence?"

"Hard to say from that. Can you see if you can pick up anything else? See if any of our sources, willing or unwilling ones, have got anything. Satellite scans. Photos. I don't care. Tap into any damn source you can. Make it a priority."

"It's done," Kurtzman said.

"Go to it, people. We want anything and everything that might be connected to this hijack. Check passengers, too. Find out who is on board that flight and download it."

HAL BROGNOLA PUT THROUGH a call to the President. He had a more or less open line to the man at the present time. With all that was going on they needed to be able to talk as and when, without delays.

"Hal?"

"You'll have heard about this hijack and the demands of the perpetrators?"

"I came out of a briefing ten minutes ago. What's your feeling about this, Hal?"

"Sir, I'm pretty convinced it's a tie-in with Mansur and his people. Don't ask me why. Maybe I'm playing one of those hunches I get now and then."

"Hal, the day you stop getting hunches we're all going down."

"Right now I have all my people working on this.

If we can get a line on any of the hijackers we might be able to tie them in with Mansur. If we can, it's a pretty sure thing this is all part of the same game plan.''

"What about your teams?"

"On standby, sir. We just need the info."

"You have my full cooperation on this. The minute you get anything you feel is relevant just get those people moving. Don't waste time asking for me to give you the nod. You have it right now. Apart from anything else we have Americans on that plane, and I don't want their lives being put in jeopardy. You do what's needed to put an end to this. Understand? I'm leaving the decisions in your hands. We'll catch the flak later if need be.''

"That gives me a good feeling, Mr. President."

"What?"

"The way you included me in the *we'll* take the flak later.''

"Hal, I've always believed in sharing."

BROGNOLA MADE HIS WAY to the Computer Room. He arrived a couple of minutes after Barbara Price. She was deep in conversation with Kurtzman and raised a hand to acknowledge Brognola's arrival.

The big Fed crossed over to where Huntington Wethers and Carmen Delahunt were poring over computer printouts.

"Anything interesting?" Price asked.

Delahunt shook her head. "Just the results of our first scan trying to pick up where Flight 291 might have gone.''

"Akira is initiating some satellite scans," Wethers explained. "We know the usual haunts of terrorist groups in the Mid East so we're starting with those. When you subtract the places where landing a 747 wouldn't be feasible, it narrows the possibilities."

"That still leaves a fair number of sites," Price said.

Wethers smiled. "Exactly."

"So you people standing around talking isn't helping to eliminate them," Kurtzman boomed across the Computer Room.

Delahunt glanced at Price, smiling indulgently.

"What a guy," she whispered good-naturedly.

Price turned away as Delahunt and Wethers returned to their stations. She crossed to Kurtzman, thumping him on the shoulder.

"My, aren't we grumpy today?" she said. "Would a mug of coffee make us feel better?"

Kurtzman turned away from Brognola.

"Could do," he said.

"Pot's over there," Price told him, jerking her thumb in the direction of the coffee station. "And you can bring one for me while you're at it."

Kurtzman made ominous threatening noises but took his mug and wheeled his chair across the Computer Room. Watching him go, Brognola couldn't help grinning.

"How the hell do you do that? If I tried it he'd run me down."

"Hal, you either got it or you don't got it," Price said. "Listen, I just talked to Hunt. He's been on the phone to some of our intelligence contacts in the Mid East. Specifically Ben Sharon. He thinks he might have something. The feeling is there's something brewing no one can exactly put a finger on. Rumors apart, Hunt's certain it has something to do with Mansur. He's keeping up the pressure, making the rounds of everyone he knows. He has a number of contacts who are coming back to him once they have any feedback.''

"Well, let's hope it's sooner rather than later," Brognola said.

CHAPTER SEVEN

The War Room

"Phoenix Force is heading to Afghanistan," Barbara Price said, sliding files across the conference table. "Your priority target is locating Waris Mahoud. We have to find out what else he might be able to tell us about Mansur's planned strike. We're running on short time here, guys, so no sightseeing."

McCarter handed out the files to his team, and they scanned them briefly.

"The Iranians are being exceptionally helpful," Manning pointed out.

Brognola smiled. "You could say that. They are cooperating with a degree of reluctance they're finding hard to hide. I think we have to thank your pal Fayed, David. Looks as if he presented a good case on our behalf. Opened doors for us with the Iranians."

"The bloke was sound," McCarter said. "He understood how this whole thing could pan out if we don't shut Mansur down."

Rafael Encizo leaned forward, his gaze directed at Kurtzman.

"What do you make of Fayed's explanation of Mansur's vision, Aaron?"

Kurtzman considered his reply.

"We see Abrim Mansur as some kind of soulless monster, willing to destroy one of our cities in an act of senseless violence. Fayed sees him from the Islamic side. He can align himself with Mansur and even appreciate the depth of his feelings because he subscribes to the Islamic mind-set. He can put himself in Mansur's place and understand what makes the man tick. Fayed sees *why* Mansur has reached the end of his patience. He most likely has a degree of sympathy for Mansur's reasoning. But give credit to the man. Fayed also views the picture from another angle. He can see that if Mansur makes his statement it could cause ripples that might reach out and drown us all."

"Hell of an answer," Calvin James said. "I'm still not clear which way you go, though."

Kurtzman inclined his head. "You can be ambivalent about a man and his beliefs. Consider the reasons for his actions. Maybe allow a little sympathy. But come crunch time, you don't hesitate to put him down for good."

Price rattled her sheaf of papers.

"Phoenix, you'll fly in to an airbase in Tajikistan. It's being used by the U.S. and British as a staging post. From there you'll be choppered in. We have intel that came from a guy who has been recommended by our people on the ground. Seems he has good credentials as a guide. He could be a help to you."

"Okay," McCarter said. "So what's the current situation on hostiles out there at present?"

"Still a lot of malcontents around," Price said. "The Taliban might have been kicked out of power and the Northern Alliance put in charge, but up in the mountains you're liable to come across hostile groups. Let's not fool ourselves into thinking that the Taliban has vanished forever. They're still around and there are enough of them to cause problems if they decide to. Mansur has followers up there as well. And don't forget the various warlords all vying for power. If Mahoud is on the run, he'll have all that to contend with. Mansur can't afford him reaching friendly territory with vital information in his head."

Kurtzman spoke up. "We'll be running satellite sweeps of the area to see if we can spot anything."

"Just to add to what Barb mentioned, the clock *is* ticking, guys," Brognola said. "Whatever else we have going for us, time isn't on our side. I don't see this mission having a long shelf life."

"Let's go and draw our gear," McCarter said.

Brognola held up his hand.

"This is for both teams. Listen up, people. We waive the rules on this one. We lose our grip here and the consequences are too severe to even consider. The President has authorized total backup for you. All military contacts will be under presidential orders to render you any and all immediate facilities and assistance. What we have here is a *possible,* and until we find otherwise we go with that premise, possible nuclear strike on American soil. It can't be allowed to happen. Find these sons of bitches and put them down for good. I don't expect prisoners on this one, but I do expect all of you back alive and well."

"WHAT ABOUT Able?" Lyons asked.

"Don't worry. You guys aren't going to be sitting around on your butts," Brognola said.

"Man's getting tetchy," Blancanales commented.

Brognola sat back in his seat, searching his pockets. He found he had run out of antacid tablets. All he did find was a cigar still in its wrapper, so he settled for that.

"Okay. We have a few things to sort yet. The tapes and CDs David brought back from London are still with our translation team. The only thing we do know is the guy doing the talking. It's Abrim Mansur. Maybe we'll get to know something once we get the English version. In the meantime we go on what we know for certain."

"The e-mail David rescued has been translated," Price said. "It's a message to a group in Russia asking for an update on their operational status. It doesn't go in for specifics, but when we add it to some other intelligence we've gathered we start to pull threads together."

"We've received confirmation from the Russians that they have a Typhoon-class nuclear submarine missing. It has SS-N-24/26 nuclear missiles on board. And a group of Russian Muslims, all navy personnel with experience in subs, has gone AWOL. Last seen in the vicinity of the Nerpichya naval base where the missing sub was based. They vanished at the same time the sub set sail for the Safonovo Navy Yard. Nothing has been heard from the sub or the navy group since."

"That's the biggest coincidence I ever heard," Schwarz said. "Or one hell of a plan coming together."

"We see it that way," Brognola said. "So does the President. He's already been in touch with the Russian president. We have an unconditional go from the White House. The President will not countenance another September 11 scenario, especially on the scale Mansur appears to be threatening.

"Able, you'll tie up with a Russian team that has information about Gabril Yasim, Mansur's fixer. Aaron traced calls from the cell phones we appropriated. He isolated some from Yasim, talking to some guy in a settlement called Govograd. That's on the Barents Sea coast. Too much happening and a lot of the players are from Mansur's camp. We need to know why."

"I don't warm to the thought of a Russian sub carrying nuclear missiles being on the loose," Schwarz said. "Those SS-N-24 missiles have a hell of a range."

Lyons caught Brognola's eye.

"What about New York?" he asked.

Brognola spread his hands.

"That's something the President is considering right now. We are talking millions here. Plus the surrounding areas. How do you get them clear? Where do you send them? Hell, Carl, where is *safe* in a situation like this?"

None of them had an answer, and Lyons was wishing he hadn't even asked the question.

Afghanistan

THE SOUND of the U.S. Army UH-60 Black Hawk helicopter faded as it turned and set a return course for Parkhar Airbase in Tajikistan, leaving Phoenix Force alone on the windswept Afghan hill slope.

"So all we have to do is meet up with this guide?" Hawkins said. He took in the desolate terrain, the folds and high slopes of barren rock. Very little vegetation. Wind blew across the landscape, picking up dust and carrying it along its path. The occasional flurry of snow warned of hard weather closing in. The sky was pale, with a hard, cold look to it. "Shouldn't be hard to find him out here."

"You want it easy?" Manning asked.

Hawkins grinned. "I love a challenge."

McCarter took out the GPS unit and established their position. According to the readout, they were within ten miles of the rendezvous point.

"Listen up, ladies," he said. "We go southwest. The satellite recon shows the meeting point pretty clear. The good news is we'll not reach the target before dark, so at least we'll have that for cover."

"See, he's making it easy for us again," James said.

"Just for that you can take point," McCarter told him.

James grinned and moved out, the others falling in line. McCarter took position behind James, using the GPS unit to keep them on track.

They were equipped for what they hoped would be a short insertion. They carried 9 mm handguns, Beretta 92-Fs, except for McCarter, who still favored his

Browning Hi-Power. Personal preference knives were strapped to legs. Each man also had an M-16 A-2 rifle, and Calvin James had an attached M-203 grenade launcher below the barrel of his. Extra ammunition for each weapon was held in pouches clipped to the web harness they wore over their cold-weather combat suits. In addition each wore a woolen cap and gloves against the expected cold of the Afghan climate. Scarves were wound around their necks as added protection. Rucksacks held a small selection of equipment and rations. Water canteens were clipped to their belts.

In order to maintain contact they were all wearing microphone and headset communication gear, powered by packs clipped to their waist belts. Each of the five carried a homing signal device that could be used to call in a pickup helicopter once they were in close proximity to the border with Tajikistan.

The terrain proved to be more than a simple challenge. It was some of the most inhospitable country Phoenix Force had encountered. There wasn't a single uniform stretch of terrain. It rose and fell in a series of ridges, deep fissures and undulating slopes. The chill wind picked up dust, swirling it around them, seeking ways into their clothing and finding every exposed portion of flesh. They were forced to wrap their scarves around their mouths to reduce the amount of dust they inhaled. The constant battle against steep slopes and the rough ground made walking an effort. Absorbing the discomfort, Phoenix Force pushed on. They took whatever the elements threw at them, expecting nothing else and accepting it as part of the job. If any of them had wanted a quiet, comfortable life, the last thing they would have done was join Phoenix Force.

McCarter called a halt after the first two hours. As the team sought cover beneath a wide overhang, the Briton took out the GPS unit and took another reading. He checked this against the map he carried and verified they were on track. With that done he joined the others.

"Look at this," Encizo said.

He indicated the area beneath the rock. There were footprints, indications that others had used the same overhang to shelter under. Farther back, where the eroded rock had opened a shallow cave, they found a scattering of shredded tobacco and some ash. Manning spotted the impression in the dust where a rifle butt had rested.

"Any suggestions?" McCarter asked. "They don't look all that old to me."

Manning agreed. "No more than a few hours. Wind would have blown all this away if it had been around longer. Footprints aren't even filled with drifting dust yet."

"They're not military boots from the pattern," Encizo said. "I'd say local boys. Not the ones we want to run into."

"How many?" McCarter asked. "I see at least three."

"Something like that," Encizo said, scanning the footprints. "Could be others in the area."

They took the opportunity to rinse the dust out of their mouths and take a drink.

"We have to expect locals," McCarter said. "Can't avoid it in the current situation. Could be pro-Taliban groups, or even Taliban themselves. These people are going to be anticipating armed incursions, so there's not going to be any pleasant walks in the sun. Over the past few months they've had covert U.S. teams in and out. The SAS as well. So any locals we come across are going to be hard-liners who aren't going to be too easy on us. Let's remember that. Unless you have a death wish, ladies, don't be too slow when it comes to defending yourselves. In this situation giving the other bloke the benefit of the doubt *will* get you killed.''

''It's times like these I can't wait for,'' James said. ''One of David's team pep talks. Always set me up for what's coming.''

''What else am I here for?'' McCarter said. ''My next text is titled, Up off Your Arses and Let's Get Moving.''

T. J. HAWKINS, WITH THE SWIFT responses of a reactive fighter, caught a shadow of movement off to his left and at a higher elevation. He swiveled his torso, bringing his M-16 A-2 with him, finger already slipping inside the trigger guard. He framed the lean figure in his sights, seeing in that frozen microsecond the autorifle braced against the man's shoulder. Behind the weapon he saw a taut, bearded face. They fired together, the sniper loosing off a single shot that struck rock only inches from Calvin James, his attention disturbed by Hawkins's suddenly spotting him. Hawkins triggered a 3-round burst, finding his target and punching ragged holes through his chest and left shoulder, kicking the shooter back from the wedge of rock he had leaned out from.

Phoenix Force scattered, each man seeking cover, and for a moment there was only the sound of pounding boots. Disturbed dust was caught by the wind and tossed about in misty spirals. Pebbles bounced as they were scuffed off the ground.

Crouching on the spot where he fired from, Hawkins scanned the slope above their position. He saw the sniper's dropped rifle lying just below the rock that had concealed the man. A flap of cloth floated into sight from behind the rock and waved like a lone flag.

Cold wind drifted in, muting the sound of the gunshots, leaving only the rattle of dust behind. Hawkins waited, his eyes narrowed. His open position, as well as leaving him exposed to enemy fire, gave him a wider view of the fire zone. Hawkins felt he should have moved, taken cover like the rest of the team. The seconds that had passed were still minuscule, no more than a span of a few breaths.

Hawkins heard the rattle of loose pebbles, followed by the unmistakable chink of an ammunition belt. He twisted and caught the outline of a black muzzle showing above a boulder no more than ten feet to his right. Hawkins flipped the selector of his rifle to single shot and brought his M-16 around, making target acquisition as the cloth-wrapped head came into view. His eyes met those of the enemy. The man realized his mistake an instant too late. Hawkins tripped the M-16's trigger and placed two close shots through the target's forehead, taking out the back of his skull as the terrible force slapped the guy to the ground.

McCarter saw Hawkins's second takedown. He was scanning the area himself, as were the others, and they picked out a few more targets as the opposition made a concerted attack, yelling wildly in an attempt to unnerve their enemy. They had chosen the wrong team to scare. The high, shrill cries were ignored as Phoenix Force returned the volleys aimed at them. The defile echoed to the sound of bullets bouncing off rock obstructions and whining into space.

Leaning against his sheltering rock, McCarter led his first target, eased back the trigger and put the man down with a single shot. The running man hit the ground on his face, the momentum of his forward motion dragging him across the ground until he came to a shuddering stop against a large chunk of rock embedded in the hard earth.

Encizo, James and Manning were similarly engaged, weapons spitting out lethal bursts as they clashed with their attackers.

The whole exchange lasted no longer than twenty seconds. Autofire and single shots blended. The hard impact of ricochets burned off rocks. Dust and gunsmoke wreathed the air, and the frantic struggle swept both sides along in its heady mix of sheer adrenaline rush and the wild fear that ran rampant during close-combat encounters. There was little time for anything other than aim and fire, turn, seek a target and fire again, all the time hoping no one had you in his sights. It ended with the survivors, still on a high, sweeping the area for any target that might have been overlooked. Sweat sheened the flesh and pulse rates surged almost to overload levels. And then, as the realization came that it was all over, came the slow descent to normality.

"ANY INJURIES?" McCarter asked.

Heads shook, each man checking his teammates to see if they were all telling the truth.

"That came out of the blue," James murmured. He dusted himself off and caught Hawkins's eye. "Hey, T.J., my man, sharp spotting there."

"Time he started earning his pay," McCarter said without a trace of a smile.

"Reckon that one should earn me a bonus," Hawkins stated.

Somebody snorted with laughter. It was Encizo.

"He wants a bonus. Hey, hombre, where you think you are? Somewhere where someone gives a damn?"

Hawkins smiled. "You don't ask, you don't get."

"At least he got the last part right," Manning said.

They checked out the fatalities. The dead men were clad in clothing for the terrain. They had carried Kalashnikovs that were far from new. The weapons had the look of hard usage about them, the metal bluing rubbed away in places to show the bright steel beneath.

"What do you think?" James asked. He was carefully going through the clothing of one of the dead men, searching for ID or anything that might indicate the owner's background.

His search did turn up a wad of currency, and some folded papers showing an image of Abrim Mansur and lines of script. James showed the papers to his teammates.

"For or against? Hard to tell with these guys. They don't seem to do much to show who they favor."

Manning checked the papers, turning them over in his hands as he studied the script.

"This could be a wanted poster for Mansur. On the other hand it could be a message urging his followers to keep the faith."

Encizo and Hawkins inspected the papers.

"I favor the last suggestion," the Cuban said. "I didn't see these guys as wanting to do *us* any favors."

McCarter was prowling the area, checking out the slopes rising ahead of them. His view was tempered by the knowledge that the sound of their clash with the opposition could have been heard by others of the same group. He wasn't nervous, simply cautious. Their presence in this part of the country wouldn't be viewed with anything less than hostility by the occupying force. Phoenix Force had a mission: to locate and, if possible, extract the Iranian undercover agent who carried information vital to the location of Abrim Mansur and his ongoing operation. On paper the operation sounded straightforward. In and out in the shortest time possible. But McCarter took the view that life had the ability to change at will. It made no concessions, seeming to deliberately present the most difficult obstacles with a perverse delight. Looking at it pragmatically, the Briton had to admit it made for an interesting, if not bloody hard, struggle.

He rounded off his check and turned back to the rest of the team. They were spaced out, each man watching a different point of the compass, weapons at the ready.

"Let's go, lads, we've spent too much time around

here. Eyes and ears on full scan. I don't want to let any more of these buggers get the drop on us."

James took up point again as they strung out, moving as fast as they could without relaxing their observation of the surrounding terrain. Manning brought up the rear, constantly checking their backtrail. They were moving deeper into enemy-held territory, looking to link up with a single individual, aware that the opposition would also be looking for them.

THE WEATHER WAS changing imperceptibly. Any warmth they had felt began to drift away, bringing a keen chill to the air. Overhead, the sky lost its sharp aspect as gray clouds began to show. The temperature began to drop rapidly. The ever-present wind touched their skin with chill fingers. Occasional flakes of snow drifted into view, followed by fierce, short flurries. On the higher slopes the snow began to build until the jagged rocks were covered with a thin layer.

"We'll need to find shelter if this keeps up," Encizo said. He was close behind McCarter.

"Don't bloody remind me," the Briton said. "Pass the word back. Any place we can find."

WARIS MAHOUD FELT the darkness closing in. The light was fading quickly and he could feel the temperature dropping. He was aware of his exposed condition. Not just to his pursuers, but to the extremes of the weather in these bleak mountains. Survival from both depended on his keeping moving. If he stopped to find shelter, he would most likely die from the cold. He had nothing to protect him from the long, cold night ahead. Those following him would be equipped for the prevailing conditions, and they wouldn't stop, either.

He leaned against a crumbling section of rock, taking a brief moment to catch his breath. Already his hands were stiff from the cold. Mahoud pushed them into the pockets of his thin jacket. Now he was still he began to feel the effects of the recent beating he had endured while in captivity. His ribs hurt and so did his lower back where someone had repeatedly kicked him. The left side of his face pained him. It was like a nagging toothache. Reaching up, he touched his cheek and felt the swelling over the bone. His fingers moved down to his ragged beard where he could feel crusted blood. The left side of his mouth was torn, the lip thick and raw.

Mahoud put his back to the rock and stared at the distant line of the mountain peaks. His wish was that he might have been closer to the border with Iran. His homeland. Fate had decreed otherwise and the line of least travel was the one that would take him to Tajikistan. He knew there were American forces based there, so if he managed to reach that far he might reach comparative safety. Not that he believed too much in the concept. What was safe any longer? The word had become almost superfluous when placed against the current world situation. Life had become a day-to-day survival test. Every twist and turn held threats and danger, there were few people to be trusted any longer, and a strange madness had infected humankind.

Mahoud pushed away from the rock, muttering to himself. Was it his weariness that was making him harbor such thoughts? He could only assume that was the reason. He was usually much more optimistic in his outlook. But events of the past days had taken much of his natural energy and left him with muddled thoughts and flitting images of doom.

He forced himself to concentrate on the way ahead, pulling his clothing closer to his body, trying to shut out the cold. He felt the touch of wet snow against his face. The chill cleared his mind for a time, allowing him to check his bearings and establish his course toward the distant peaks. He tried to work out time and distance, but the calculation eluded him. Mahoud finally gave up. He would move on, with the mountains as his marker. If God willed it, he would reach the border—if not he would have to accept that as well.

"WE ARE NOT GOING TO FIND him before dark," Ashok said bitterly. "If he keeps moving, he might reach the border before we get to him."

No one said anything. They could see that Ashok was becoming angry, and when he was angry it wasn't wise to contradict anything he said or did. In this case he was most likely correct. The fugitive, Mahoud, had eluded them during the daylight hours, and with the onset of night tracking him would prove to be both difficult and fruitless. The rocky foothills, giving way to the steeper slopes and ravines, were hard enough to negotiate during daylight hours. Once it was dark, searching for something as small as a single man would only add to the problem.

Ashok took another few moments to study the map of the area again. He bent his head over it, tracing invisible lines with his finger, crisscrossing the area they were trying to cover.

"We know he is deliberately staying away from the regular trails," he said. "That will make his journey longer and the terrain will slow him. Unfortunately that applies to us, as well. Mahoud knows the territory, possibly better than we do."

Ashok folded the map and stuffed it back into a large pocket in his coat.

"We'll move on, set as fast a pace as we can." He made sure all his men could hear him. "Make sure you have everything you need. Get what you want from the truck. We leave it here. Two men stay with it to maintain radio contact with us and base. Go and gather your equipment. We leave in twenty minutes. Forget anything, and you will have to do without it."

Ashok beckoned to his second in command.

"Pick two to stay with the truck. Make sure the men have what they need."

The man turned away. Ashok thrust his hands deep into the pockets of his heavy combat coat, hunching his shoulders against the cold. Snowflakes brushed his face. He raised his eyes to the dark peaks of the mountains, wondering where Mahoud was at the moment. One thing he could be sure of. Mahoud would go on until he dropped through sheer exhaustion, or was caught. Ashok had admiration for his dedication. Mahoud was the enemy, but at least he was a worthy one. If it became necessary, Ashok would kill the man without hesitation. But that didn't prevent him from respecting his quarry.

Ashok was in the lead when they moved off, cradling his AK-74 against his chest as they pushed up into the foothills. Shadows were starting to slide across the landscape, bringing more cold wind and heavier snow. Ashok had calculated they had less than an hour before it would be completely dark. That time would bring them closer to Mahoud. He might not be carrying as much equipment as they were, but he didn't have protective clothing, or weapons, and he would be affected by the lowering temperature faster than they would. The extreme cold would slow him down.

Ashok reminded himself of the possibility they might run into the American commandos who had been infiltrated into the area in an attempt to find Mahoud. He hoped that they were intercepted before that happened. That was up to Shakir, who was on his way to meet them. The Americans believed Shakir was sympathetic to their cause. It would be a great surprise when they learned that Shakir was one of Mansur's followers, working as a double agent.

THE MEN of Phoenix Force kept moving until the changing weather and the darkness forced them to halt. Snow was sweeping down off the higher peaks, clinging to them as the cold froze it on their clothing. The swirling flakes cut their field of vision down to no more than ten to twelve feet in any direction. When McCarter checked his GPS unit, he saw they were still on course, but had not made as good a time as anticipated.

McCarter glanced at his watch. It was almost 8:30 p.m. He pulled his insulated glove back over his hand and turned to bring the others to him. He had to call into his mike a couple of times to attract James, who was yards ahead.

"No point trying to go much farther in this," he said. "Someone is going to fall off one of these bloody drops. We'll just have to sit this out until it eases. We won't be any help to anyone if we end up with broken legs."

"What about Shakir?" Encizo asked. "He's going to be in the same position."

"If he's out in this, I hope he has the sense to take cover," McCarter said.

"I think I saw a place we can use as shelter," James said. "Just ahead when you called me."

He led the way and they spotted what he was indicating. Not so much a cave as a scooped-out hollow with a narrow projection jutting overhead. The team crowded into the shelter, each man finding himself a spot.

"This is going to be cozy," James muttered.

Encizo took off his backpack and unzipped one of the side pockets. Slipping off his gloves he pulled out an aluminum can, upended it and pressed the plastic base, shaking the contents, then sat back to wait for the result. The can contained coffee, now undergoing the process of self-heating. Phoenix had been offered a supply of the cans by the U.S. task force based at Parkhar Airbase in Tajikistan. Sitting in the dark on a snowy slope, Encizo felt the can warming up in his hands. He clasped it, feeling the heat against his skin. The process took about three minutes. By then the coffee had been heated significantly. Encizo popped the tab and took a drink. The coffee was hot and very welcome.

The others watched this with interest.

"Is it okay?" Manning asked.

Encizo nodded. "Go for it,"

"Pity they can't do a Coke that chills itself in the can," McCarter said as he waited for his drink to heat up. He sat watching Manning struggling with his own can.

"Just can't please some folk," James said. He shook his head. "Chilled Coke."

Manning took a swallow of coffee. "Not bad," he said.

"All the comforts of home," James commented.

"You really live like this?" Encizo asked. "Cal, I know bag ladies with a better lifestyle than this."

McCarter chuckled to himself. He studied his team, knowing that he was looking at the finest group of operatives any commander could have under him. They took on anything and anyone, never stepping back from any challenge, no matter how dire it might be. On mission after mission, Phoenix Force went into action against disparate groups who were attacking, on different levels, the very core of Western society. The reason might be political. Religious. Created from sheer greed, or a deep-seated grievance that could, from the opposition's viewpoint, only be solved through brutal violence against their fellow man. None of the reasons fazed Phoenix Force. When the word went out, and the call was received, the Force reacted. In the time honored way of the fighting warrior they accepted their lot, good, bad, or indifferent, and stayed the course, making every second count.

Like now. Sitting on a freezing Afghan mountain in the dark and making light about the usage of self-heating coffee cans.

And they call me crazy, McCarter thought.

HARD WIND DROVE the snow across the empty slopes with maniacal fury. It sought out every nook and cranny, peppered the sheltering men of Phoenix Force and, despite the cold-weather gear they wore, the cold got through. The five-man team sat it out with bitter determination. The mission was all. It was their responsibility and carrying it through was uppermost in their minds. Cold. Uncomfortable. Deep in hostile territory. None of those conditions made any difference to their objective. If Mahoud was alive, if they reached where he was being held, if they succeeded in freeing him, then some physical discomfort could be accepted.

It was well after midnight when the storm abated to the point where Phoenix Force was able to break cover and take up its forced march. The ground was hard underfoot, covered in places with a brittle layer of frozen snow. In other places the wind had pushed the snow into drifts. The air they breathed was sharp, icy cold, and it stayed that way as they trudged through the darkness. Heads down, weapons cradled to their chests, they moved across the barren, unfriendly landscape in edgy silence.

McCarter checked his GPS unit a number of times. They were still on course, though now hours late. There was nothing McCarter could do about that.

There had been no point in trying to keep moving during the height of the storm. They would have become lost in the white fog of snow swirling back and forth across the mountain slopes. That would have achieved nothing.

Dawn was on them when Phoenix Force approached the meeting place. Pale light showed the surrounding terrain. It was layered with snow now, the ground underfoot hard and icy.

McCarter called a halt. He stepped up alongside James and they scanned the area.

"What do think?" McCarter asked.

"Too quiet. Too still," James said. "I didn't expect a brass band, but there's something wrong here."

"You said it, chum," McCarter said. Via his mike he warned the others to spread out. "Start to ease back to those rocks. Sooner we reach cover the happier I'll feel."

James looked around casually, then began to stroll back the way he'd come. Facing the rest of the team, he used his concealed left hand to indicate they should keep backing off. The others picked up James's signals, except for Hawkins, who had been moving in toward McCarter from the far right. For some reason he seemed to have missed McCarter's radio call. He also missed James's signals as he approached McCarter. The Briton spotted him too late to warn Hawkins.

Moving shapes some distance ahead of McCarter and Hawkins alerted them to unexpected company.

"Bloody hell, T.J.," McCarter said.

"What's going on, boss?" Hawkins asked.

McCarter nodded in the direction of the armed figures emerging from the cover of rocks just ahead of them. "I'll let you figure it out," he said. He spoke quickly into his mike, warning the other three to stay well away until he established what *was* going on.

Moving in the front line of the armed figures was the man McCarter recognized from the file photo he'd been shown back at Parkhar Airbase.

Shakir.

The man who was supposed to be here to lead them to Waris Mahoud.

Shakir raised an arm and shouted a command. Smoke canisters were lobbed in the direction of the Phoenix Force pair, thick white clouds starting to form, cutting McCarter and Hawkins off from the rest of the team.

"You can die right here if you wish. Or you can surrender," Shakir said. "It is your choice."

CHAPTER EIGHT

Shakir had double-crossed them. He was with the op-position. McCarter knew this was always on the cards when dealing with go-betweens. It was an acceptable risk, but when it did happen that did little to ease the anger.

"You have to give up," Shakir yelled. "Now."

The thick smoke billowed, isolating the Briton and Hawkins from the rest of the team. McCarter swung around and checked to their right. It looked clear. He was aware their options were being reduced quickly. Combat wasn't a static situation. Movement between combatants was liable to sudden, unexpected change, and the trick was in being able to flow with those changes.

"T.J., with me," he called.

Hawkins responded without question, tracking McCarter while still keeping an eye on the converging opposition.

They cleared the immediate area, stepping into an open area of flatland streaked with snow. On the far side a line of ragged stone, man-high, enclosed the area. McCarter preferred to view the rocks as a possible line of cover. A gust of wind came sweeping in and dragged some of the drifting smoke between McCarter and Hawkins and the advancing opposition. The Briton yelled to Hawkins to make a direct line for the rocks. There was no telling how soon the enemy might appear from the smoke, but they had to make the best use of that time in their effort to avoid confrontation in such an open piece of the terrain.

They were yards from the rock, boots pounding the ground, breath gusting from their lungs, when armed figures stepped into view from their intended cover. McCarter counted at least six, with autorifles held ready. Shakir was still in the lead. They had anticipated McCarter's move and had blocked it.

The Briton had to fight back the temptation to put a shot through the man's grinning face. He held back. Now wasn't the time. But he wasn't going to forget.

Other armed men came out of the smoke, converging on the Phoenix Force pair. Behind them the rattle of autofire told them the rest of the team was putting up strong resistance to the appearance of Shakir's men.

"Son of a bitch," Hawkins said bitterly.

"My thoughts exactly, mate," McCarter said, lowering his weapon. "T.J., don't give them the satisfaction. They need us alive. If they didn't, we'd be dead already. Leave it alone." Under his breath he added, "For now."

Into his mike he said, "Withdraw, team. They've got us cold. That's an order. No point all of us catching it."

Hawkins aimed the muzzle of his M-16 A-2 toward the ground. He did it with a great deal of reluctance. Like McCarter, he was a man who hated giving in to the enemy. It went against his nature, but despite that he was able to see the other side of the coin. Any resistance at this moment in time would only get him killed, with the chance that McCarter might be included. Hawkins wouldn't allow that to happen.

"This I don't like, boss," he whispered.

"How do you think I feel? Holding up my hands to these miserable bastards isn't doing my image much bloody good."

Shakir moved out to confront them. He was still smiling, and he seemed to be enjoying the situation.

"Not so high and mighty now," he said. "And you imagined you were going to walk in and make fools of the simple local peasants."

"Only one," McCarter said, "by the name of Shakir."

The smile vanished. Shakir yelled something McCarter didn't understand, then lunged forward and lashed out, the knuckles of his left hand catching McCarter across the cheek. The blow had enough force to push the Briton off balance. As McCarter pulled himself upright, he tasted blood inside his mouth where a tooth had cut into his cheek. He could feel the cold air against the spot where Shakir had hit him.

Shakir was flexing his left hand. McCarter could see that he had split the skin over three of his knuckles. The sight gave him a little satisfaction.

Shakir called his group to him. He ordered McCarter and Hawkins to be disarmed and searched for additional weapons. Their headsets and microphones were stripped off. McCarter watched as they were thrown aside. Once this had been done their hands were tied behind them. Shakir took the GPS unit and studied it carefully. He glanced at McCarter, holding up the unit.

"Very clever," he said, then turned and hurled the unit at the nearest rock, fracturing the casing and the screen. "Think you could find your way without it?"

"Every time you open your mouth you just prove what an idiot you are," Hawkins said.

"You wanted to see where Mahoud stayed?" Shakir made an exaggerated gesture. Looking away then back again. "You can have the cell next to his. I suggest you don't get too comfortable. You will not be staying long."

THEY TREKKED through the snow for twenty minutes before they reached a temporary campsite, where more armed men waited. They had a battered Toyota pickup with an open back. As McCarter and Hawkins were recognized as Westerners, some of the waiting men came up to them, shouting abuse and waving their arms. They launched a short but painful physical attack on the Phoenix Force pair before Shakir stepped in and ordered them back. He was taking pleasure in seeing McCarter and Hawkins being hurt.

"Be careful how you treat them," he said to McCarter and Hawkins as the two men were roughly pushed into the rear of the Toyota. "These men have lost family and friends from American bombing."

At least six of the armed fighters crowded into the pickup. They shoved and kicked McCarter and Hawkins to the wet, filthy floor as the vehicle's engine was coaxed into life. The pickup swayed and rattled down a long, rocky slope, sending up a dirty spray of snow as it sped along a barely visible trail. Any springs it might have once boasted were badly worn, as were the shock absorbers. The pickup bounced and jolted with increasing severity. Lying facedown on the floor, McCarter and Hawkins were on the receiving end of every hard bounce the truck made. They endured the discomfort in silence, knowing that their captors were just waiting for them to protest. As it was, they were repeatedly kicked and jabbed with autorifles the entire journey.

The ride lasted for over an hour. By the time the pickup arrived at its destination McCarter and Hawkins were aching from head to toe. Under their clothing their bodies were bruised and battered. As soon as the Toyota ground to a stop, they were dragged out and thrown to the ground. It was cold and wet, the earth under the snow as hard as iron. The pair were made to stay on their stomachs while there was a heated argument. McCarter could only understand a little of what was being said. He worked out that some of the men wanted to stand him and Hawkins against a wall and shoot them. Shakir had to convince them that their prisoners had possible information that might be of help. They had to be kept alive so they could be questioned.

The discussion ended. McCarter and Hawkins were hauled to their feet and directed toward a stone building that appeared to be the focal point of the ramshackle encampment they had arrived at. Tents and small huts made up the rest of the place. There were stacks of wooden boxes that McCarter took for weapons and ammunition supplies. To one side he spotted a couple of D-30 Howitzers and an MRL-24. There was also a multiple rocket launcher fixed on the back of an old Soviet truck. Some distance away stood another truck. The Briton glanced across at Hawkins, who nodded. He'd seen the ordnance himself.

A thick wooden door was opened and they were shoved inside the stone building. It was badly lit inside and possessed a stench that washed over the Phoenix Force duo the moment they entered the place.

Shakir spoke to his men. Somebody laughed. Without another word they moved on their prisoners. A rifle butt caught Hawkins alongside the head, dropping him to his knees. McCarter fared little better. He was sent reeling from a barrage of blows that pushed him against the wall. The Briton stood his ground, resisting the brutal attack for as long as he could before the sheer ferocity knocked him off his feet. The beating stopped as quickly as it had started. McCarter felt himself being dragged across the rough earth floor. He managed to lift his head, peering through half-closed eyes as he was pulled to his feet. They were in a short passage. To their right a stone outer wall. On their left a wooden door. McCarter felt the rope being removed from his wrists. One of his captors opened the door and McCarter was hurled into the room beyond with enough force to bounce him off the far wall. He fell to the floor where he lay, stunned and silent. He heard a harsh scuffle followed by the sound of blows. Hawkins's angry voice could be heard as he fought against his captors. McCarter heard his partner being thrown to the floor. The door was closed with a crash, bolts being slammed home.

Silence enveloped McCarter. Under his breath he swore forcibly, angry at being so neatly caught unprepared, angry at Shakir's betrayal. McCarter felt he had walked into Shakir's trap with his eyes wide shut. He felt like a rookie, straight out of boot camp. The Briton wallowed in self-pity for a full five seconds, then turned that feeling into cool, controlled anger. Determination overwhelmed his basic need to take Shakir's skull in both hands and crush it like an eggshell, and McCarter set himself the task of evaluating his and Hawkins's position and how to get out of it. He had no intention of letting Shakir get away with his traitorous actions. Justice would be swift.

A GROAN OF PROTEST erupted beside McCarter. The Briton pushed himself into a sitting position and leaned against the wall, swiveling his head to look in Hawkins's direction. The younger commando had managed to sit up himself. He had his head in his hands, shaking it gently. McCarter could see blood on Hawkins's hands.

"T.J?"

"Not so damn loud, boss, my head hurts," Hawkins muttered. "What the hell was that all about?"

"We have been thoroughly shafted, my son," McCarter said. "Caught, plucked and well and truly fucked."

"Shakir." Hawkins forgot his aching skull, dropping his hands from his face. Blood was smeared across one cheek from a raw gash and Hawkins's mouth and nose were running red. "Looks like he had everybody fooled."

"I guess the opposition pay better."

"He'd better spend it before I get my hands on him," Hawkins said. "That mother is dead."

"Hey," McCarter chided. "You get in line, mate. He's mine."

Hawkins shoved to his feet, favoring his left side where someone had laid in with a hard boot. He wandered around the small, grubby room, kicking old newspapers out of the way. There was only one window and it had a heavy iron frame secured to the wall. He turned his attention to the door, only to discover that it was constructed from thick, solid wood.

"This is not good, boss," he said. "They don't want us to get out of here."

McCarter climbed to his feet and took in the room. He was rubbing his wrists where the rope had burned his skin.

"I think you're right, mate. Looks like we're going to have to wait for our chance to get out of this dump."

Hawkins slumped against the wall, sleeving blood from his face.

"This happens every time I get partnered with you," he said. "Why?"

"Lucky, I guess," McCarter said.

"I don't fell lucky."

"I was talking about me. I could be stuck here on my own."

"Keep talking like that and *I'll* go over to the other side."

McCarter made a tour of their prison. He crossed to the window and peered through the grille. He looked out on a bleak, empty landscape with little to offer if they broke out. Which was McCarter's intention. The terrain was rough, a layer of snow covering the hard ground. Little cover, so if they did get out of their cell they were going to have to move pretty fast to shake off their captors.

"Hey, what are you thinking, boss?" Hawkins asked.

McCarter turned away from the window.

"That we'll need to move bloody fast once we break out of this place."

"If they leave us alive long enough to get the chance," Hawkins said. He paused. "What the hell *do* they want?"

"That's the point, T.J. They must think we have something to tell them. They know we came to get Mahoud out. So I'm guessing they'll want to find out how much we know about whatever it is Mansur has planned. If they weren't thinking that way we'd be dead already. They wouldn't waste time keeping us alive. So we've got an edge."

"A pretty thin one," Hawkins said.

"I don't give a damn how thin as long as it keeps us breathing. And gives us the chance to get out of here as well."

Hawkins sighed. "Boss, this just keeps getting better and better."

SHAKIR SENSED TENSION in the room when he entered. He glanced from face to face. Of the three men in the room Zarinder was the only one to hold his stare. Shakir sat down and waited. Finally Zarinder let out a slow breath.

"How many more are becoming aware of our plans, Shakir?"

"I told you from the start it wasn't going to be easy keeping this secret."

"I will have a medal struck in your honor," Zarinder said dryly, "to show how right you were."

"This is no time for levity," Sharif said from his corner of the room.

Shakir held up his hands. "You mean he was being funny? And there I was thinking he meant it. Life can be a bitch."

"I believe we should be considering the consequences of this incident," Medin said. "If these men are American agents, then how many others have information about us? And how detailed is that information?"

"We don't know for certain that they know very much," Shakir said. "They came to break Mahoud out of here. For all we know they want to question him as much as we do. Perhaps their information is as poor as ours."

"Well why don't we go and question Mahoud," Zarinder said. "Oh, I forgot. You let him escape, Shakir, so even we can't ask him anything. Have you forgotten why we came here? It was so that we could escort Mahoud back to Mansur for questioning. That will not be possible unless you recapture him."

Medin banged a fist on the table to get attention.

"Can we discuss matters of importance?" he said.

"Arguing among ourselves is not helping. Let us view a few points. We now know Mahoud was infiltrated by the Iranian security force. He was undercover long enough to learn a great deal about the operation. When he realized he might be discovered, he made a telephone call to a relative in New York, telling him something was going to happen. He also let his people in London know. Then he made his escape. He almost made it to safety before our people caught up with him and brought him here.

"Warning his people in London and also giving them Khalil Hassad's name seems to have started this whole affair. Hassad is dead and the Iranian team in London has been dealt with, but now we have this damned American-sponsored team looking for Mahoud as well as ourselves. It seems to me that the Americans do not have a great deal of information because they have not been in direct contact with Mahoud. And unless Shakir has informed them otherwise they still believe he is here, locked up in a cell. Am I right?"

Shakir nodded.

"They are not aware he has escaped."

"Fine. Then let us look at another option. Disregard the intention of this team coming to Afghanistan. Consider who we have in our hands. Two people we can use if the need comes for bargaining. Or as propaganda material. These men have come into this country as agents of the U.S.A. Not as legitimate military but as covert operatives. Something for us to exploit I think."

Sharif smiled. "He is right. We can make use of

these men. A little more productive than just taking them out and shooting them.''

"Whatever you decide," Shakir said.

"We need to concentrate on the problem with Mahoud," Medin said. "If that traitor manages to reach the border and return to Iran, we could have more than just a pair of Americans to worry about."

"Should we send out more people?" Sharif asked.

Zarinder shook his head. "Too much time has passed. Our main hope is Ashok. He is already out there. If anyone can get to Mahoud before he reaches the border, it is Ashok."

"I'll go and see if we can reach him on the radio," Shakir said.

He left the room and made his way to the radio room. The operator was monitoring transmissions. He glanced up as Shakir entered.

"How long since you spoke to Ashok?"

"At least a couple of hours."

"Make contact and find out if they have had any success."

The operator nodded. He set his transmission and gave the call sign. He had activated the radio's external speaker so that Shakir could hear what was being said.

"Commander Ashok and the main team left during the night."

Shakir took the handset and spoke to the away team.

"This is Shakir. Has Ashok been in contact since they left?"

"About an hour ago. Nothing to report. They are hoping to make better headway now it is light."

"Call Commander Ashok again. Tell him we need results. Mahoud must not get across the border into Tajikistan."

Shakir didn't wait for a response. He leaned forward and broke the contact, passing the handset back to the operator.

"If anything comes through, let me know immediately."

MCCARTER HADN'T SPOKEN for some time. As far as Hawkins was concerned, it could only mean one thing. The Briton had something on his mind. He would stay with it, like a dog gnawing at a bone, until he reached a satisfactory conclusion.

"You going to tell?" Hawkins asked.

"Remember what Shakir said about Mahoud?"

"Which part?"

"He said, 'you want to see where Mahoud stayed?' Then he moved on pretty quick. Said we could have the cell next to Mahoud's."

"Okay, you've got my interest."

"T.J., he said 'stayed.'"

"Slip of the tongue?"

"I might have thought so until they tossed us in here."

"Still listening, boss."

"There is no cell next to this, T.J., I have a sneaking suspicion Mahoud has vacated the premises. He isn't here."

"He's gone over the wall?"

McCarter turned and grinned at his partner. "Too bloody right."

"You figure he's out there somewhere?"

"And heading for the border."

"Which is what we want," Hawkins said. "Isn't it?"

"Not this way. If Mahoud is on the run, you can bet Shakir and his mates will have someone on his trail. They're not going to let him go without a try at getting him back."

"And our guys don't know that," Hawkins said.

"So the sooner we get out of here the better," McCarter said.

"I hear you, boss, but saying isn't doing."

"We're not dead yet, T.J."

THE OASIS PROVIDED PEACE and isolation for Mansur. Surrounded by the eternal desert he was able to consider his options and evaluate the information that came to him from a number of distant sources. This place, almost holy in its tranquility, allowed him the time to come to the decisions that would dictate the progress of the operation already under way. Here he was able to sit in the shade of the palms, on the very edge of the pool of clear water, his reflection gazing back at him while he mulled over the data he had received.

He had been informed of the deaths of Khalil Hassad and Razak. He mourned their passing, accepting that, in the case of Hassad, he had lost a vital member of his group. Not only had Hassad been a strong presence within the group, his advice and counsel had been something Mansur had found of great importance. Now his brother had gone, his incisive mind and clever planning lost for all time. Razak, too, in his way would be sorely missed. Long established in England, Razak, as well as being a manipulative financier, had been instrumental in setting up the British cell. Now with the uncovering of his London base, the planned campaign within England had been shut down, albeit only for the time being as far as Mansur was concerned. He still had plans for the island nation, but they could be resurrected at a later date. The importance of the current planned strikes was still paramount.

One other matter still troubled Mansur. Since the incident in London, he hadn't heard from his man, Jafir. No contact either way. Mansur had tried to get in touch via cell phone but he had been unable to raise Jafir. With the London cell broken up there was no one else Mansur could contact. His concern had grown with the passing of time. Had Jafir been killed? Or taken captive? The material in Jafir's possession was what really concerned Mansur. If it fell into the wrong hands, it could interfere with his ongoing operation. Mansur considered his options, deciding to carry on. There was nothing else he could do until clearer information came his way. The loss of contact with Jafir left many unanswered questions. In the face of uncertainty the only option left to Mansur was to go forward. Too much had already been committed. Matters had progressed now, and the point of no return had been passed.

Of greater concern to Mansur had been the unsettling news that his group had been infiltrated by an undercover agent. It was known now that he was Iranian. Not that nationality made any difference. What did concern Mansur was the ongoing problem with the man—Waris Mahoud. He had preempted being discovered and had fled, though not before contacting a relative in New York to advise of a possible strike against the city. The relative had contacted the American authorities, even as a trio of Mansur's business associates had traveled to the city and enlisted the help of their drug suppliers in tracking down the relative. The kidnap of the man had been foiled by U.S. agents and in a follow-up to that the New York base of the drug dealers had been raided. In the ensuing gun battle Mansur's three associates had been shot and killed and the relative of the undercover man taken into protective custody. The Americans had taken him off the streets to some undisclosed safehouse.

Had Mahoud revealed details on the actual method of the proposed strike against the city? Mansur felt certain the agent hadn't done that, because he hadn't been allowed to gain that degree of knowledge during his time with the group. Of course it was possible he had found out more by simple subterfuge while in the presence of the group. Listening in on conversations, perhaps checking computer databases. Though he accepted these things were possible, Mansur felt reasonably confident that Mahoud had collected only basic information. To be certain it had become necessary for Mahoud to be caught and interrogated. To that end Mansur's people on the ground had tracked Mahoud to northern Afghanistan, where he was attempting to reach the safety of the border with Tajikistan. They had even succeeded in capturing the man. Mansur had sent three of his qualified people into Afghanistan to use their considerable skills to extract anything Mahoud might know, but before that happened Mahoud made a dramatic escape from the isolated encampment. The local supporters of Mansur's cause had sent out a retrieval party. Mahoud was on foot, ill-clad for the terrain and the bitter weather that engulfed the northern mountains. If he did manage to elude his pursuers, Mansur felt sure he would die somewhere in the mountain wilderness. If that happened, then his knowledge would die with him.

But now Mansur had learned that an American team of specialists had been infiltrated into the area, seeking Mahoud. This information came to Mansur from the man called Shakir. He was one of Mansur's people, working as a double agent, who had been accepted as a guide for the team of American agents. His mission brief was to lead the Americans into an arranged rendezvous with Mansur's people and capture at least one or more of them. Their capture might provide insight into how much American intelligence knew of the operation.

Mansur thought about these setbacks but refused to allow them to disturb his composure. There had always been risks associated with the operation. Until he knew for certain that any of them had created significant obstacles, the operation would move forward. He didn't relish the possibility of disruption and it remained as a nagging thought at the back of his mind, even as he contemplated the successful elements of the operation.

The American airliner had been brought safely to

earth. It stood on the resurrected runway of the abandoned airfield on the edge of the Somalian desert. Already the demands of the hijackers would have been sent to the Americans, and while that was being negotiated, the nuclear device would have been covertly loaded into the luggage compartment of the aircraft. If the plan was carried through, the hijackers would finally agree to let the plane continue on its journey to New York's JFK airport. The moment it touched down the device would be detonated by Mansur's man on the aircraft. He would die a martyr's death, along with the millions who lived in the city.

Simultaneously, the Russian Typhoon-class submarine, now in the hands of Russian Muslim dissidents, would launch its SS-N-20 missiles at the Russian oilfields.

By the time some kind of control was reestablished in Moscow and Washington the world would still be in a state of total shock at this cataclysmic attack on two of the largest nations in the world, and the Islamic world would have its long-awaited justice. The whole affair was so simple, to Mansur's way of thinking. He had known for years that this day would come. He had worked at building his power base for a long time, his quiet patience drawing a loyal and devout following. His outward calm and his subdued words had convinced so many that his was the right way, and when they saw what he had achieved his promises would be vindicated. With those two bold strikes at the heart of America and one of its new allies, Islam would be able to hold up its head and stand firm against any enemy.

Mansur's intent was also to retain control of the

submarine and its arsenal of SS-N-20 missiles. Even after the strike at the oilfields there would be four missiles remaining, armed and ready to be used. The where and when would remain a threat. Mansur wanted the West to understand that it was dealing with a group that was capable and willing to strike again. He had further strikes to make at pinpointed targets, and he would have no hesitation in issuing the order for those targets to be hit.

Mansur stepped out of the cool building he used as his personal dwelling. The bleached bricks, cast so long ago, were dusty and crumbling, but the interior of the small structure gave him shade and the opportunity to contemplate the future. He stood and watched his people moving around the oasis, busy with their individual tasks. A few hundred yards out from the oasis stood the helicopter that had brought Mansur in from the coast. It was covered with a light camouflage net that helped to conceal its presence. Not that Mansur felt any concern over being discovered. He had many sympathetic friends in Somalia. A number of his followers were from the country. Their offer of sanctuary had been welcome when Mansur had made his previous visit here before his exile in Paris. On his return his base had been provided and the airfield given over for his needs. Equipment had been installed by Sadiqi and supplies brought in.

Some distance away he could hear the muffled sound of the generator that provided electricity for the encampment. It allowed for communications and light.

Mansur crossed the sandy compound until he reached the building that actually housed the communication set up. He stepped inside and spoke to the team operating the radio. They reported that all was well at the hijacked plane site and also passed on a brief message they had deciphered. It had originated from the Russian submarine. Varic, the leader of the boarding party, had informed them that the submarine was on course for its rendezvous with the freighter bringing them the man named Seminov, who had arming and launch codes for the submarine's missiles. There would also be additional supplies for the men on the submarine that would allow it to remain submerged for a great length of time. Once the missiles had been programmed there was little anyone could do to prevent them from being used.

"Has there been any further contact with Shakir? Anything from Afghanistan?" Mansur asked one of the operators.

"Nothing. Shall I contact them and ask for an update?"

"Yes. Do that and inform me when you have their answer."

The man nodded and turned back to his communications desk.

Mansur stepped outside and stood with folded arms, deep in thought. He was concerned about the situation in Afghanistan. If the man, Mahoud, did escape and passed along any information he had obtained during his time within Mansur's group, then they might have problems. His planned attack on New York depended on secrecy. If his intention was relayed to the Americans there would be no chance of flying the nuclear device into U.S. airspace. Flight 291 would be shot down before it got within reach of the U.S. coast. If his man on board still managed to detonate the bomb, the effect would be minimal. An explosion over water would dissipate the capabilities of the nuclear device. Nothing would be achieved if that happened. Mansur felt a stirring of disappointment growing inside. If the Americans learned of his intention and prevented his carrying it out, a great deal of time and effort would be wasted. The long-term planning, the careful choice of people, and the great expense would all be for nothing.

Mansur walked slowly across the encampment, pausing at the edge of the water hole. When he stared down at the surface of the water it looked black and seemed to reflect his own dark thoughts. The desert wind had deposited a thin film of dust over the usually cool, tranquil water. At that moment the oasis failed to revive his somber mood and he turned away sharply, trying to understand why his God appeared to have deserted him in his moment of anticipated triumph.

CHAPTER NINE

Stony Man Farm, Virginia

Able Team sat in the War Room, facing Brognola and Aaron Kurtzman.

"The three guys you came into contact with in New York were associates of Gabril Yasim," Brognola said. "Ergo, a solid connection to Abrim Mansur."

"Still doesn't point us to what he's up to," Schwarz said. "All I do know is they were damned hostile."

"Listen up," Brognola said, nodding at Kurtzman.

"The computer David hauled all the way from England looked to have all data wiped from it," Kurtzman stated. "I gave it to Akira and let him loose with one of our programs. It's been designed to go into the hard drive and retrieve any information still in there. Most people believe that if you erase data you're safe. Not true. Fragments of information can be lost in a kind of cyberlimbo in the hard drive, even though they've been deleted. Needs some coaxing, but there are ways of bringing it back. It isn't always a hundred percent, but generally there's enough to piece together."

"And?" Lyons prompted.

Kurtzman smiled. He tapped at the keyboard set on the conference table and displayed data on one of the wall monitors.

"This is the original mess we retrieved."

As far as Able Team was concerned, they might as well have been looking at text in Serbo-Croatian.

"We cleaned it up," Kurtzman added.

He tapped in new commands and the screen displayed more data. This time it was in English.

"Still looks like spaghetti pie to me," Lyons grumbled.

"Okay," Kurtzman said. "We have a freighter named the *Red Star*. Very Russian and very tacky. Runs around the coast of northern Russia along to Finland and Sweden at one end of its limit and then as far as eastern Siberia at the other. Takes on cargo here and there, drops it off likewise. Nothing spectacular. The data we found refers to the identification of the vessel.

"Once we had the name I did some further checking on the *Red Star*. She's a coastal rust bucket. Small crew. Diesel powered. Owned until last year by a family concern who it appears were in financial difficulties. They sold out to a guy who came up with the asking price. Since then *Red Star* has changed hands twice. Each time to individuals who came out of nowhere. So more checks showed they have one thing in common. Paid cash up front. When you look at it, who would want to buy a no-hope ship like *Red Star*?"

"Change of ownership so regularly says someone might be funding the payroll for their own purpose," Blancanales suggested. "Like getting their hands on the ship without being known? Change of papers. Cash buy. Real owner stays in the background and just throws money around."

"Right on the button, Pol," Kurtzman said. "So you'll like this. The current owner is a guy named Kataya Numbar. He's a Somali warlord with his own territory in the east of the country. We took a sneaky peek into CIA files on this guy, and he has a bad rep even among his own kind."

Brognola, watching the reaction to Kurtzman's revelations, caught his eye.

"Mind if I jump in, Aaron?"

"Go ahead."

"Aaron is on the right track here. What he's detailed is the background based on the data picked up from the computer. It might not make sense on its own, but a clearer picture emerges when I tell you what we found on Kataya Numbar. Our Somali warlord is one of Abrim Mansur's loyal buddies. Big time it seems. He has also had visits from Gabril Yasim in the last few months. Each visit coincided with the registry of *Red Star* to a new owner."

"Do we take that to mean Yasim was bringing money to Numbar?" Blancanales asked. "Helping with the purchase of the *Red Star* by a separate party?"

"What the hell does an African warlord want with

a freighter trading along the Russian coast?'' Lyons asked.

"It's just a smokescreen to hide the fact Mansur now has control of *Red Star*. One of the data bits Aaron's team found on the computer hard drive was a list of new crew members. It looks as if they have put their own people on board."

"This is all going to tie in with a missing Typhoon-class sub and a crew of Russian Muslim sailors going AWOL," Schwarz said. "Am I right, Aaron?"

"You're getting there."

"And now we have a freighter that makes regular runs across the Barents Sea off the Russian coast in Mansur's camp," Lyons added.

"Hard guesses," Kurtzman agreed. "But there's too much happening to be nothing more than chance."

"The *Red Star* makes an unscheduled stop somewhere out at sea? Meets up with sub?" Schwarz looked around the table. "Any suggestions why?"

"Exchange the crew from the sub?" Blancanales said. "Deliver something to the sub?"

"Or someone," Lyons said. He snapped his fingers impatiently, repeated the move a couple more times.

"He's going to sing something out of *West Side Story*," Blancanales said. "The *Jet* song."

Lyons's scowl could have blistered paint.

"The missiles," he said, glancing across at Brognola. "The hijackers will need launch and arming codes for the missiles."

"Not so easy to get," Schwarz pointed out.

"The right amount of money can get you anything," Blancanales said.

"I feel bad news coming on."

Kurtzman keyed in an image of a square-jawed man in his forties, with thinning gray hair and heavy spectacles. He'd been caught against a blurred background talking to a man they all recognized from the file photograph.

Gabril Yasim.

"Taken by an agent of the FSS. This is an agency of the Russian Federation, and one of its functions is counter-intelligence," Brognola said. "The man with Yasim is Viktor Seminov. He vanished four days after the photograph was taken. Just before the FSS moved in to arrest him. Seminov had been under suspicion for some time. The FSS had let him run on a long leash so they could identify his contacts. Seminov was suspected of trading in military information. Had bank accounts in Switzerland apparently. The day after Seminov vanished, a clerk who worked in one of the Russian navy departments was found dead in a Moscow back alley with his throat cut. The same day the FSS found that launch and firing codes for SS missiles had been taken from a file in the office of the naval commander responsible for the Northern Fleet out of Nerpichya."

"So we could be looking at a rogue submarine with armed nuclear missiles running around...anywhere," Blancanales said.

Brognola slumped back in his seat.

"Sums it up pretty neatly."

"So do we assume this is Mansur's threat?" Schwarz asked.

"Only part of it," Barbara Price told them as she entered the War Room. She had a video cassette in her hand. "This is one of the tapes of Mansur. Our translators have wiped his voice and replaced it with an English voice-over of the message they worked out."

"Let's hear it," Brognola said.

Price slipped the cassette into one of the War Room's players and keyed the play button. The TV monitor flickered into life, Mansur's image fading up from darkness. He sat facing the camera, dressed in severe black robes, his face expressionless. The background was neutral, giving no indication where Mansur had been at the time of the recording. His lips began to move as he spoke, moving out of sync with the flat, direct narration of the translator.

"When you listen to this message, the deed will have been done. You will all be witness to the results. New York will be no more. There be no rising from the ashes this time. Now you will understand what it is to have your world taken from you, your people reduced to specks of dust. In the space of seconds you will have been reduced to what my people have had to endure for decades. Your need for domination and the love of your almighty dollar has blinded you to the plight of my people. Your lack of understanding, your need to control our destiny, has split apart the nations of Islam. Look at us and see how we bicker among ourselves. You have pushed us to this, refusing to even consider what we wanted, what mattered to us. You made the choices, established the boundaries, selected who should be the stronger. For so many years I watched and prayed that things might change, that time would bring wisdom to your actions. But nothing has changed, so I have made the change in your name. America will no longer dominate in a world order that has been altered for all time. Your suffering will be with you each day. And take heed that it was the small people who delivered this to you. The might of the U.S.A. no longer means anything. We have taken back our birthright.

"At this time of change you will also have seen what we have done to your Russian friends. They, as you, have been party to the selections made around the conference tables. Not content to simply dismantle their own nation, they now cling to you, offering assistance and begging to be allowed to become another dominant force with their influence and their weapons. So as New York was struck, so were the Russian oilfields. Destroyed by their own weapons now in the hands of Russian Muslims. Nuclear missiles from a Typhoon-class submarine under the control of our brothers have delivered a telling blow to the Tyumen oilfields. Production will have already ceased and the area will remain contaminated for many years.

"I considered the repercussions of these acts for a long time. Even as the preparations were taking place I hoped a change of heart from the U.S.A. might allow me to cancel my plans. However, I saw no such change, so it became inevitable that matters were allowed to continue.

"I am Abrim Mansur. I will not hide myself away, pretending to disassociate myself from what has happened. My intent was to show the people of Islam that we need not hide in the shadows, cowering in the dark, fearful of the wrath of the Americans and Russians. There will be many who will deny I have done this for Islam, and they have the right to that view. In carrying out this deed I will have killed many of my own people who lived in New York. For that I do not apologize. In all acts there is a degree of sacrifice that is decided upon by one individual, regardless of the consequences. America should understand only too well. I took that decision. My own life has held little purpose for a long time. If I am hunted down and killed by those who will come after me, then so be it. My death means nothing, because I have achieved my goal. I decided to sacrifice New York and all who lived there for a purpose far higher than my own existence. I do not ask forgiveness or understanding other than that which says it was necessary."

The image faded. Price switched off the monitor.

"The tapes David found were in a number of languages," she explained. "Each one had been independently shot. One in French, English, Hebrew. The content was the same in each one. The CDs contained similar messages. We believe that these were to be distributed by Jafir in the wake of the attacks Mansur has been preparing."

There was a protracted silence. No one seemed to

have much to say in the aftermath of Mansur's message.

Brognola cleared his throat.

"We've been lucky," he said, "to have these tapes fall into our hands. It gives us something of a head start. We know what Mansur is planning."

"Still fuzzy around edges," Lyons said.

"We go with what we know," Brognola said. "No choice. That sub needs neutralizing. Mansur's tape threatens the Russian oilfields. That's bad enough, considering what the aftermath will be. What I'm concerned with is the fact that there are ten missiles on board. If Mansur uses a couple against Russian oilfields, what's he going to do with the other eight? He can target Europe, even the U.S. if they escape detection and get within range. We need to put a full stop to this sub. If it's going to meet this freighter, it could be our one chance to do it. Able, you'll fly to Ramstein, then pick up a Russian transport that will be waiting for you there. You'll be met at the other end by Andrei Lipov. He's in charge of the Russian undercover team based around Govograd."

"One final piece of information to add," Kurtzman said. "I wanted you to hear everything else first. These few fragments were on their own. Looked at in the context of the main story I think you'll like what they say."

He flashed the data on screen. Kurtzman's assessment was correct. The individual words on their own didn't convey a great deal. Brought into the briefing as a whole they took on new strength.

...dock Govograd...cargo...Seminov...with care... vital...Bortai...

"Andrei Lipov will be able to pin that down for you," Brognola said.

"Suit up, guys, and don't forget your thermals," Price stated. "It'll be cold where you're going."

Blancanales pushed his chair back and stood.

"Barb, that's the last thing I need to know right now."

Northern Russia

"AND I WAS ALWAYS LED to believe Chicago was a cold place," Blancanales complained.

Able Team was waiting for its Russian contact to show. The small airfield the team had touched down at was basic in the extreme. It had a small control tower, two run-down hangars and a wooden hut that served as shelter for passengers. The facilities it offered were basic, but at least it was warm inside.

By the time an hour had elapsed Able Team was tired of drinking the mugs of hot Russian tea that were constantly passed around.

The door opened and a man stepped inside the hut. He was in his thirties. He wore civilian clothing, leather coat and thick pants, and his blond hair was cut short. He gazed around the hut until he spotted Able Team, then made his way across to them.

"Lipov," he said by way of introduction. "You are Hanks, Newman and Redford?"

Lyons nodded. "I'm Hanks."

"Time for introductions later. We have to move quickly to catch the train that will take us to Govograd. I have transport outside. Until I give you the signal please do not speak. Especially English."

The men of Able Team picked up their gear and followed the Russian outside. There was a mud-streaked pickup waiting, smoke curling from the exhaust, the engine rumbling unsteadily. They all climbed in, and Lipov said something to the bearded driver, who nodded and ground the gears as he moved off. The pickup lurched across the uneven ground as it jolted its way from the airfield. Lipov sat up front with the driver. He said nothing to Able Team the entire drive, only conversing with the driver when it was impossible to ignore the man. The drive took just under a half hour, coming to an end when the pickup pulled up next to a small wooden structure alongside a single span of rails. They all got out. Lipov spoke to the driver and handed him some money. The man wound up his window and drove off without a backward glance.

The train showed within a couple of minutes, smoke streaming from the stack as it rolled in toward the halt. The blackened locomotive was hauling eight cars. They had all seen better days. Every coach had a chimney stack poking out of its roof, with smoke issuing from it.

The moment the train drew to a clanking, hissing stop, Lipov led the way toward the rear. He climbed up into the second last coach, pushing open the door. Able Team followed him along the corridor until Lipov slid open a door and motioned for them to go through.

They were in a large compartment with a cast-iron stove resting on a steel plate at one side. The stove threw out heat that was a pleasure after the exterior cold. Lipov slid the door shut. He crossed to the stove and held his hands out to feel the heat.

Able Team put down its gear. They felt the train shudder, couplings clanging as the locomotive started to move. The halt vanished behind them.

"Now we can speak," Lipov said. His manner changed as he went from man to man, shaking their hands as he familiarized their cover names. "My name is Andrei Lipov. Please call me Andrei."

"Any update since we left?" Lyons asked.

"Viktor Seminov is in Govograd. He is staying at what I think you would call a boarding house." The Russian smiled. "Not that he has much of a choice. Govograd is not what you would call overrun with hotels."

"The *Red Star?*"

"According to our intelligence, the ship docks sometime tomorrow. Refueling should take a few hours."

"We need to be on board when she leaves. It's the only chance we have of getting to that sub. Right now I don't give a damn if we have to swim out to the thing, long as we end up on board."

Lipov smiled. "You are one of these crazy Americans I have heard about. Am I right?"

Blancanales leaned forward. "You got that right, Andrei. This is the original California crazy man."

"I have heard so many things about California," Lipov said. "Is it true that sun shines all the year around?"

Schwarz grinned. "Except when it's raining, or the smog hides everything beyond the end of your fingertips."

Lipov looked at him, not sure whether to believe Schwarz.

"This is true?" he asked Lyons.

Carl Lyons leaned against the hard back rest of the seat. "I'll let you decide that, Andrei. Right now I don't want to deal with this pair of clowns."

Lipov shook his head. "I don't understand your American sense of humour."

Blancanales actually laughed out loud. "He doesn't have a sense of humour, Andrei. That's why we have to keep reminding him."

"And you trust one another in a firefight."

Blancanales glanced across at Schwarz, who simply looked back at him.

"Truth is I never thought about that. Hey, boss, do you trust us?"

"You don't want me to answer that do you?"

Schwarz inclined his head at Blancanales. "Do we?"

Blancanales stared out the window.

"No, don't answer that," Schwarz said. "I'd rather be ignorant and happy on that point."

"You know what I think?" Lipov asked. "I think you are all bloody crazy."

Blancanales sighed. "Didn't take him long to figure us out."

Lipov located a cupboard and took out a large kettle. He filled it with water from an urn on the floor and set the kettle on top of the stove. The cupboard also provided tea and thick mugs.

"Tea, my crazy friends?"

THE TRAIN EASED into the halt just after dawn. The stop was little more than a deserted hut alongside the tracks, identical to the one where they had boarded the train. Able Team and Lipov climbed down from the car, bleary-eyed from sleep. They emerged into a cold, overcast day. Rain clouds were already forming out at sea, slowly moving toward land. The sky was gray and bleak. Beyond the shore the sea rose and fell with a restless motion that hadn't changed in thousands of years. Blancanales, zipped up to the collar in his parka, stamped around, kicking at the iron-hard earth. He took a long look at the empty landscape, shaking his head in disbelief.

"Welcome to Mother Russia," he muttered.

"You are very welcome," Lipov said.

The train pulled away from the stop and disappeared in the distance, leaving Able Team and Lipov alone.

"I'm not sorry to see that go," Blancanales said. "Those damn seats we slept on were harder than Hanks's heart."

The sound of a diesel engine alerted them to the

approach of a battered panel truck. It drew to a stop and a huge, bearded man climbed out and joined them. He wore a thick leather overcoat that added to his bulk.

"At last," he said to Lipov in Russian. "I began to think you had decided to take that office job they offered you."

Lipov embraced him. "And miss seeing your ugly face? Now let us speak in English for our friends."

Lipov turned to Lyons.

"Hanks, this is Yorgi."

Lyons took the Russian's huge hand, feeling Yorgi grip him tightly and put on the pressure. The Able Team leader resisted the viselike grip and stared Yorgi in the eye.

"Yorgi, none of your damn games," Lipov warned.

Yorgi grinned through his beard as Lyons squeezed back.

"Very good," he said in accented English and let go.

Lipov introduced Blancanales and Schwarz.

A frown crossed Yorgi's face. "Why were you all named after American movie stars?" he asked.

Even Lyons had to grin.

"They are cover names," Lipov explained.

"Why? Are their own names like girls?"

"Yorgi, let us get in the truck and go."

The ride to the Russian undercover team's base took just under an hour.

It consisted of a long, low timber building with a few smaller outbuildings dotted around the area.

Smoke rose from a tin chimney stack. Yorgi parked the panel truck beside the building and they all climbed out and trooped inside.

Welcome heat blasted out as Yorgi shoved open the door. At the far end of the long room was an open stone fireplace. A blazing log fire threw heat into the room.

"That's the best thing I've seen since we got here," Schwarz said, making for the fire.

"And that's the second," Blancanales said softly, as a young woman, clad in dark pants and a thick sweater, appeared from the far side of the room. She was beautiful, with dark hair reaching her shoulders and warm, brown eyes that could have melted the frozen ground outside.

Lipov held out his arms and the woman walked into his embrace.

"Danielle, these are our American guests," Lipov said, introducing Able Team.

"Have you come to rescue us?" the woman asked.

"If it's a rescue mission, it's for all of us," Lyons said. "We don't stop these people, we're all in trouble."

"Danielle has been gathering intelligence reports and putting together as much information as she can," Lipov explained.

"And I also make the best tea you can get in this frozen piece of hell," Danielle said. "Andrei, have any of you eaten today?"

"No. There was nothing on the train for us."

"Good. Then we'll eat first and talk after. Does everyone agree?"

Blancanales expressed what they were all thinking. "I don't think I can refuse an offer like that."

"Good," Danielle said.

She moved to the far end of the room, where a huge, old, cast-iron stove burned fiercely. A number of blackened cooking pots were issuing steam as they bubbled from the heat.

"So how do you explain your presence here?" Lyons asked.

Lipov grinned. "We're a survey team looking at the local environment. Our cover is we're looking at ways to restart the community businesses. The locals tolerate us because they would welcome anything that might improve their lives. The criminal element do the same but for another reason. They try to stay in the background so they can carry on with their activities without being bothered. We've been here for a couple of months now. This area has been under suspicion for a long time. It's pretty isolated, and there's no law enforcement you can speak of. The local police force in town is made up of no more than a half dozen men, and from what we can figure out they're likely to be on the payroll of the organization."

"You have any trouble with law?" Schwarz asked.

Lipov shook his head. "We showed them our Department of the Environment authorization when we arrived. They didn't like it but they can't do much about it. They're suspicious because we are supposed to represent the government. There's still a lot of fear of authority from the old days. It takes a long time to go away and works in our favor.''

''Must be handy when you don't want to be bothered,'' Blancanales said.

''It helps.''

''Do you like fish stew?'' Danielle called. ''Bad luck if you don't because it's all we have.''

''Fish is very good for you,'' Blancanales said solemnly.

''You haven't tasted it the way Danielle cooks it,'' Yorgi said.

''For that I'll give you a double helping.''

Yorgi rolled his eyes and held up his hands in mock terror.

''He says that because he actually likes it,'' Lipov said. ''It's the only way he can get enough.''

''We'll give it a try,'' Lyons said.

''Never had fish stew for breakfast before,'' Schwarz said.

''Never had fish stew period,'' Blancanales added.

The stew when it came wasn't as bad as they might have expected. Danielle had added some local herbs and plenty of boiled dumplings. There were chunks of potato, some chopped cabbage. There was also a bowl holding wedges of coarse black bread. It was grainy, with a rough texture, but freshly baked.

''This is the only reason we bring her along,'' Yorgi said. ''She can cook.''

Danielle swiped at him with her wooden ladle, just missing his head.

''I love your fish stew,'' Yorgi grinned.

Lipov produced a couple of bottles of vodka. There were no glasses so they all drank it out of mugs.

"Wow." Blancanales said. "Some bite."

The three Russians laughed at his watering eyes and flushed cheeks.

"This is not the refined baby water we export," Lipov said. "This is the local brew. Full strength. This will take rust off girders if you dip them in it."

"I believe you," Lyons said.

They completed the meal in a better frame of mind. After they had cleared away the remains they gathered around the big fire. Danielle had made a huge pot of tea, which they spiked with the vodka.

On a low table Danielle spread out a diagram of the dockside. She explained the layout for Able Team.

"The refueling dock is the end one. Here. It is a little distance from the main dock and warehouse area simply for safety. There are three large fuel-storage containers at the end of the dock. There will be a crew of about six, maybe seven men who will operate the pumping station."

"What about security?" Lyons asked.

"There may be a police presence. Usually no more than two in a patrol car. They are always around if a vessel is running contraband. They keep an eye out for rival gangs who might try to steal whatever has been brought in. The police will receive a consideration for their services."

"Who runs the criminal element in Govograd?" Schwarz asked.

"Fellow named Bortai. Record longer than the national debt," Danielle said.

"Another connection," Lyons murmured.

"You know the name?" Lipov asked.

"It came out of the data we located on a computer we picked up in London."

"Andrei mentioned the refueling should take around three hours?" Blancanales said. "Do you agree, Danielle?"

The young woman nodded. "It's an average figure. Sometimes depends on the weather. If there are high winds and rough sea it slows the process. It has taken up to six hours in bad weather. Unless we get a severe change in weather conditions the sea should be fairly calm tomorrow."

"What we can't anticipate is the degree of security on board the ship," Lyons said.

"That thought had crossed our minds," Lipov said. "Do you think a distraction might help?"

"Such as?" Lyons turned to look at the Russian.

"There is a warehouse at the far end of the dock. Right now it holds a supply of weapons and explosives. If that warehouse was set on fire, it should provide enough of a spectacle to distract even the most devoted security man. Don't you think?"

Blancanales raised his mug of tea. "Andrei, you're the man."

CHAPTER TEN

McCarter paced the cell, restless, waiting for his chance to make some kind of break. Hawkins watched in silence, knowing it was safer to keep his thoughts to himself. He sensed the Briton's mood, sympathized with it, but accepted that there was nothing to be done until the opportunity presented itself.

Eventually McCarter settled down. He squatted at the base of the outer wall, his gaze fixed firmly on the door, hands shoved deep in the pockets of his combat jacket, and waited.

He remained there until pale dawn light filtered in through the window and pushed the shadows out of the cell. Pushing to his feet, he began to pace the cell again, working his cramped muscles. Seeing the sense in that, Hawkins did the same and they moved around the cell, warming themselves up in readiness for any upcoming action. Neither spoke. They still carried the bruises and cuts inflicted by their captors the previous day, and the injuries were enough to illustrate the mood they were both in. At that precise time words didn't matter.

The rattle of the bolt on the door told them they

were going to receive visitors. McCarter glanced at his partner.

"We'll only have the one chance," he said. "Don't let's waste it. Follow my lead."

Hawkins nodded. He moved to the side of the cell and leaned back against the wall in a submissive posture.

The door was pushed open and Shakir stepped into the cell. An armed guard moved in behind and slightly to his left. The guard carried an AK. A second guard, identically armed, stood just inside the open doorway.

Shakir stood with folded arms, looking from McCarter to Hawkins, then back to the Briton.

"So, now you have had time to consider, I believe we need to talk. About what you know of Mansur's plans."

McCarter actually grinned at the man.

"You clowns amaze me. I would have thought you had enough to do chasing after Waris Mahoud, not wasting time in here with us."

Shakir's eyes widened. For a moment he seemed lost for words.

"What are you talking about?"

"Come on, Shakir, you don't have him. Mahoud has gone. Fled. He's over the wall, you idiot."

"Who told you…"

"You just did," McCarter said.

This time Shakir reacted with an angry yell. He lunged forward, his right hand clawing for the auto-pistol holstered at his waist. McCarter stayed exactly where he was, allowing Shakir to lift the weapon clear before he moved. When he did, it even caught Hawkins off guard.

McCarter's left hand shot out and his fingers clamped around Shakir's wrist, forcing the weapon down. In the same instant McCarter's right hand, palm out, struck at Shakir's exposed under jaw. The full force of the blow shattered the lower bone, taking Shakir's jaw out of its sockets. The man's mouth was slammed shut, breaking a number of his teeth. He stumbled back, blood frothing from his lips, and banged into the guard standing behind him. Shakir offered no resistance as McCarter reached across with his right hand and snatched the pistol from his slack fingers. Leaning forward, the Phoenix Force leader pushed the pistol under Shakir's left arm and triggered two shots into the chest of the guard as the man tried to moved away from Shakir. The impact of the bullets at close range spun the guard, and he fell against the wall. McCarter put a third shot into the back of his head, then turned and slammed the heavy pistol across the side of Shakir's skull, driving the man to his knees.

The instant he saw McCarter hit out at Shakir, Hawkins made his own move. Pushing away from the wall he raised his booted foot and drove it against the open door. The heavy door slammed into the second guard, numbing his right shoulder. Hawkins followed up by putting his full body weight behind the door, the force knocking the guard off balance. His AK became wedged between his own body and the door frame. The guard reacted by pushing against the door, managing to clear his upper body. McCarter saw his chance and brought up the autopistol. He fired once, putting his shot into the guard's head. The man sagged against the door frame, the AK slipping from his fingers.

McCarter tucked the pistol inside his jacket, then bent to scoop up one of the AKs. Hawkins retrieved the other rifle. Both weapons had second magazines taped to the ones in use for quick reloading.

The Briton dragged the door open and peered into the passage beyond. He could hear raised voices. Glancing across the passage, he saw an open window. There was no frame or glass, simply an opening. He could see falling snow swirling past the opening. Turning, he indicated the exit to Hawkins.

"Let's go, T.J.," he snapped.

An armed figure stepped into view at the far end of the passage. McCarter didn't waste any time. He raised the AK and triggered a short burst that took the man in the right shoulder, tearing away a chunk of bloodied flesh and muscle. The wounded man pulled back out of sight. McCarter fired off a second burst, the slugs splintering chips of stone from the corner wall.

"Go!" McCarter said.

Hawkins took three long steps across the passage and flung himself through the opening. McCarter fired another warning burst, then followed suit. He cleared the window, landing hard on the frozen ground.

"Need a minute to catch your breath, boss?" Hawkins asked, a trace of sarcasm edging his words.

"Cheeky sod," McCarter muttered.

He nudged Hawkins and pointed to a truck standing

some thirty feet away. It was one of the vehicles they had seen on their arrival.

"Let's hope they haven't drained the bloody battery," he said.

The Phoenix Force duo ran hard for the truck. With only yards to go a robed figure, brandishing an assault rifle, stepped into view from the front of the truck. He started to yell out warnings, lifting his weapon. Hawkins fired at him on the move, laying down a short burst that ripped into the robed figure and knocked him off his feet.

"See if this thing runs," McCarter said, turning about as he saw more armed men edging out of the building they had just exited.

Hawkins grabbed the rifle from the man he had shot and climbed into the cab. He laid both weapons on the seat as he settled behind the wheel, running his gaze over the controls. He flicked on the ignition switch and made sure the gearshift was in neutral. He jammed his foot on the floor starter and heard the big engine grind as it turned over, grateful it wasn't a diesel that would have needed to warm up before it fired. The engine kicked in almost immediately. Hawkins worked the gas pedal, feeling the power build.

"Let's go, boss," he yelled, dipping the clutch and shifting into first gear.

Gunfire was crackling in the crisp air as McCarter hauled himself up into the open cab, returning fire and scattering the robed figures spilling out of the building.

Hawkins took off the brake and floored the gas pedal, feeling the truck's heavy tires bite, then skid. He hauled the big steering wheel around and the truck lurched forward across the bumpy, iron-hard ground. As it slewed around, Hawkins spotted the Toyota pickup that had brought them to the encampment. Armed men were pulling open doors and climbing in. Racking the gear into second, Hawkins pulled on the wheel, rolled the big truck across the compound and plowed into the side of the Toyota. The smaller vehicle was lifted off its wheels and turned on its side under the weight of the truck. Men scrambled to get clear. Some failed and were crushed under the Toyota as it was sent spinning across the ground.

"Very clever," McCarter said. "Now get us the hell out of here."

Hawkins worked his way up through the gears, piling on the power from the massive engine. He knew he was driving recklessly considering the weather conditions, but the alternative was just as threatening. Both he and McCarter could hear bullets bouncing off the truck's thick metal body and chassis.

"Just as long as they don't hit the bloody gas tank," McCarter said.

"Nothing in the book that says you can't fire back," Hawkins reminded him.

"Right," McCarter said. He swung onto the step and hauled himself onto the open body of the truck, bracing himself against the frame as he lifted his AK to push shots at the encampment. Something moved under his feet. McCarter looked down to see what was in his way and gave a yell that startled Hawkins.

"Boss?"

"Only some bloody RPGs," McCarter yelled back. He picked up one of the Russian rocket launchers and laid it across his shoulder. He tracked in on the encampment and triggered the weapon. Nothing happened.

"Shitty Russian duds," he grumbled.

Tossing the launcher over the side of the truck, McCarter picked up a second one. The same thing happened. His third choice launched successfully. The fiery missile streaked toward the encampment. It struck just short of the main building, scattering armed figures as it detonated. McCarter tried a fourth launcher. He took his time and when he fired the rocket curved in a deadly arc that ended when it struck the side wall of the building. When it exploded there was a second, larger blast. The blast expanded out and up, a large ball of fire and smoke engulfing a greater part of the compound. Debris was hurled across the encampment. Running figures were struck down in midstride.

"Whoa, boss, what did you do that time?"

McCarter climbed back into the cab. "Buggered if I know. Maybe they had a store full of fireworks to celebrate Mansur's birthday."

The encampment vanished from view. Hawkins pushed the truck on, gripping the vibrating steering wheel as it fought to free itself from his hands. The steering was in need of alignment, causing the wheel to pull constantly to one side. It took all of Hawkins's strength to keep the vehicle on track.

"This thing could do with a heater," Hawkins said.

The open cab meant they were exposed to the cold and the falling snow.

Hawkins eased off the power as the ground began

to climb. They were moving back into the hills where their incursion into Afghanistan had been located. Somewhere in the misty, snow-shrouded distance the rest of Phoenix Force was still on the loose.

And so was Waris Mahoud.

At least McCarter hoped he was.

While Hawkins drove, McCarter kept watch, scanning the terrain around them. At this moment he and Hawkins were free and clear. How long that would last was anyone's guess. Knowing the way things tended to happen, McCarter was sure that condition might not last long.

SINCE THE CLASH with Shakir's force, James, Manning and Encizo had endured a long, cold night in the Afghan hills. When they realized McCarter and Hawkins were gone, even their radio setups disconnected, the Phoenix Force trio regrouped and discussed their options. They made an attempt to pick up the trail left by the retreating force, but the oncoming darkness and the falling snow and wind made tracking nearly impossible. Common sense prevailed, and the trio found themselves a place to weather the storm and wait for the light. They took turns standing watch, allowing the other two to rest and catch some sleep. The hours were long, the temperature low. By dawn they were ready to move on, attempting to pick up the trail.

Manning did some calculations, based on star sightings during the night, which he transposed to the map he carried in one of his pockets. He admitted he was extrapolating to a great degree, but the Canadian was an outdoorsman, having spent a great deal of his personal time trekking in the Canadian forests. If anyone in the team could get them back on track it was Gary Manning.

"This is where we came in," he said. "We moved in this direction while David had the GPS unit. When we met up with Shakir and his team I figure we were here. I fixed our position last night. We're going to get back on track if we move south and west. The sun rose at our backs so we need to head in this direction."

He indicated the way they had to go with a raised finger.

Encizo glanced across at James. "You buy that?"

James smiled. "Sounds good to me. I'm not going to argue with the last of the living trailsmen."

"You guys just don't have faith," Manning said.

"Has nothing to do with lack of faith," Encizo said. "I just don't want to end up doing a full circuit of Afghanistan."

James took point again, leading them out of their cover. It was still snowing, the high wind sweeping down off the peaks and turning the fall into a white mist. Clinging snow quickly crystallized on their combat gear.

For the next hour they kept moving, following Manning's guidance. The drawback to trekking through the Afghan high country was the featureless terrain, fold after fold of slopes and ravines that seemed to go on forever. It was close to impossible to find a distinctive spot to establish a focal point. With the white mist of swirling snow eddying back and forth, it was difficult to see far ahead.

Toward the end of the hour the wind rose dramatically, hurling snow at the Phoenix Force trio. It was becoming difficult to stay upright. And then, just as swiftly as it had arrived, the wind dropped. It eased off, calming until it was little more than a gentle breeze. With the decrease in wind power the falling snow became less of a threat. The wind-chill factor dropped too.

"Somebody just have a wish granted?" James asked.

"I don't give a damn why, I'm just glad it happened," Manning said.

Encizo appeared to be ignoring his partners. The Cuban had moved aside, gazing off into the distance, his attention drawn to something the others had missed.

"Rafe?" Manning asked.

"You hear it?" Encizo said.

"What?"

"Gunfire." He raised a hand, pointing. "Over that way."

Manning and James joined him. Concentrating, they listened, and Manning was the first to acknowledge that Encizo was not mistaken.

"I hear it."

James nodded in agreement.

"But who is it?" he queried.

"Only one way to find out," Encizo said.

THE TERRAIN WAS PROVING too much for the truck. It bounced across the rocky ground, springs groaning in protest at the rough treatment. As it swayed from side to side, McCarter and Hawkins were forced to brace themselves against being thrown from the open cab. Their bodies were shaken and jarred as the lurching vehicle bounced against an outcropping. Hawkins's arm and shoulder muscles were screaming for relief as he fought the heavy steering wheel.

"Boss, I don't think we're going to get much more out of this tin can. She's struggling. We hit anything much bigger she is going to lie down and di—"

His words were cut off as the front of the truck rose, then dropped with a solid thump. Hawkins trod on the gas pedal and heard the engine fade. He juggled with the pedal, getting nothing but harsh rattling sounds. And then the engine shut down completely. Hawkins didn't even try to start it again.

"You were saying?" McCarter asked.

Hawkins shrugged. "She got us this far."

They climbed out of the stricken truck, taking their weapons with them. Hawkins took a look under the front end. Oil was still leaking out of the cracked engine casing where the truck had dropped onto a large wedge of rock.

"We walk from here," he said.

McCarter tugged up the collar of his jacket, peering into the misty distance. He had noticed a drop in the wind velocity. It would make moving around a little easier now that the swirling snow had been reduced to a minimum.

"Shakir's buddies are going to be on our trail, T.J., so let's keep moving."

HAWKINS MOVED to a section of higher ground and took a look around. The falling snow restricted his ability to see very far back the way they had come. He finally accepted defeat and rejoined McCarter.

"So which way do we go now? If Mahoud is out here, do you really think we can find him? David, it was bad enough before Shakir shafted us. Now we're out on a limb, looking for one man. Hell, we're not so far off being lost ourselves."

"My old granny used to say, 'you're only lost when you don't know where you are.'"

Hawkins stared at the man, trying to make sense of his remark. "Meaning?"

"How the hell do I know, she was as crazy as a loon."

Hawkins shook his head. "Must run in the family."

"T.J., would I be stuck out here with you for company if I was sane?"

Hawkins held up a silencing hand. "Maybe I'm going the same way you are, but I reckon I hear gunfire. Coming from up there."

McCarter nodded. "You're right on both counts. Let's go see if it's the guys, or another bunch of Mansur's trusty acolytes."

CHAPTER ELEVEN

They reached the settlement about a half hour before midnight. Lipov, driving the battered pickup, brought them in as close to the docks as he dared without arousing suspicion. A thin, cold rain was drifting in from the dark waters beyond the shore.

Able Team was kitted out in blacksuits, and for the close-quarter work they envisioned they were carrying 9 mm Uzi SMGs, as well as their handguns. Each man had a small backpack holding additional equipment, including fragmentation, stun and gas grenades. Schwarz had a couple of HE packs. They wore night-vision goggles around their necks that would enable them to operate in the dark if they needed to. Lipov had provided them with short-range radio communicators so they could stay in contact during the diversion and their move to get on board the freighter.

''We will drop you off on the edge of the docks,'' Danielle said. ''Then we will drive to the far side of the loading area and make our way to the warehouse.''

The Russian team had weapons in the pickup as well as a couple of incendiary packs they were going to use to set off the explosives stored inside the warehouse.

"We should synchronize watches," Lyons said.

When they had done so Lipov said, "We will give you ample time to get into position. When you are ready, radio the go-ahead. As soon as the warehouse goes up, you can make your move."

"We drop you here," Yorgi stated, pulling the pickup into the shadows of a derelict store shed. "There is plenty of cover to get you to the perimeter fence at the dock."

"Any security stuff to look out for?" Lyons asked. "Sensors on the fence? Around the dock?"

"Nothing like that," Danielle assured them. "Just armed thugs. I have been inside the dock a number of times. These people don't go in for that kind of protection. They have the locals under watch and no one is going to be foolish enough to try and breach their docks."

"Oops," Blancanales said. "What does that say about us?"

"These people are extremely violent," Danielle said, "and they have a way of asking questions *after* they have done harm. You understand? Don't have sympathy for them. They won't for you. These men are criminals."

"Shoot first, ask questions later?" Blancanales suggested.

"Yes. I couldn't remember the correct way to say it."

"Near enough," Lyons said. "Let's do it."

"Good luck, my friends," Lipov said. "To us all. You remember the radio frequency?"

Lyons nodded.

"We will be waiting to hear from you," Danielle told them.

"You don't let those bastards escape," Yorgi advised.

Blancanales gripped the big Russian's hand. "No chance, Yorgi."

Able Team exited the pickup and merged with the shadows. The truck drove away, following the rutted road that would take it through Govograd and allow them to reach the far side of the mainly derelict dock.

Lyons took the lead as they eased toward the dock perimeter fence. Their approach was made easy by the scattering of rundown buildings, rotting hulls of a number of vessels that ranged in size from a small rowboat to a full fishing trawler. Empty oil drums and timber crates were lying around in abundance.

"Never win a prize for coastal community of the year," Blancanales muttered.

They came up on the sagging perimeter fence, which had seen better days. The chain links were warped and sagging, even the concrete posts supporting them were broken and corroded by long exposure to the bitter climate and the sea water.

Able Team hunkered down behind an overturned wooden hull. Lyons pulled his night-vision goggles into place and scanned the immediate area beyond the fence. The green image showed him things he might have missed using normal vision—such as the armed man wandering in their general direction, his Kalashnikov cradled in his arms as he folded his hands inside his thick coat. The guard wore a thick fur-trimmed cap that had ear flaps pulled down and tied under his chin. Lyons watched the guard for a while, following his line of travel. The man wasn't patrolling in any regimented sense of the word. He was simply moving around aimlessly, probably wondering just what he was doing outside on a miserable night like this. He stopped twice, once to adjust the collar of his coat and again to relieve himself against an empty oil drum. Blancanales, who had joined Lyons, stared at the guard through his own goggles and couldn't resist a low chuckle.

"What?" Schwarz asked.

Blancanales dropped back down beside his partner. "Guard over there taking a pee. I wouldn't chance it in this temperature. Imagine it freezing and snapping off in his hand."

"At least this guy has something worth snapping off," Lyons remarked.

"For that cutting remark I will never let you see me in the shower again," Blancanales said peevishly.

"*Again* already?" Schwarz said. "Again?"

Lyons joined them, ignoring Schwarz. He checked his watch.

"Time we moved," he said.

They reached the fence and located a break large enough for them to slip through. Lyons had kept the guard in sight and with the man moving away from them, they were able to cross the dock area and conceal themselves beneath the nearest of the jetties that pushed into the dark, choppy waters of the Barents Sea. Freezing water lapped against their boots as they crouched in the shadows, with the wet timber pilings providing cover.

They were able to see the adjoining dock. This was the one where the fuelling tanks were located. The huge steel structures, supported on metal and concrete cradles, were bathed in the glare of powerful lights. The sound of diesel pumps rocked the night air and the shouts of the operators reached the men of Able Team as they surveyed the vessel they had come to Russia to locate.

The *Red Star* wallowed in the swell of the tide. Thick flexible fuel pipes connected the shabby freighter to the pumping station as it fed fuel into her holding tanks. The length of the dock the ship was moored to seemed to be lit from end to end. Able was able to identify at least four armed men on the dock itself. They seemed to be waiting for someone to appear.

"Seminov, I'll bet," Schwarz suggested.

"Hey, look over there," Blancanales said.

They followed his finger and saw a large Japanese 4×4 roll along the dockside and come to a stop at the head of the fuelling dock. Two large men climbed out and flanked the rear door of the vehicle. They were both wielding guns. One opened the door and a broad, stocky man wearing a leather coat with a thick collar stepped out. It seemed as if his head had been positioned directly on his shoulders, with no hint of a neck. His exposed head was devoid of hair.

"That looks like the local crime czar," Blancanales said. "Bortai. Just like Danielle described him."

"Yeah?" Schwarz said. "And when was this? Not another shower episode I haven't heard about?"

"Nothing like that," Blancanales said. "We were just talking."

"That's your problem," Lyons snapped. "You talk *too* much. Now shut up."

They watched as two more men climbed out of the 4×4. The bright lights covering the dock showed the men clearly.

"Yasim and Seminov," Lyons said. "Looks like all the guests are here. Time we joined the party."

Able Team used the time Yasim and Seminov were escorted along the dock to the gangway slung down the side of *Red Star*. The black-clad trio made its way along the edge of the rocky strip of beach that led directly underneath the fuelling tanks. The noise was deafening and the stench of diesel filled their nostrils. They emerged on the far side and used the bracing timbers of the dock supports to bring them closer to the *Red Star*.

Lyons, braced against one of the thick timber pilings, took out his handset and activated it.

"Andrei, you read me? Over."

The response was instant. "Yes. Are you in position? Over."

"Good as it's going to get. Hit that button, Andrei. By the way, Seminov and Yasim are going on board right now. Bortai just brought them to the *Red Star*. Over."

"Be ready. Good luck again. Out."

Lyons put the handset away and nodded to Blancanales and Schwarz.

"Heads up," he said. "Party time..."

LIPOV, DANIELLE and Yorgi had left the pickup in the shadows cast by a deserted metal workshop. Armed and carrying the explosive packs, they approached the warehouse housing the cache of weapons and explosives from the blind side. The entrance to the building faced the docks, and Lipov knew there would be at least three guards. They would be armed and equipped with communicators that linked them to Bortai.

Crouching in darkness beside the warehouse, Lipov peered around the edge of the wall. His assumption had been correct. Three of Bortai's armed thugs were walking the concrete apron fronting the entrance to the warehouse. Lipov drew back, touching Yorgi's arm.

"There are three of them. All armed. We need to dispose of them without making too much noise."

"Give me something difficult to do," Yorgi said.

He pulled his weapon into view, a suppressed autopistol. Yorgi had carried the weapon for a number of years, especially since joining the special operations group under Lipov's command. The pistol had been specially built for him by an armorer who had once worked with the KGB's assassination bureau. The armorer, a man who lived to create his special weapons, crafted the 9 mm pistol to fit Yorgi's large hands. The butt grips had been premolded to the contours of Yorgi's palms and fingers, the trigger set to his own preference. Even the magazine had been constructed from scratch and was able to hold twenty cartridges. The large suppressor had been balanced by adding weight to the rear of the pistol so that it did not pull the muzzle down to any great degree. The weapon was heavy to handle for anyone but Yorgi. In his massive hands it was like a derringer.

"Let us do our work, Andrei," Yorgi said, easing himself into position.

He watched the three guards for a little while, estimating distance and taking into account the wind factor. Satisfied, he eased off the safety and pulled back the slide to push the first round into the breech.

The three guards were standing yards apart. Two were positioned behind the third, their backs to him as they stared out across the dock in the direction of the floodlit fuelling dock and the freighter. Yorgi could hear their muted voices as they discussed some women they had encountered in one of Govograd's bars.

Raising his pistol, Yorgi used both hands to support and steady the weapon. He sighted in on the lone guard, aware that the man might turn and rejoin his comrades at any moment. Yorgi held his aim, then made a slight adjustment before he stroked the feather-light trigger. The pistol coughed discreetly, its soft sound drowned by the wind and rain pattering against the side of the warehouse.

The 9 mm round cored in through the target's skull just above the left eye. The guard stiffened, then dropped to his knees without a sound. His AK was slung from a shoulder strap, so it didn't clatter to the ground and attract attention.

Yorgi put his sights on one of the other guards. He placed two quick shots through the back of the man's skull. Although the shots were on target the remaining man was alerted when warm blood jetted from his partner's face and struck his cheek. He turned to see the stricken man falling, saw the bloody mess where the 9 mm rounds had burst out of the man's face, and spun. His own weapon was swinging into the firing position when Yorgi's pistol coughed again.

The first guard toppled forward on his knees and struck the concrete face first.

The man who had taken two shots through the back of the skull was still falling when Yorgi's final shots hit the third guard over his heart. Yorgi fired three times, his trio of 9 mm slugs hitting in a tight cluster. They cored through his chest, ripping into the beating organ and tearing it apart. The man fell hard, his AK clattering noisily as it bounced on the concrete.

Lipov moved out of cover, heading for the warehouse, ignoring the huge sliding doors as he headed for the small access door set in the wall. He tried the handle and felt the door open. With the others close on his heels Lipov stepped inside.

The interior of the warehouse was poorly lit, though not so bad that they were unable to see the stacked merchandise in the center of the dusty, trash-littered floor. Some of the wooden crates had been opened, and when the three Russians reached them they saw that the open crates held 9 mm Uzi SMGs. Another crate was stacked with new Kalashnikovs. From markings on the sides of other crates they identified grenades, plastic explosive, rocket launchers, handguns and boxes of assorted ammunition for every weapon in the place.

"Let's do it," Lipov said.

While Yorgi stood watch Lipov and Danielle placed the explosive packs in position. They set the detonators, which would be activated by a small control device Lipov carried, switched on the power and extended the short aerials that would receive the signal, then exited the building and returned the way they had approached the warehouse.

It was as they reached the pickup that Lipov's handset emitted a beep that indicated an incoming call. He took the set out of his pocket and pressed the receive button.

The conversation with the American called Hanks was brief. As soon as it was over, Lipov cut the connection.

"Well?" Danielle asked.

"They are on board the freighter," Lipov said.

Then he turned and looked back at the warehouse.

Lipov switched on the control device, extended the aerial and pressed the button.

THEY HEARD the first explosion within thirty seconds. Shouts of alarm came from the men on the dock. Able Team heard running feet pounding on the thick timbers of the dock over their heads. And then the second explosion came, ten times louder than the first. The night lit up as huge gouts of fire rose into the sky. The blast rocked the *Red Star*. The ship swayed in toward the dock, making the timber groan. The impact almost shook Able Team from its positions. The tremendous explosion was followed by a series of lesser, but still spectacular detonations. More men ran down the dock so they could get a better look.

"Let's move," Lyons said. He swung himself out from where he was standing and reached for the wooden rungs of a service ladder fixed to the side of the dock. He went up fast, peering over the edge of the dock. He could see a cluster of excited figures at the head of the dock. Checking the end that jutted out into the water, he was relieved to see it deserted.

"Move," he said as Blancanales and Schwarz joined him.

The three moved quickly along the dock, keeping close to the dark hull of *Red Star*. They didn't hesitate or look back. This was their only chance to get on board the ship. If they were discovered before they managed it, then all hell was going to break loose in Govograd. They had an open chance to board the vessel in the next couple of minutes and they were going to make the most of that opportunity.

Near the bow Lyons spotted a steel ladder welded to the hull of the ship that followed the curve of the hull down to the massive steel ring surrounding the anchor. Lyons figured it had to be a maintenance ladder to allow access to the anchor itself. He wasn't about to go into the particulars of ship construction, but he was going to make use of it. He went up the ladder hand over hand, pausing briefly at the top to peer over the rail. The foredeck was deserted. Lyons scrambled over and dropped to a crouch behind an air-vent cover. Blancanales and Schwarz joined him.

"Hatch cover open there," Blancanales said, pointing it out. "Should take us down into the bow hold."

They cut across the wet deck and checked out the open hatch. Another steel ladder dropped into the shadowed depths of the hold. They went down one by one, moving away from the base of the ladder and into the musty, damp area of the hold. It held a number of steel freight containers and roped-down packing cases. It was a dirty, stale-smelling area. The steel decking moved constantly under their feet.

"I was never cut out to be a sailor," Schwarz said. "I like my floor to keep still when I walk around."

Aware of time slipping away, Able Team checked out the hold.

"Hey, can I ask a stupid question?" Blancanales said.

"Go ahead," Lyons said.

"What do we do if they secure the hold cover and the hatch we got in here by? Isn't that what they do on ships. 'Batten down the hatches, Mr. Christian?'"

"He has a point there," Schwarz said. "We sit here while they rendezvous with the sub and yell, 'come on guys, give up, we got guns in here.'"

Lyons led them across the hold and indicated a large hatch set in the side of the hull.

"That lets cargo out straight onto a dock. They use it when they don't have those dockside cranes. You can drive a forklift directly inside the hold, and they are opened from inside by those lock bars."

"You sure it's above the waterline?" Blancanales asked.

"If it wasn't, the ship would sink every time they opened it."

Blancanales shrugged. "Okay, you got me there."

They worked their way to a corner of the hold away from the entry hatch and into a narrow space behind one of the large freight containers.

Before they settled Lyons checked to see if the con-

tainer was secured to the deck of the hold. Satisfied
that the container wouldn't move even if the ship was
riding out heavy seas, Able Team made themselves as
comfortable as they could and began their long wait.

Stony Man Farm, Virginia

HUNTINGTON WETHERS watched the satellite image
fill his screen and set a disk to record everything he
was about to view. It had taken him some time to
break into one of the remote birds circling the globe,
and now that he had it Wethers was going to use it.
His fingers flew across his keyboard as he instructed
the satellite to alter course and trajectory. The coordinates he fed into the bird's onboard computer were
decoded. The satellite imperceptibly changed course
and began to scan the area Wethers had ordered.

The rugged coastline of northern Russia swam into
view and as Wethers maintained his control over the
satellite he used the digital camera to start plotting a
run that would, he hoped, pick up the freighter *Red
Star*. A message had been received three hours ago
that the freighter had left Govograd, heading out to
sea in a northerly direction. The Russians assisting
Able Team had reported that the Americans had managed to board the freighter and call in that they were
on board. After that there had been no more calls from
Able Team. As dawn began to lighten the sky, Wethers brought his satellite surveillance online.

Using his control over the satellite, Wethers scanned
the Barents Sea, following the northerly course the
freighter had taken. He used a long-range tracking

scan until he isolated a small image out in the open. Wethers brought the digital camera in for a closer shot, keeping up the zoom until he had the screen dominated by a small freighter moving steadily north. He dropped the image lower and moved back so he could pick out the stern of the vessel and waited until the rising swell of the sea lifted the vessel on the crest of one large wave. His fingers manipulated the camera, keeping the image in focus, and in the brief seconds the stern was raised Wethers read the name. *Red Star*.

Wethers smiled in quiet satisfaction. He locked the satellite onto the vessel and keyed in the commands for a position scan that would tell him exactly where the ship was. As long as he had the satellite within range, Wethers was going to maintain his watch over the *Red Star*.

He picked up his telephone and called Brognola's office. The phone rang but no one answered. Wethers let it ring for a while, then tried Barbara Price's office. She answered on the first ring.

"Hunt?"

"I've got the *Red Star* on satellite scan... Oh, yes, she's the one. I tried to get hold of Hal but he's not answering... Okay, I'll leave it with you."

Price put down her phone. She sat back for a moment, her gaze wandering around the office, then she took a deep breath and pushed up out of her seat. She left her office and made her way down the corridor until she was outside the office Kurtzman was using. She tapped and heard the acknowledgment. Stepping inside she saw Kurtzman behind his desk, surrounded by paperwork and peering at his computer monitor.

"I just had a call from Hunt," she told him. "He's located the *Red Star* on satellite and is keeping track of it while he has a window. You know where Hal is?"

Kurtzman shook his head.

"I've been in here the last hour or so."

"At least we have that damn ship in sight."

"Won't do much for Able, but at least we'll know where they are."

"Any more from our contacts?" Price asked.

Kurtzman shook his head. "Nothing yet. But I haven't given up. How about you? Heard from Phoenix?"

"No. The problem with their mission is we can't put a time scale on it. Looking for one man in the Afghan mountains is no cut-and-dried exercise."

CHAPTER TWELVE

As McCarter and Hawkins moved forward, weapons locked and loaded, the gunfire increased.

"That way," Hawkins said. "Over the ridge."

They pushed up the steep slope, their lungs starting to burn as they sucked in the icy air. The ground underfoot was slippery with loose snow, and their movements were hampered by the rocks that littered the area.

They reached the top of the slope and dropped to a crouch, checking out the way ahead. The ground fell away in a series of serrated smaller ridges. Movement caught their attention and they saw armed men, wearing thick protective clothing, skirting the edge of a wide stream that was heavy with melted ice and snow. The rushing water was foaming against the banks. The armed men were shooting in the direction of a cluster of rocks.

McCarter spotted a dark shape behind the rocks. The attackers were too far to the right of the rocks to be able to see the sheltering figure. The fugitive looked to be in a bad way, and McCarter saw a splash of red on his left shoulder and upper arm. The man wasn't wearing cold-weather clothing.

"Mahoud?" Hawkins asked.

"Whoever he is, these blokes are making a big thing about getting their hands on him."

Hawkins looked beyond the fugitive's cover and saw three more armed figures moving into view. He recognized them instantly and nudged McCarter's arm.

"We've got company, boss."

McCarter saw the newcomers. "Bloody hell," he said, as Manning, James and Encizo came into view. "Always the last to show."

ASHOK CAUGHT SIGHT of the three armed figures moving across the slope behind Mahoud's cover. His frustration increased when he recognized the weapons they were carrying—M-16 rifles. The American commando unit who had come looking for Mahoud. He and his men had spent the past two nights, with a day in between, tracking Waris Mahoud. For almost thirty-six hours they had struggled against the severe weather, the freezing cold, barely pausing for rest as they searched for the man. Despite their efforts, he had eluded them until a short time ago. Unarmed, poorly clad and without food or water, Mahoud's determination to avoid recapture had proved successful.

They had spotted him no more than an hour ago, still running, still heading for the border. They had opened fire, hoping to wound him enough to bring him down. A single shot had hit him in the left shoulder, yet Mahoud struggled to his feet and stayed there. He seemed to be possessed by some inner determination to remain free, to not let his pursuers get to him. Ashok's team had kept up the chase, and just when it seemed they had him cornered the damned Americans had shown up.

"Don't let those Americans reach Mahoud," Ashok yelled at his men. "Kill them all. Every one of them."

He turned his Kalashnikov in the direction of the three men coming down the slope, bullets kicking up gouts of freezing earth. Ashok ran forward, screaming at his team as they turned their weapons on the advancing Americans. The three men separated and lost themselves in the uneven hollows of the slope.

"Find them," Ashok roared.

McCARTER SHOULDERED his AK and settled the sights on one of the men firing at his partners. He took his time, leading the target before he stroked the trigger. He saw the bullet impact between the man's shoulders, punching through into his chest cavity, kicking him forward. The man dropped to his knees, his own weapon falling from his hands, and then crashed face-first to the ground.

Hawkins, down on one knee, began to fire off single shots. He put down two men before the rest of Ashok's team realized they were under attack from behind as well as in front. They began to scatter, some of them splashing through the flooded stream as they sought cover themselves.

With the main force drawn away from them, Manning, James and Encizo broke cover and fired down at the opposition. They caught Ashok's team in a deadly cross-fire. The opposition hadn't envisaged such a fierce assault. They held for a short time but

Phoenix Force, now reunited, gave nothing away as they maintained their attack.

Ashok saw his force being depleted by the extreme fire coming from the American team. He saw his men falling, torn and bloody from the enemy fire, writhing in agony, bodies gouged and raw from extreme wounds. One man flopped loosely into the icy stream, his body floating with the swift flow, blood staining the water as the body was turned and twisted.

Ashok himself, apart from a slight gash on his cheek from flying stone chips, was unhurt, and ignoring the personal risk pushed forward. There was no way he was going to recapture Mahoud, so he attempted at least to kill the man. He ran, stumbling, then pulling himself upright. His dash for the rocks behind which Mahoud had hidden shortened the distance quickly. As he closed on the rocks, he took a final leap onto the closest, his feet threatening to topple him as they fought to keep a grip on the wet surface.

For a long moment Ashok stared down at Mahoud. The Iranian returned his enemy's gaze with utter contempt. Even in his unprotected position the man maintained his defiance of his enemy.

The muzzle of Ashok's AK dropped to settle on Mahoud. With his finger on the trigger Ashok knew that supreme feeling of power over another human being. All it would take was a gentle squeeze.

He felt something strike his left side. A solid blow that wrenched the breath from his lungs. Twice more he felt the stunning impact, this time higher up his body. He felt himself tumbling back, all control gone from his body. He heard his rifle fire as his finger jerked against the trigger. And then the world began to close down around him. Everything dissolved into a silence. When Ashok's body hit the hard ground, he barely registered the impact. He was already slipping into the quiet cocoon of near death, all sight and sound and feeling spiraling down to absolute nothingness....

Rafael Encizo's 3-round burst had caught Ashok in the ribs and chest, coring deep. The M-16's power had knocked Ashok back off the rock he had stepped onto. The little Cuban's killing burst had the required effect, but Ashok had got off a single shot before he fell, and that hastily triggered round had still hit its target, the bullet tearing into Mahoud's right side, shattering ribs before it exited out of his back, taking with it lacerated flesh and shards of bone.

By the time Phoenix Force reached Mahoud he was wedged in among the smaller rocks, bleeding heavily and trying to stop himself drifting away from reality.

"Waris Mahoud?" McCarter asked as he crouched beside the man.

Mahoud could only nod.

"Might be hard to believe but we've come to get you out of here."

"How did...?" Mahoud managed to whisper.

Calvin James, on his knees beside the wounded man, was opening up the Medi-kit he carried. He ignored what was being said and concentrated on helping Mahoud.

"Long story," McCarter said. "Lot of it is down to your old mate Fayed."

Manning had the homing device out. He activated

it, sending out the call for the U.S. helicopter to come and lift them out of Afghanistan.

"You understand why we had to find you?" McCarter asked.

"Mansur's strike against New York?"

"We're going to get you out of here. Might take a little time for the ride to arrive.

Mahoud nodded. He was drifting off. McCarter could understand why. The Iranian looked in a bad way. Apart from the bullet wound he looked as if had been through some rough treatment. His face was badly bruised, sections swollen. There were signs that his exposed hands might be suffering from the previous night's low temperatures. The skin had that pale, frozen look that suggested tissue damage. And he had obviously undergone some rough treatment before his escape from Shakir and his people. After that he had spent almost two days on the run. Poorly dressed, with no weapons or food, the Iranian had endured the hostility of the bleak Afghan mountain country. He had been shot and even now he was expected to pass information to McCarter. The Briton felt a brief twinge of conscience at having to keep on at the man, but he had to obtain whatever Mahoud was carrying in his head just in case he didn't make it.

"Anything we need to know about Mansur? Anything you didn't pass along to your cousin?"

"Only what I learned after I spoke to him and before I had to break my cover."

"Did it have to do with a hijacked airliner?"

"Yes. Has that happened?"

McCarter nodded.

"Mansur plans to have a man on board the hijacked airliner with the detonator for the nuclear bomb they will conceal in the luggage hold. After the negotiations reach an agreed compromise, Mansur's people will allow the plane to continue to New York. The moment the plane lands at JFK the man will detonate the bomb."

"Looks like we guessed right," Encizo said.

"Only thing we don't know is where the bloody plane is," McCarter said.

Mahoud reached out to grip the Briton's arm. His fingers dug in hard as he fought off a sudden escalation in the pain. Blood began to trickle from the corner of his mouth. His eyes closed. McCarter glanced at James. The slow shake of the medic's head told him what he suspected. James's hands were red with the blood that was coming from Mahoud's wounds. He was desperately attempting to staunch the flow, but the results he was achieving were negligible.

The fingers clamped on McCarter's arm slackened for an instant, then dug in even tighter. Mahoud's eyes flickered open and he stared at the Phoenix Force leader.

"Listen, my friend. The plane is in Somalia. An old airstrip near the coast. Mansur has an ally, a local warlord sympathetic to Mansur's cause. He is called Kataya Numbar."

"That's all we need, Waris," McCarter said. "Now you take it easy, chum. We have a chopper coming to get us out of this mess. No time at all you'll be in a U.S. field hospital."

"And in the hands of my accursed enemy," Mahoud whispered, and he actually smiled at the joke in the few seconds remaining of his life.

The grip on McCarter's arm slackened, the hand slipping away.

James bent over the still form, feverishly working on the open wounds, reaching for extra medication.

"Hey, Cal," Manning said gently. "He's gone."

"No," James snapped. "Dammit, no. I can—"

"Cal, you tried," McCarter said.

"He was hit too bad," Encizo added.

"But I—"

Hawkins put his hand on James's shoulder. "I ever get hit when we're out, buddy, I just hope you're around. I wouldn't want anybody else to treat me."

James looked up at the younger man.

"Bullshit," he said.

"True, though," Hawkins told him.

James sank back against a slab of rock. "Mansur has a lot to answer for," he said, glancing down at Mahoud. "One man like that is worth the whole of Abrim Mansur's crew."

"You just keep remembering that," McCarter said, "and we'll deal with them."

The Briton scanned the snow-laden sky, searching for the rescue helicopter. He knew it could be some time before it showed. The sooner it did find them the better because he needed to contact Stony Man and relay the information Mahoud had passed on before he died. Before Mansur's hijack plan moved to its next stage. Whatever else happened, Phoenix Force had to stop the airliner from taking off. It wasn't just the fact that it would be carrying a nuclear device. There were the innocent passengers on board. If the plane did leave the ground and head toward America, there would be only one way to stop it. That would be to destroy it while it was in the air, probably over the sea, and that would seal the fate of the passengers as well as removing the potential threat to New York.

Not if we can help it, McCarter thought. No bloody way.

Stony Man Farm, Virginia

KURTZMAN PLACED his information on Brognola's desk at the same time David McCarter was relaying details about the hijacked airliner to Kurtzman. The computer expert's feedback from his Middle East contacts had finally come through.

"We have a number of known Mansur faithful taking off from various points around the area," Kurtzman pointed out as Brognola read the details. "No one had any information as to where they were going, but all my contacts are certain their destinations were out of the Mid East."

Brognola's telephone rang. He picked up and listened. "Okay, Hunt, go ahead and start your sweeps. We'll be along shortly." He put down the phone, a thoughtful look on his face.

"What?" Kurtzman asked.

"That was Hunt. David was just on the radio link from Parkhar."

"Did they find Mahoud?"

"Yes, but he died from wounds received during the firefight. Not before he gave them information he'd

picked up before he had to break cover and run. The
hijacked airliner *is* Mansur's doing. The hijackers intend to load a nuclear device on board before the plane
is allowed to continue to New York. The vital part is
the location of the plane. It's at an old airstrip near
the coast in east Somalia.''

''Kataya Numbar's territory?''

Brognola glanced up from sorting out the papers on
his desk. ''Yeah.''

''His name came up from a couple of my sources.
It appears Numbar has had meetings with Mansur's
people on a number of occasions. He's looking to
make a name for himself in his own backyard and
must believe tying in with Mansur is going to give
him status.''

Brognola stood, papers in his hand.

''Looks like he might have made a mistake there.
Now let's go see what Hunt has for us.''

KURTZMAN'S TEAM was busy, working flat out.

Barbara Price was checking out the availability of
Air Force transport for Phoenix Force, out of Parkhar
to Somalia. It hadn't been put into actual words, but
they all knew what was in the cards for the five-man
commando team.

Akira Tokaido was waiting for a satellite link up,
intending to check the status of the *Red Star*. A digital
readout in the corner of his monitor screen was click-
ing off the minutes to when the satellite would come
on stream so he could pick up his search pattern from
the previous scan. The position of the freighter from

that last scan had been logged, and the oncoming satellite would be able to pick up from those coordinates.

Huntington Wethers and Carmen Delahunt, working in partnership, had Kataya Numbar as their target. Wethers already had his bird on stream and was searching for the hijacked airliner along the eastern coast of Somalia. Waris Mahoud's information, though helpful, hadn't pinpointed the exact location of the plane, so Wethers was having to do a detailed scan. The satellite's digital search capabilities were working alongside Wethers's human skills. Together they would find the airliner.

Delahunt, calling on her FBI knowledge, combined with data extracted from NSA and CIA data banks by the back door, was building a profile on Numbar. It wasn't the first, nor would it be the last time that Kurtzman's infiltration program had helped Stony Man with information it might otherwise not have been privy to.

The picture she was seeing wasn't pleasant. Kataya Numbar had a bad reputation even among his fellow warlords. In the volatile atmosphere of Somalia, Numbar ran his own piece of territory with a ruthless disregard for anything and anyone he took a dislike to. He was one of the old school. A man trained in England in military matters, he had returned to his native land, and when the country began to fall apart, both literally and morally, Numbar stepped in with his own brand of nationalism and created his army of armed followers.

What Delahunt's information didn't tell her were Numbar's deep inner feelings about Abrim Mansur and his cause: Numbar was a Muslim who had followed Mansur ever since he had attended one of his rallies in the former Palestine. It had been a strictly low-key, unpublicized meeting. People had heard about Mansur and were intrigued by his philosophy and his almost pacifist ways. Numbar, despite his following, still retained his hard-line attitude when it came to preserving his own regime of feudalism. When Mansur came to him at the outset of his planned strike against the West, Numbar had been both pleased and in his heart relieved that Mansur desired to employ a violent protest. He offered everything he could to the planned strike. He didn't like the Americans himself and anything that might throw fear into their hearts sat well with him. He agreed to help when Gabril Yasim came to him with large amounts of cash and asked for Numbar's help in purchasing the *Red Star*. The deceit involved was something Numbar enjoyed. He had a highly duplicitous nature, so anything on that level appealed to him. When he heard that Mansur was looking for a secluded airstrip where he could land his hijacked airliner, Numbar came up with the strip that was within his fiefdom. The area was desolate, with practically no inhabitants, and if there were they lay under Numbar's control.

So the elements were brought together and Kataya Numbar became an important part of Abrim Mansur's grand plan to strike against America.

Delahunt saved and printed out her information on Numbar, making copies for Brognola and Price. She had just completed that when Brognola stepped into the Computer Room, with Kurtzman close behind.

"What have we got?" the big Fed asked, stepping up behind Delahunt.

"A big chunk of real estate," Delahunt said. "This Numbar controls a big area. The guy is a warlord plus. Hunt is running his scans now. If that airstrip is there, we'll find it."

"Keep at it, people," Brognola said. He was reading through Delahunt's details on Numbar. "Sounds like a sweet guy."

"That's being generous." Kurtzman had scanned the pages himself.

"Carmen, get this stuff through to Phoenix. They're still at Parkhar. I need to arrange transport for them. It looks like they're not going to get much rest before they make the jump to Somalia."

"You're going to be one popular guy," Price said.

Brognola smiled wearily. "When they offered me the job they said there'd be days like this."

"Hal," Price called, "we can work this transport easily enough."

Brognola joined her and she showed him the details she had noted down.

"Phoenix can be airlifted from Parkhar and taken to Oman. Airlift Command has a C-130J they can use. They can outfit from supplies at Parkhar and get some rest during the flight. We'll be able to talk to them in flight. All we need is for some presidential string-pulling via the British PM. The UK has a good relationship with Oman, politically and militarily. I'm sure the PM can talk to someone and get us clearance for the Air Force to land and offload Phoenix. At the same time we also need landing clearance for the C-5 Galaxy already airborne to deliver Jack and *Dragon Slayer*. The guys are going to need a ride into Somalia and removal once the party is over.''

Brognola nodded. ''I'll call the Man right now.'' He paused. ''How far is it from Oman to Somalia?''

''I already thought about that. *Dragon Slayer* is having extra tanks fitted while she's in flight. The extra fuel will get her most of the way, then Jack can drop them and switch to his normal supply. He'll have ample fuel for whatever he needs to do over Somalia. When he pulls Phoenix out, he'll fly out and land on a Navy carrier in the Indian Ocean. The Navy has already diverted the carrier. I used our presidential leverage to get things moving.''

''Nothing left for me to do,'' Brognola said.

''You have to let the President know he'll be getting some calls from the various command centers I spoke to in his name.''

''This time around there won't be any hassle. Remember he already gave me the green light for anything we wanted.''

''Just checking.'' Price grinned.

Brognola crossed over to pick up one of the phones that would give him direct access to the Oval Office. Within a few minutes he had the President on the line.

''You'll have your landing permission by the time those planes reach Oman,'' the President said. ''And tell Ms. Price I've already had the Navy on asking if what she told them was correct.''

''It's called command initiative, sir.''

The President chuckled. ''Tell the truth, Hal, that

young lady scares me the way she takes control. I'm just glad she's on our side.''

"I know what you mean, sir."

"I'll talk to the British PM soon as we finish. By the way, Hal, any news from Able Team?"

"Nothing since we got the word they were on board the *Red Star*."

"Keep me posted."

"Will do, Mr. President."

Brognola put down the phone.

CHAPTER THIRTEEN

Aboard the Red Star

They took it in turn to keep watch. One on while the others rested. Not that rest was easy. The deck of the cargo hold was hard and cold. It moved constantly under them as the freighter plowed through choppy waters. There was an ever present smell of diesel fuel in the air, and some sea water found its way in through the cargo hatch in the hull, despite the tight seal.

Blancanales found himself checking the hatch regularly. Despite the assurances from his partners, he couldn't rid himself of the image of tons of water pounding at the hatch, even though it was above the freighter's water line. He just felt uncomfortable.

"Pol, Pol," Schwarz said out of the blue. "Did you see that hatch move? I'm sure it moved."

Blancanales scanned the hatch, his eyes searching for more water coming in, and then he heard Lyons's stifled snigger.

"Very funny," he said. "I hope you bums are enjoying this."

"I am," Lyons admitted. "Makes a change for you to be on the receiving end."

"Oh, I see. This is a revenge campaign? Just because my ex-buddy and I had a few laughs at your expense. This is different. If that hatch bursts open you won't be laughing."

Schwarz cleared his throat. "No, you're right there, Pol. It won't be a laughing matter. I can see that now. No time for laughing when you're drowning."

Lyons stood and walked up and down their confined space. They all did the same every so often so their limbs didn't stiffen.

They fell silent for a moment, each caught up in his personal thoughts. Blancanales was the first to notice the change in the beat of the freighter's diesel engines. He stood, moving along the side of the container until he could place his hands against the cold steel of the hull.

"We're slowing down," he said.

The others joined him.

"Damn right," Lyons said.

They could feel the freighter vibrating. The engines had reduced power, then began to pick up again. The *Red Star* wallowed as the propellers were put into reverse, the motion stalling the ship's forward movement. The vessel began to settle in the water, the heavy beat of the engines slowing to a gentle murmur as power was removed from the drive shafts.

"Who wants to bet we'll have a damn great submarine moored alongside any time?" Lyons said. "Time to get ready, we've got a party to crash."

"WE ARE AT THE COORDINATES you requested," the navigation controller said.

"Good. Surface now," Varic ordered.

The helmsman glanced across at Rashenski. His action enraged Varic. He moved up behind the helmsman and struck him across the back of his head.

"When I give an order you look at me! Not him. Rashenski is no longer master of this vessel. *I am.* Understand?"

The helmsman, still defiant, muttered, "If you say so."

"I do say. You bastards should listen. We are not playing games here. Do you think we took this submarine so we could ride around for pleasure?"

Rashenski lost his patience for the first time since Varic and his boarders had taken over.

"We don't have any idea why. All you do is make threats and tell us you can do what you want. Maybe that is so, Varic, but I think we are all getting tired of your bragging. Either tell us what you want or shut your damn mouth."

The hijacker called Kerim stepped forward and used the butt of his autorifle to hit Rashenski in the ribs. The blow dropped the sub captain to his knees, gasping for breath and clutching his side. Kerim moved in closer and hit him again, this time across the back of the skull. Rashenski fell forward, facedown on the deck plates. As Kerim made to strike him again, Varic stepped in to stop him.

"I think he understands. I think they all understand.

Arrange to have Captain Rashenski taken away. Place him with that other hero. Let them swap stories.''

Once Rashenski had been removed from the control room Varic turned back to the helmsman. His hand rested on the butt of his holstered handgun.

''Do we have an understanding now?''

The helmsman nodded and bent to his task. Orders were given and the submarine's depth readouts showed that the vessel was rising.

''Hold at periscope depth,'' Varic ordered.

The sub came to a stop minutes later.

''Periscope depth.''

Varic moved into place as the periscope rose into position. He gripped the bars and leaned in against the eyepiece. He began a 360-degree sweep, his movements steady and precise. He had almost completed his circle before he halted and held his position.

In the periscope's view screen he could see the gently rolling *Red Star*. The freighter was motionless except for its rise and fall on the restless, fairly calm sea.

''Kerim, get on the radio to the freighter. Use the frequency we arranged.''

Kerim crossed to the communication station. He gave the operator the frequency he wanted and waited until it had been selected. He picked up the handset and gave the recognition signal. He waited until the freighter responded, then spoke to Varic.

''I've got them.''

''Tell them we will be surfacing shortly. On their

port side. We need to make this exchange as quickly as possible.''

Varic turned back to the helmsman. ''Surface now.''

Checking the periscope again, Varic saw figures moving on the deck of the freighter. They were throwing cargo nets over the side of the ship. Ropes were tethered between both vessels to prevent drift.

''Kerim, get your team ready. Once we're alongside get them outside and ready to bring Seminov and Yasim on board.''

Kerim nodded and spoke into his com set.

Varic checked his watch. For the first time since boarding the submarine he experienced a sense of apprehension. This would be the time they would be most vulnerable, exposed on the surface and defenseless to a degree.

''We've surfaced,'' the helmsman informed him.

''Bring us alongside the ship,'' Varic ordered, ''and hold your position.''

ABLE TEAM FELT the slight but solid bump as the submarine was run alongside the *Red Star*.

They ran a final weapons check as they moved out from their hideaway and crossed the hold to the hatch in the hull. While Blancanales stood watch, Lyons and Schwarz cracked the lock handles and loosened them slightly. Some seawater seeped in around the seals, and Blancanales heard it splash on the deck.

''Watch that,'' he said. ''Damned if I'm bailing us out if you flood this hold.''

Once the locking handles had been freed Lyons and Schwarz were able to ease the hatch open a few inches. The massive bulk of the sub floated alongside the freighter. The dark curve of the huge submarine almost dwarfed the ship.

"Great," Schwarz muttered. "Now what? You want me to poke a hole in the thing with my knife?"

"Only way we're going to stop that thing is to keep it from submerging again," Lyons said.

"Blow any hatches they open?" Blancanales said. "Get up on the hull and plant one of the explosive packs against the hinge mechanism of the hatch. Blow the thing off."

"When he does speak he talks sense sometimes," Schwarz said.

Lyons had leaned out through the hatch. He saw the cargo net hanging down the side of the ship. Crew members from the *Red Star* were making their way down it to the hull of the submarine. Movement on the boat caught Lyons's eye, and he spotted armed figures up on the conning tower. A hatch on the sub's flat hull top swung open, a man's head and shoulders coming into view. The man wore a headset-microphone and carried a Kalashnikov.

"Let's do this before we get too many on deck," Lyons said. "I'll go first. Pol, you next and cover us from the ship's crew."

Schwarz had one of the explosive packs in his hands. He set the timer for eight seconds. Before they moved Lyons showed him the open deck hatch.

"You realize this is crazy?" Schwarz said.

Lyons had that wild gleam in his eye as he grinned back at his partner.

"Hell, yes," he said and hauled himself up onto the hatch frame, then took a lunging spring that took him onto the curving hull of the submarine. The rubber soles of his boots gripped the surface. Lyons pushed upward, his legs powering him up the sub's hull to the flat deck above.

Schwarz followed, his 9 mm Beretta pistol in his right hand, while he carried the explosive pack in his left, tight against his body.

Last man out of the hold, Blancanales leaped onto the sub's hull, hauled himself to the top and dropped to a crouch, his Uzi turned toward the conning tower.

Lyons was fully aware of the implications of the submarine's potential. A free-ranging, nuclear-powered submarine, with near-stealth capabilities that would enable it to stay undetected for a long time, was something out of a living nightmare. Added to that was the threat from the nuclear missiles it carried within its hull. It had become a no-choice decision. Able Team was on the spot, and they had little choice in what they had to do...

A shouted warning from the ship drew the attention of the figures on the conning tower. Able Team had been spotted.

The men on the conning tower followed the waving arms of the men on the freighter.

"Damn!" Blancanales muttered and turned his Uzi up at the tower. His initial burst sent the figures ducking out of sight.

Lyons kept moving forward, keeping the man in the hatchway in sight. The man himself twisted his upper body, saw the advancing American and hauled his Kalashnikov around to target Lyons.

The Able Team leader triggered a short burst that put holes in the man's skull, sending dark flecks flying across the deck plates. The man gave a shocked grunt, his AK jerking in his hands. He lost his footing and fell back down the hatch.

"Go, go, go!" Lyons yelled at Schwarz.

As his partner ran past him, someone opened fire from the deck of the freighter. Slugs hammered the deck of the sub, missing Schwarz by inches as he made his dash for the open hatch.

Turning his Uzi up at the ship, Lyons let go another burst, raking the area with 9 mm slugs. The crewmen fell back, one yelling as a single slug ripped through his left shoulder.

Spotting movement on the conning tower again, Blancanales let fly with another burst, his slugs clanging against metal.

Reaching the open hatch, Schwarz dropped to his knees. He aimed the Beretta into the opening and triggered three shots down into the sub as a warning to anyone contemplating climbing the metal ladder. Hidden from the ship by the raised hatch plate, Schwarz took the explosive pack and wedged it against the hinge mechanism. He flicked the switch and saw the digital readout on the detonator start to fall... 8...7...6....

"Fire in the hole," he yelled and put three more

shots down the hatch before turning and running back to where Lyons was trading shots with the crew of the freighter.

Schwarz jammed his Beretta back in its holster and grabbed his sling-suspended Uzi. He joined Lyons in driving the crewmen back from the ship's rail as they retreated along the vessel's deck, then threw themselves flat, along with Blancanales in the final couple of seconds...2...1...0....

The explosion was sharp, and the force of the powerful plastic compound tore the hatch free from its hinges, mangled the open hatch rim and sent red-hot chunks of metal flying across the deck of the submarine. The blast reached out and impacted against the side of the freighter. It shredded the cargo net hanging down the side of the ship and turned the crewmen clinging to the net into charred corpses.

"Hit that conning tower," Lyons said, pushing upright as the noise of the blast began to fade.

He took out a fragmentation grenade and pulled the pin. Lyons hurled the bomb and watched as it curved up and over the lip of the tower. The detonation threw a swirl of smoke into the air. A wailing voice rose as the blast faded away.

Armed figures erupted from the damaged hatch, weapons swinging up as they spread across the deck of the sub—and ran directly into Lyons's and Schwarz's Uzis. The crackle of autofire was the only sound to be heard. The sub hijackers might have gained the deck of the sub, but their ill-timed attack hadn't allowed them any chance to bring their weapons online. Bullet-ravaged figures tumbled to the deck, others slid, bloody and hurt, down the sloping hull and into the icy waters of the Barents Sea. One had the added bad luck of tumbling into the narrow gap between the sub and the freighter. Plunged into the cold water, already severely wounded, he had time for a moment of rising horror as he sensed the bulk of the great submarine swinging toward him, then his life was terminated as he was crushed between the two vessels.

"Around the far side of the tower," Lyons yelled. "It'll cover us from the freighter."

Able Team sprinted along the deck. As they passed the ruined hatch, Blancanales dropped an activated tear-gas grenade down the opening. He followed on the heels of Schwarz and Lyons, pulling himself behind the cover of the conning tower as a hail of bullets came from the freighter's deck.

They moved around the base until they were able to look across at the *Red Star*. Schwarz saw that the crew was dropping another cargo net over the side. Armed crewmen began to climb down. Schwarz raked the area with autofire, dropping one man to the deck of the sub. The others scrambled back up to the ship, except one who hung from the net, his right side torn and bloody.

Lyons reversed his taped double magazine and cocked his Uzi.

"Remember what Lipov said. The captain of this sub is Petre Rashenski. We could use his help if we locate him."

Blancanales held his gaze for a moment. "We're going inside? Right."

Lyons glared at him for a fraction of a second. "What do you expect us to do? Tap on the hull and ask them to surrender?"

"Might save some time," Blancanales said. "We'll try your way first."

He glanced over his shoulder, pointing at a circular hatch set in the deck toward the stern of the submarine.

"Our way in," Lyons said.

He took a couple of smoke grenades from his backpack and placed them on the deck, pulling the pins. Thick white smoke began to escape from the canister and form a shifting screen between Able Team and the freighter as they made a dash for the stern hatch. Blancanales paused once, briefly, to place an additional smoke canister on the deck. The smoke wasn't the most dependable cover, but under the circumstances it was better than nothing.

PETRE RASHENSKI RAISED his aching head and listened. He was sure he had heard…yes, they were gunshots. Had the navy found them?

The Russian sat up, ignoring the ache in his body. The back of his head was still pulsing with pain from the wound opened by the butt of Kerim's rifle. Rashenski overrode the hurt. This wasn't the time to worry about a few bruises. He had to do something to help regain control of his submarine. To take it back from the traitors who were now in command. He glanced across at Berin. The young submariner swung his legs off the bunk and moved toward the door. The bandage covering one side of his face was dark with dried blood. Rashenski had found it necessary to attend to the wound a number of times since the day of the hijack. Berin had been in agony for some time, but he had rested as much as he was able, and though the wound was still raw it had started to heal over slightly. Rashenski followed him. They paused at the door, listening. They were able to pick up the sound of voices. In the distance they heard shouting, then an explosion that came from the front section of the submarine.

"Permission to do something, sir?" Berin asked.

Rashenski gripped the younger man's shoulder. "Granted."

Berin eased the door open and peered into the passage. The hijacker who had been guarding them was standing a few feet away, speaking into his headset. It was obvious he wasn't receiving good news as his voice rose in anger. Berin and Rashenski checked out the length of the passage in both directions. The hijacker was alone. Berin slid the door fully open and without a moment's hesitation he stepped into the passage, moving up behind the hijacker.

As Berin closed in on the man the hijacker broke his contact with whoever he had been arguing with and started to turn back to his former position outside the cabin door. Berin wrapped his left arm around the hijacker's neck, placed the palm of his right hand against the back of the man's skull and increased the pressure by pushing the hijacker's head forward. The man began to choke, struggling against Berin's encircling arm. Rashenski stepped out of the cabin and moved alongside the hijacker. Without a moment's hesitation the submarine captain reached down and slipped the combat knife from the sheath on the hijacker's leg. He stepped around to face the hijacker and thrust the knife into the man's chest, the keen blade severing flesh and muscle as it sank deep into his beating heart. For a brief moment the hijacker stared into Rashenski's eyes. There was a mounting expression of terror in the hijacker's gaze, then he expelled a deep sigh, his body going rigid. He thrashed about for a moment, still held upright by Berin, and then his body slackened and he became a deadweight in the submariner's arms.

"Get him in the cabin," Rashenski said.

Between them they carried the corpse into the cabin. Berin closed the door. When he turned back Rashenski was removing the dead man's weapons. He handed the Kalashnikov to Berin, along with the extra magazines in the terrorist's pouches. He took the pistol for himself, noting that it was a SIG-Sauer P-226. He found two additional magazines for it.

"Get to the engine room," Rashenski said. "If you can free our crew members there, perhaps we can take control of the sub again."

"Where are you going, Captain?"

"To try to contact whoever it is who has boarded us. I'll use one of the rear deck hatches."

Berin turned and eased open the cabin doors. The passage was empty. He turned briefly.

"Good luck, Captain."

"For both if us. Berin, remember that these terrorists took our submarine by force. No hesitation if you meet any of them. You have your weapon. Use it."

Berin nodded. A moment later he was gone. Rashenski waited for a couple of minutes, then slipped out of the cabin and began to make his way toward the stern, negotiating the narrow passageways. He was counting on the disturbance keeping the hijackers busy. He was heading for a deck hatch. If he could get outside, contact the boarding party…

Movement ahead caught his attention. Rashenski flattened against the bulkhead. He could feel the ever present, slight vibration that coursed through the submarine's steel construct. It came from the powerful turbines, the very heart of the vessel. He thought briefly about Berin. The young man had courage, and if anyone could reach the reactor room and free the crew from the hijackers it was he.

The movement Rashenski had noticed became an armed figure. One of the hijackers. He was moving in Rashenski's direction, his Kalashnikov cradled in his arms. Rashenski pulled himself into an alcove, in among the thick pipes and cables that snaked through the hull. He waited until the hijacker had moved on by, then stepped out and raised the pistol in his hands. Rashenski pressed the pistol's muzzle against the back of the man's skull and pulled the trigger. The 9 mm pistol cracked sharply, sending a bullet into the terrorist's skull. The man lurched forward, dropping to his knees, then onto his face. As Rashenski bent over the man, taking his handgun and tucking it into his belt, he saw blood spreading out from under the man's head, creeping across the deck plates.

Turning, Rashenski hurried along the passage. He took risks, making no attempt to conceal himself now. Time would run out soon once the hijackers organized themselves. Surprisingly, he reached the stern hatch without encountering any of the hijackers. He would have expected them to at least check access points in case the boarders came in by a back door move. Their lack of foresight became Rashenski's good fortune. He went up the steel ladder, reaching for the locking wheel with his left hand, bracing himself with his right arm hooked around the ladder. The locked-down wheel refused to budge at first. Rashenski felt sweat pop out on his face as he gripped the wheel and tried to loosen it. When it released, the movement almost made him lose his grip on the ladder. He jerked the wheel again, felt it slacken. Rashenski spun the wheel and heard the seal ring creak as the pressure slackened.

As the hatch was freed, Rashenski put his left hand against the steel disk and pushed to raise it.

From below he heard booted feet running along the passage he had just used. Someone shouted a harsh command. He had been discovered.

Rashenski put all his strength into raising the hatch. Somehow he didn't believe he would be able to climb to safety in time.

The hatch was suddenly jerked fully open. Rashenski blinked as daylight poured down into submarine. Then a dark shape blocked the light and Rashenski was staring up into a man's face. Blond hair, disturbed by a slight breeze. Hard blue eyes that looked at, then beyond Rashenski.

"Get him out of the way," the blond man yelled in English.

Strong hands reached down to grab Rashenski's clothing. He was hauled up and out of the hatch. The blond man leaned to one side, cursing in a steady tone as he thrust an Uzi SMG past Rashenski and opened fire, sweeping the passage below the hatch with autofire.

Though he wasn't aware of it, this was Rashenski's introduction to Able Team.

CHAPTER FOURTEEN

Oman

Phoenix Force took advantage of the flight to Oman by sleeping most of the way. McCarter roused himself toward the remainder of the trip and spent some time in the communications section, seated at a desk as he spoke with Hal Brognola over the satellite link via a visual setup.

"You've looked better," the big Fed said when he was confronted by McCarter's bruised features.

"That's what you get when you complain about the rooms in Afghan boardinghouses," the Briton replied casually.

"Sorry to hear Mahoud didn't make it."

"That was one tough bloke," McCarter said. "He stayed alive until he gave us what we wanted."

"I don't know whether it helps but that information has paid off. Aaron and his team have located the airstrip and the hijacked plane. He's working on the data now. By the time you touch down in Oman he'll have images he can download into *Dragon Slayer*'s computer. We got some good images for you."

"Anything else we need to know?"

"Background stuff mostly. Aaron received information from his Mid East contacts. The cell phones and computer we got our hands on have come up with calls between the principal players. That ties them all together—Gabril Yasim, Seminov, Hassad. It took some digging, but Aaron got into the phone records and traced the calls. We even managed to pick up more connections via the three guys Able tangled with in New York. It's all coming together piece by piece and should give us definite leads on people we need to follow up on when the main event is over."

"Make sure that happens, Hal. No more trade offs for political expediency. Too many bloody decent people die in these things and the bastards responsible slip through the net because of bleeding hearts and liberal do-gooders. We get our arses kicked and the bad guys walk away to do it again."

"The President agrees. That's why he gave us an open ticket on this. Do what you have to."

Brognola looked off screen as someone joined him. He adjusted the vid-cam and McCarter saw Kurtzman.

"We identified the passengers on the hijacked plane from passports," Kurtzman said without any preamble. "They all check out except for two. One guy going under the name of Hanni Amir. When we checked further it turned out his real name is Hanni Basur. We linked him to Mansur."

"Half-hearted attempt at hiding his identity," McCarter commented.

"Some people have no imagination," Kurtzman agreed. "Now the second guy almost slipped through, but I picked up something from the NSA files. We came up with a full folio on this guy. Real name is Yusef Kasim. He's traveling on a French passport that has him down as Mustapha Safir. He is a proved Mansur follower. I've got you photographs of both men. I'll download them into *Dragon Slayer*'s main computer for you.''

"Thanks for that," McCarter said.

"As soon as we get more satellite access, I'll work on providing you with a live update on the hijack site," Kurtzman said.

"What's the state of the negotiations?" McCarter asked. "Can we keep up the dialog so the hijackers keep the plane on the ground long enough for us to go in?"

"Lucky for us the hijackers are playing the whole thing pretty calmly. I think it's deliberate on their part. Whatever the outcome they're going to have to keep up the pretence of negotiations for a reasonable time so we don't become wary. That makes it easier for our people. Their instructions are to keep the thing going. Let the hijackers believe they're getting somewhere without reaching any deals.''

McCarter checked his watch. "We should be touching down in just under an hour. We need to move out ASAP. I hope Jack will be ready for us.''

"He will be," Brognola promised.

THE MOMENT the C-130J landed at the Omani air force base it taxied across to a section of the desert base to where *Dragon Slayer* sat on the concrete next to the C-5 Galaxy that had flown it in from the U.S. The first thing McCarter noticed were the extra fuel tanks fitted under the helicopter's stub wings. They would use the fuel in them for the flight in and then Grimaldi would dump them, switching to his main fuel supply for the remainder of the operation. McCarter went up to the flight deck and had a brief word with the pilot and co-pilot before he led Phoenix Force off the aircraft and out into the hot, dry Omani afternoon. It wasn't the first time McCarter had been to Oman. In the past his visits had been into combat situations. Despite that, he had good memories of the place.

Jack Grimaldi climbed out of *Dragon Slayer*'s cockpit and came out to met Phoenix Force.

"Hi, guys. I hear you're looking for a discreet charter to run you into Somalia."

McCarter took the pilot's hand. "That's right, chum. I heard they couldn't find anyone to fit the bill so they kicked your arse out of bed instead."

"Been polishing up your diplomatic skills I see."

Grimaldi led the team across to *Dragon Slayer* and opened the passenger hatch. "Ready when you are, girls."

The team climbed inside. Grimaldi closed the hatch. It sealed itself shut and the commandos settled in the passenger seats, enjoying the flow of cool air from the chopper's air-conditioning unit.

McCarter had occupied the co-pilot seat beside Grimaldi's.

"Did Aaron send along the data he promised?"

Grimaldi nodded. He activated the main computer screen and brought up the images of the two men Kurtzman had told McCarter about.

"This pair belong to Mansur," McCarter said.

"They were on the flight under assumed names. Until we move on the plane we won't know whether they're still there as part of the bomb threat. When we go on the plane to look for these two, if you see them, take them out. No messing about. Just do it. We have to make sure the passengers aren't put under any more threat than they already are."

"Other thing is we have no way of knowing whether there are other terrorists on board," Manning said.

"I agree. And we aren't going to know until we actually get inside," McCarter said. "No amount of planning could tell us that because we don't have intelligence from inside the plane. Look, I'm not making any predictions here. We're walking into it with minimal data. I don't like it any more than you blokes."

"Is he whining?" James asked out the corner of his mouth. "The way he's talking, you'd half believe he always considered every move he ever makes."

"He's trying to make his position look difficult," Manning said. "Must be after a pay rise."

"Bloody transfer out of this squad of misfits is more like," McCarter said. "Jack. Next picture."

Grimaldi brought up the satellite scan image. It showed the airstrip and the hijacked 747 in sharp detail. The team studied the photo, taking in every detail it showed them, and committed the images to memory.

"Plane here," McCarter said. "Three machine-gun posts, all of which have an effective sweep of fire covering the plane and the surrounding terrain. With the plane in the center we have those machine guns at the northwest, south and east. All within the immediate perimeter of the encampment.'' He moved his finger to the lower right of the image. ''Three of the original buildings of the airfield. Control tower here, showing a satellite dish and aerials. Communications center. To the left and slightly behind are two more buildings. To the right of the control tower five tents. There's a chopper to the far left of the tents. Between the chopper and the main buildings three vehicles. On the perimeter of the field, west side, is another vehicle. Larger than the others. I'm guessing it's a fuel tanker.''

''We need to shut down those machine-gun posts,'' Hawkins said. ''As long as they're operational, we have problems.''

''They have to be neutralized without alerting the rest of the camp,'' Encizo said. ''Minute the shout goes up, we lose our advantage.''

McCarter nodded. ''Any suggestions?''

''Wait until it's dark. That's our best time. Three of us to take out the machine guns then go for the plane,'' Hawkins said. ''The other two can get into position and hit the other buildings and the tents, keep the rest of the terrorists out of the way.''

''Sounds easy when you lay it out like that,'' Encizo commented.

''Nothing about this is going to be easy,'' McCarter admitted. ''Just keep in mind what we're going to be there for. To make sure that plane doesn't leave the ground. As long as Mansur's people have that nuclear device, it's a threat. It has to stop on the ground. Any more questions?''

''No.'' James said.

"Okay. T.J., Cal, Rafe. You take out the machine-gun posts. Decide which one you want between the three of you. Gary, you'll be with me."

The Canadian nodded.

"Jack, backup as usual. Maintain silent contact once we move out but come running the minute you get the call."

"You got it," the pilot said.

"Let's do it," he said. "Jack, what's the in-flight movie this time?"

"If there was, it would be *Groundhog Day*," Grimaldi said.

"Hey," James said, "irony from the pilot."

"We'll need to watch him," McCarter said. "He'll be learning to read next."

East Somalia, Midnight plus thirty minutes

THE SATELLITE DISPLAY was live now. Kurtzman had brought them a night image, the ghostly detail shimmering from the infrared source. Clustered around the monitor Phoenix Force discussed the layout, each man offering his suggestions as they formulated their approach.

Grimaldi had brought them in north of the airfield, at high altitude. He had circled around to land west of the airfield, switching to *Dragon Slayer*'s silent mode, the mufflers reducing the beat of the engines as he put the mat black helicopter down in a depression two miles from the airfield. He cut the engines as soon as *Dragon Slayer* had landed.

While the rest of the team made final weapons and

equipment checks prior to EVA, McCarter entered co-ordinates into the GPS unit Grimaldi had brought along. The Briton saw Hawkins watching him and couldn't hold back a grin.

"I know. I lost the last one, T.J."

"Did I say a word, boss?"

"It's his age," Manning said. "He gets forgetful when the drugs wear off. I'll keep an eye on him."

Grimaldi activated the com-link with the headsets Phoenix Force was wearing. He ran an individual check with each member of the team to make certain each unit was operational. He also had a lock on the locators that were integrated with the com units.

"Okay, guys I've got you all tagged."

"Time to move," McCarter said.

"Take it easy, guys," Grimaldi said and opened the hatch.

He watched as the five-man team exited the helicopter and vanished into the moonlit Somali night.

JACK GRIMALDI CLOSED the hatch as the last member of Phoenix Force jumped to the ground. He pulled back into his seat. Scanning the console, he affirmed that the com-link that connected him to Phoenix Force was active. Down one side of the panel five lights showed green, indicating that each man had his comset switched on. As he looked at the display, a red light next to one of the green lit up. Grimaldi touched his own comlink and heard David McCarter's voice in his headset.

"Phoenix One to DS. Do you read?"

"Affirmative, Phoenix One."

The other four all called in, one after another, establishing that the com-links were functioning. After the final check the radio link fell silent. Grimaldi wouldn't hear from any of them again unless something went wrong, or they were calling for him to move in for the pickup.

He touched control buttons and brought up the computer image map. Grimaldi spent the next few minutes going over the map grid, checking position, distance, and fed any changes he made into *Dragon Slayer*'s memory. Once he was in the air and heading toward the airfield, the onboard electronic system would guide him in, alerting him to any deviation from the optimum course it would have chosen and advising him of any alternatives.

Grimaldi activated *Dragon Slayer*'s external sensor array. It would warn him of anyone in close proximity to the chopper. All he could do now was wait. It was the part of any operation Jack Grimaldi hated.

CHAPTER FIFTEEN

Russia

"Captain Rashenski?"

Rashenski stared up at the blond American.

"Yes."

"You understand English?" Lyons asked.

"Of course," Rashenski answered. "Do you speak Russian?"

"Debate later," Blancanales suggested. "Right now we need to get your sub back from these hijackers."

There were questions crowding Rashenski's mind, but he had the sense not to ask them. That would come later, when he was back in control of his submarine.

"Move it up," Schwarz said. He was crouching at the base of the conning tower, keeping an eye on the smoke that was providing cover, albeit temporary, from the men on the freighter and also any who might still be in the tower above their heads.

"How many hijackers?" Lyons asked.

"There were twelve originally. Two are dead inside."

"We hit at least four. Maybe a couple wounded," Lyons said. "They could still be a danger."

"Don't forget the freighter's crew," Schwarz called, "because they haven't forgotten us."

There was a sudden rush of dark shapes in among the rolling white smoke from the canisters set on the deck as a half dozen men from the freighter swarmed across the sub's deck. As they emerged from the smoke, searching for Able Team, they were met by a burst of fire that scattered them. Two fell instantly, bodies punctured by the gunfire. One man clutched an arm, where one of Rashenski's bullets caught it. As the man tried to regain his balance, the sub captain triggered a second and a third time, the bullets punching into his chest. The man fell back, rolling across the sub's deck. One of his companions jumped to miss tripping over his body and stumbled. Before he could recover Blancanales caught him with a burst from his Uzi, spinning the moving figure onto his face.

"Rashenski, with me," Lyons yelled.

As the sub captain turned to join him, Blancanales and Schwarz combined their efforts in pushing back the attacking sailors from the freighter, their autofire cutting into the men. The group faltered and began to retreat. The problem was there was nowhere to go on the sub's open deck.

Lyons and Rashenski reached the hatch the captain had used to exit the sub.

"THERE MIGHT only be a few left," Rashenski said, "but two of them had explosive satchels with them. The leader, Varic, threatened to use them if things didn't go his way."

"At least they wouldn't be able to use the missiles. Would they?"

Rashenski glared at the American. "I am finding it hard to like you at the moment."

Lyons grinned. "Stay that way and you'll fight harder."

"Very funny," Rashenski muttered.

"Well, let's go and do it while you can still laugh."

Lyons went down the metal ladder first, with Rashenski close behind.

"This way," the Russian said. "Control room. That bastard Varic is going to do whatever he can to stay in charge. I want him off my submarine, whether you sink it not."

"How do we recognize these hijackers?"

They were moving toward the control room now, Rashenski leading the way.

"They are all dressed in black," he said over his shoulder. "Just like you."

A figure appeared ahead of them, clad in black and brandishing a Kalashnikov. He turned when he heard the sound of Lyons and Rashenski approaching.

"Down!" Rashenski yelled, turning to push Lyons aside.

The passage echoed to the crackle of autofire. Bullets struck the bulkhead, some piercing the metal. Rashenski gave a soft gasp, stumbling, then dropping to his knees.

Lyons was already crouching. He raised his Uzi and fired in the direction of the hijacker, then he pushed to his feet, leaning over Rashenski's hunched figure, and fired a second burst. The rounds caught the hijacker in the upper chest. He fell backward, missed his footing and went down with a hard sound, his rifle rattling against the deck plates. Lyons stepped over Rashenski and advanced along the passage. As he neared the fallen man, he saw him move. Lyons laid another short burst into the guy, saw him arch his back before he lay still. Turning back, the Able Team leader saw Rashenski pushing to his feet, his back to the bulkhead. The Russian had his left hand pressed to his side. Blood was seeping through his fingers.

"Yes, I am all right," he said testily.

They moved on. Rashenski paused when they reached the dead hijacker. He crouched beside him and dragged a square pack that was hanging from the dead man's shoulder into view.

"There is another like this."

"Are we close to the control room?" Lyons asked.

"Yes. Why?"

Lyons pulled a canister from his pack.

"Tear gas. Couple of these in the control room should ease the situation. Are there some of your crew in there?"

"Three only."

Lyons nodded.

They proceeded along the passage until Rashenski tapped Lyons on the shoulder. He indicated the hatch that led directly into the control room. Lyons pulled the pin on the tear-gas grenade and released the lever. He waited until the last moment before rolling the grenade into the control room. It detonated with a soft thump and started to issue the gas. He repeated the maneuver with a second grenade, throwing this one in a separate direction.

"Give it a minute," he said to Rashenski.

THE SECOND THE FREIGHTER'S crewmen started to retreat, Blancanales and Schwarz advanced on them, firing. All but two of the crewmen remained on the deck of the sub, sprawled in bloody poses. As the Able Team pair emerged from the drifting white smoke, someone opened up from the rail of the freighter, bullets hitting the sub's deck.

Schwarz dropped and rolled, coming up on one knee. His Uzi tracked in on the figures at the rail and he fired off two short bursts. He saw one of the men stumble back, clutching at a shoulder that had burst open under the impact of 9 mm slugs. The man screamed as he saw the mess the bullets had made of flesh and muscle, catching his fingers on the jagged splinters of bone protruding from the pulpy wound. Schwarz's second target, turning to see what had happened to his partner, was hit in the side of the face by the second burst and he went down screaming, clutching at his bloody cheek and shattered jaw.

Blancanales ran by his partner and took a run down the sub's hull, then leaped for the open hatch in the side of the *Red Star*. He almost lost his footing as he landed. Regaining his balance, Blancanales jumped down into the hold, then crossed to the metal ladder that gave access to the deck of the ship. He went up the ladder, all the time hoping that the upper hatch wasn't secured. When he reached it and put his shoul-

der against it, the metal flap lifted. Blancanales raised
it far enough to allow him to check out the deck area.

He saw a couple of bodies on the deck near the rail.
He also saw the two men Schwarz had recently hit.
They were clutching their wounds, all interest lost in
the fight.

Making sure he had a full magazine in his Uzi,
Blancanales pushed the hatch fully open and stepped
onto the deck, glancing back and forth. He could hear
voices, some of them raised in an argument, but no
one was in sight. He moved across the deck and stood
with his back to the nearest bulkhead, listening. The
voices were over his head, on the upper deck. Blancanales went to the rail and peered over. Schwarz was
still where he had last seen him. When he caught his
partner's eye, Blancanales signaled for Schwarz to join
him. His partner nodded and immediately headed for
the freighter's hatch.

Blancanales heard footsteps. A number of people
were coming down the steps from the upper deck, still
arguing. When they came into sight, Blancanales
counted five of them. Three were obviously members
of the crew, all carrying AKs. The other two wore
civilian clothing and Blancanales recognized them
from the file photos he had seen. They were the two
men he had seen board the freighter when it was being
refueled in Govograd—Viktor Seminov and Mansur's
man Gabril Yasim.

Seminov seemed to be doing most of the talking.
He was obviously agitated. Probably unnerved by the
sudden turn of events, and most likely he was starting
to have second thoughts. His anger was focused on

Yasim. It looked as if Seminov was blaming Yasim for the attack on the sub.

Gabril Yasim stopped in his tracks, turning to glare at Seminov. He began to berate the man, his composure gone. He placed a hand against Seminov's chest and pushed the man against the bulkhead. The blow was hard and Seminov's glasses almost slipped from his nose. Seminov's face paled and he raised a hand to ward Yasim off.

And as he did he caught sight of Schwarz emerging from the open hatch behind Blancanales.

He jabbed a finger in Schwarz's direction and screamed a warning at Yasim.

Yasim glanced over, and when he spotted Schwarz, his hand darted inside his jacket and came out holding an autopistol. He snap-aimed and fired.

Blancanales had caught a glimpse of his partner emerging from the hatch. The moment he heard Seminov yell he stepped out from the cover of the bulkhead corner, his Uzi coming on track as he saw Yasim in the moment of firing.

The slug from Yasim's gun hit Schwarz in the fleshy underside of his left arm and shoulder. The impact knocked him back, and he caught his legs against the edge of the hatch cover, going down.

Blancanales's Uzi exploded with sound, sending a stream of 9 mm slugs into the group around Seminov and Yasim. The Able Team commando held his trigger back until the weapon exhausted its magazine.

Seminov and Yasim suffered multiple hits, bodies jerking under the impact. Blancanales eased the spitting muzzle of the SMG around, catching the three crewmen as they began to bring their own weapons into play. Two went down on the deck, the third catching only a couple of slugs in his side. He staggered but stayed on his feet and lifted his Kalashnikov in a sustained effort to take on his attacker.

The Uzi locked on empty. Blancanales let it drop, suspended by the strap looped around his neck, and reached for the holstered Beretta. The moment he had the weapon out, safety off, he took quick steps in the direction of the wounded crewman and triggered three fast shots that impacted against the man's skull, just over his left ear. The bullets cored into his head, cutting their way through his brain to emerge out the opposite side in a mushroom of bloody bits. The crewman hit the bulkhead and slid down it to the deck, trailing blood as he fell.

The scrape of a shoe on the deck brought Blancanales around. He found himself face-to-face with Gabril Yasim. The terrorist was bleeding badly. More ran from his mouth as he stared at Blancanales and then realized he still had his pistol in his hand. He started to raise it. Blancanales shot him twice in the chest and put him down permanently.

Crossing the deck, the Able Team commando bent over Schwarz, who was sitting on the hatch frame, his hand pressed tightly against his wound. He was saying something under his breath that Blancanales couldn't make out until he leaned in closer and caught his partner's litany.

"...fuck...fuck...fuck..."

Blancanales smiled indulgently. He had been shot himself before and he knew how much it hurt. It wasn't a time for poetical responses and Schwarz's expression fit the moment exactly.

"Go for cover," Blancanales said, grabbing Schwarz by his good arm and half-dragging him away from the hatch toward the bulkier cover of a ventilator housing.

They moved behind the steel housing, Schwarz crouching and pulling his Beretta.

"How many are there in this crew?" he asked.

Blancanales looked up from inserting a fresh magazine into his Uzi, scanning the empty deck.

"Not as many as there were when they arrived," he said.

"What the hell kind of answer is that?" Schwarz asked.

"Best I could come up with at short notice."

Movement on the bridge attracted their attention. A figure with an autorifle leaned over the surround and opened fire. The bullets clanged against the ventilator housing.

"You able to handle that pistol?" Blancanales asked.

Schwarz nodded.

"Get that guy to back off then," Blancanales said.

Schwarz watched him pull a fragmentation grenade from his pack and pull the pin.

"Go."

Schwarz laid a trio of single shots at the bridge housing. The moment the rifleman pulled back Blancanales stepped from cover and lobbed the grenade up and over the surround. It hit the decking and detonated. The force shattered glass in the bridge housing and a shower of debris spouted up from the point of impact.

Schwarz waited, his Beretta held steady. As the grenade's smoke drifted away, the figure of the rifleman lurched into view. The left side of his face and body was tattered and bloody. He still held the rifle in his right hand. Schwarz's Beretta cracked once, the 9 mm bullet hitting the wounded man in the chest, knocking him back out of sight.

"You want to keep covering me?" Blancanales said.

He took a selection of smoke and fragmentation grenades from his pack tossing several along the deserted deck. The explosions and the thick smoke created a feeling of devastation. The last fragmentation grenade was thrown up at the bridge. This dropped the grenade in through the shattered front window. Contained within the steel structure of the bridge the explosion was loud and the concussion blew out all the remaining windows. Smoke and flame billowed, and as the sound of the blast diminished the Able Team duo heard the wail of an alarm. The sound was taken up by more alarms that came from other sections of the freighter.

"Now you've gone and done it," Schwarz said.

The alarms galvanized the remainder of the freighter's crew into action. They began to appear on deck, coming out of the smoke, their sense of survival overriding any concerns about the submarine. Remaining behind their cover, Blancanales and Schwarz witnessed the crewmen launching a lifeboat from the starboard side of the *Red Star*. The moment the lifeboat hit the water the crew pushed off and rowed away from the ship until they were well clear.

Blancanales slipped his backpack from his shoulders and set it on the deck. He dug inside until he located the small Medi-kit he carried. While Schwarz kept watch, Blancanales worked pressure pads over his partner's wound, securing it with the bandages from the kit. He pulled Schwarz's clothing back in place, then fashioned a sling to keep the arm immobile.

"No running, jumping, or other kinds of strenuous activity. Doctor's orders."

Schwarz stared at him. "You're joking?"

"Combat situations notwithstanding, no dangerous moves."

"Pol, go find a radio. See if you can contact Lipov. Tell him to send the cavalry."

"You okay?"

"No. I hurt, and if you ask any more lamebrain questions I'll throw up all over you."

Blancanales crossed the deck and made sure he had the metal bulkhead at his back. He worked his way along to the closest hatch and slipped inside. He was directly below the bridge and figured he couldn't be too far from the radio room. He checked out the passage. Open doors led to deserted cabins. Blancanales tried to shut out the persistent clamor of the alarms that were still clanging. He located the radio room and peered inside. It was empty. There was a mug of tea or coffee on the table that held the communications array. Steam still rose from the contents. Blancanales sat in the operator's seat and checked out the radio. All the operating legends were in Russian but the Able

Team commando wasn't fazed. Radios were radios. He slipped on the headset and heard music coming from some distant station. He reached out and began to change the frequency to the one Lipov had given Able Team. The radio wasn't a current model, and Blancanales had to make the change manually. He watched the readout and finally saw the correct frequency displayed. He locked it in and pressed his transmit button.

"American Eagle to Russian Bear. Are you receiving? Come in. Come in. Over."

The hiss of static was the only reply when Blancanales hit the button. He made his call again. After a few empty seconds a voice came through.

"This is Russian Bear. I have you. What's your condition? Over."

Blancanales recognized Andrei Lipov's voice the moment he spoke.

"The party is in full swing. We have partial control and are ready for assistance. One of our team is wounded, so we would appreciate medical assist. On a positive note, Seminov and Yasim are both dead. Over."

"Can you give me your position? Over."

"Best I can do is to leave this connection open. Can you locate us via the radio transmission? Over."

"Yes. Can you maintain status for the next few hours? If possible we will get assistance sooner. Over."

"If we can't you can bury us at sea. Over."

"One more small thing. The paperwork Seminov

would have with him? Locate and destroy. Agreed? Over.''

"Understood. Will comply.''

Blancanales left the connection open, laid the headset on the table and stood. He left the radio room, closing the door behind him and retraced his steps to the deck. Recalling what Lipov had asked, he went to where Seminov lay and checked out the man's pockets. The sheet containing the arming-launch codes was in an envelope inside Seminov's thick parka. Blancanales studied the sequences of numbers. On paper they didn't seem much more than what they appeared to be. Nothing more than printed numbers with little significance. In reality they were the catalysts that in the right hands would become the precursors of mass destruction.

Moving along the deck, Blancanales saw a number of packing cases that had been part of the deck cargo. One of his grenade explosions had shattered the cases and left them burning. Blancanales screwed up the list in his hand and dropped it into the flames, watching it ignite, burn and turn into black ashes.

Then he returned to where Schwarz sat nursing his shoulder and watching the lifeboat holding the surviving crew members of the freighter.

VARIC RESISTED the urge to rub his streaming eyes. He tried to move away from the misty gas that was swirling around the control room, but there seemed to be more of the damned stuff. Close by, Kerim was suffering from the same irritation, as were the members of the sub's crew.

Varic could hardly believe the way things had suddenly turned about. One minute he and his team were in full control of the submarine, the next his whole chain of command was falling apart. He had been unable to make a full count of his men, but he was sure that he had already lost a substantial percentage of them.

Explosions, gunfire, then the tear gas. It had all erupted so swiftly. Too fast for him to do anything about it. The men he had sent up to handle the attack had been beaten back, killed or wounded. He had received a garbled report about one of the open hatches being disabled by the explosion he had heard. It was impossible for the hatch to be closed, which meant the submarine wouldn't be able to submerge without taking on a crippling amount of water. It might have been possible to isolate the flooded section, but there was also the risk of sea water getting into the missiles compartment. If that happened and the missile solid fuel came into contact with sea water, the combination could create a toxic gas that would kill any human who breathed it in.

Varic's confidence had been shaken by the sudden turn of events. All the careful planning and preparation had been swept aside. The precise hijacking of the sub and the underwater voyage to rendezvous with the freighter had been interrupted by...whom exactly? The thought occurred that he didn't even know who the attack force were. He dismissed the thought.

What did it matter?

It *did* matter that someone had attacked the submarine and seemed to be gaining control. Varic felt his anger rising.

Anger. Yes. Time to show them he wasn't finished yet.

"Kerim," he called, blinking the tears from his stinging eyes.

"I'm here."

"Let's find these bastards and show them who they are up against."

Varic brought his Kalashnikov into view, turned and made his way across the control room. His streaming eyes and burning throat irritated him, adding to his anger and frustration.

Behind Kerim the helmsman pushed up from his seat, lunging at the terrorist. His full weight slammed into Kerim and drove the man across the control room. Off balance, Kerim stumbled and fell, crashing to the deck with the helmsman on top of him. He caught hold of Kerim's hair and yanked the man's head off the deck, then slammed it back down again. He kept repeating the action until Kerim's face had become a crushed, bloody mask and his twitching body had stilled.

LYONS SAW Varic as the hijack leader reached the exit hatch from the control room. The man carried a Kalashnikov at the ready. The moment he made out Lyons's shape through his watering eyes Varic opened fire. The steady crackle of the AK echoed along the passage, slugs bouncing off the steel bulkheads.

When Rashenski recognized Varic, he raised his pistol and fired. The slug clipped Varic's left shoulder, knocking him back against the hatch. Varic turned the AK in Rashenski's direction, but Lyons fired first, triggering his Uzi at the black-clad hijacker. The long burst tore into Varic's lower body, shearing through flesh and muscle and into his organs. Some of the slugs blew out the side of Varic's torso, splintering a number of ribs. The hijacker felt himself pushed backward by the impact. He threw out his hands to keep from falling, his weapon forgotten as it dropped to the deck. He slumped against the hatch, feeling the pain start to flare as his body reacted to the damage caused by Lyons's autofire.

Rashenski leaned toward Varic. "Now I take my ship back."

Varic managed to lift his head to stare up at Rashenski. He saw the muzzle of the man's pistol moving in close to his head, felt the cold metal touch his forehead. And then Rashenski pulled the trigger, blowing Varic's brains across the gray-painted metal of the bulkhead.

"Captain."

Rashenski turned as he heard Berin's voice. The young submariner was running along the passage. He still carried his Kalashnikov.

When he saw Lyons he began to raise the weapon. Rashenski waved him to stop. As Berin didn't understand English Rashenski spoke in Russian. "This is a friend. An American. Part of a team who boarded us and fought off the hijackers."

"We have retaken the engine room. The hijackers who stayed to guard us when the others went to fight are both dead. And we have the explosive pack."

"Varic is also dead," Rashenski said.

The helmsman appeared in the hatch. He carried a Kalashnikov. His hands were very bloody and the front of his shirt was streaked with more.

"The one called Kerim is also dead, Captain."

"I believe that between us we have taken back the submarine," Rashenski told Lyons.

FIVE HOURS LATER a Russian navy ship arrived and the transfer of any remaining hijackers and crew members of the freighter took place. A Russian medical orderly dealt with Schwarz's wound. He underwent an operation to remove the bullet still lodged under the skin of his shoulder and remained in a bunk for the return trip to Govograd.

Before Lyons left the sub, which would return to its home base, he spent some time with Rashenski. The captain of the submarine, his own wound attended to and bandaged heavily, was in the control room with his own crew again. They were preparing to get under way.

"You realize that by blowing that hatch we will be forced to sail back on the surface?" the Russian told Lyons.

"Well, I'm all cut up about that, Rashenski," Lyons said. "At the time we had no choice."

Rashenski smiled suddenly. "My friend, I am making a joke." He put out a hand. "You saved my life and my submarine. I cannot stay mad at you forever."

Lyons took the offered hand. "Next time be careful who you let on board."

"There may not be a next time," Rashenski said.

"The talk is that the Typhoon class may soon be scrapped. So I may be out of a job. What then? Who wants retired submarine captains?"

Lyons was still debating that point when he returned to the Russian navy ship. His train of thought was broken by Blancanales.

"They found a big cache of weapons in those containers," he said. "Autorifles, explosives, rocket launchers. Varic's bunch looked like they were ready to start a full-scale war."

"So what's new?" was Lyons's terse response.

CHAPTER SIXTEEN

Somalia—2:00 a.m.

"As soon as we've all confirmed we're in position, we go," McCarter said. "Cal, T.J., Rafe, you take out the machine guns. When you've given the all clear head for the plane. Gary and I won't move until we get the call you're inside."

Phoenix Force was on the perimeter of the airfield, gathered in a dusty depression that allowed them a clear view of the area. They had checked out the terrain, watching patiently until they had confirmed that apart from the machine-gun posts only three armed sentries moved around the area. The presence of the sentries meant that James, Hawkins and Encizo were going to have to make a wider sweep around the edge of the field before they could close in on their individual targets.

"We set?" McCarter asked.

Once he received confirmation McCarter nodded and watched the three Phoenix Force commandos slip away into the shadows.

ALL CONTACT HAD BEEN LOST with the submarine and the freighter *Red Star*. Mansur's attempts to speak to his contact in Govograd had also been negative.

Since the breakdown in communications, Mansur had been unable to settle. Too many coincidences for it to be cast aside lightly. First losing his people. Then the escape of the undercover man, Mahoud. Attacks on his followers in Afghanistan. So many things going wrong. Now the possible loss of the Typhoon submarine. Mansur had no proof that was what had happened, but his instincts told him he was not far from the truth.

All he had left now was the hijacked airliner and the nuclear device that would now be in the luggage hold. That part of his plan *had* to go right.

It had to.

Mansur stepped outside. He looked beyond the oasis, toward the east where the dawn had begun to lighten the sky. There was a fresh coolness in the air, and he took a cleansing breath. The encampment was still. Only the guards moving about on the perimeter. He walked to the pool and stared down into the tranquil water. What he sought was still not there. His own dark reflection was all he saw.

In that still part of the new day Mansur knelt and immersed himself in prayer. He felt the fine grains of sand touch his robe, lifted by the gentle breeze that had sprung up. At this reflective time he felt as one with the sand. He was like a single grain. On his own he was nothing. Weak and unable to achieve anything. But when he was with his brothers and they combined their strength, like the many grains of sand, they could change the face of history. That was Abrim Mansur's destiny. To change the world and leave his mark in such a way that it would never be forgotten.

When he had completed his devotions, Mansur woke the helicopter pilot and told him to ready the aircraft. He wanted to fly to the airstrip and be on hand when the operation moved to its next phase.

Something within had told him he had to be there.

JAMES WAS CLOSE ENOUGH now that he could even make out the features of the man behind the 7.62 mm FN MAG machine gun. The gunner was seated on the sandbags that encircled his post, his back to the 747.

The Phoenix Force commando remained flat on the ground, no more than ten feet from the relaxed guard. He wanted to make sure the machine gunner was alone. In the long minutes he studied the area James saw nothing. Satisfied that the gunner was on a lone vigil, James reached down and slid his sheathed knife free, the handle fitting snugly against his palm. Easing forward, James snaked his lean form across the sandy earth, never once taking his eyes off his target. He stopped and remained motionless a couple of times when the guard stirred. On one occasion the man stood, stretching lazily to ease cramped muscles. James waited until the guard resumed his seat.

Closing in on the sandbag enclosure, James pushed up off the ground, rising to his full height. A final step brought him up behind the guard, and he didn't hesitate. His left hand reached around to clamp over the guard's mouth, his left knee rising to jab into the lower back. James pushed forward with his knee, using his clamped left hand to jerk the guard's head back, stretching the flesh taut across the throat. Bringing around his knife, the Phoenix Force warrior placed the razor-keen blade against the throat. He made a deliberate and deep cutting motion, drawing the blade from left to right, severing flesh, tendons and arteries. The guard struggled as he felt the blade slice into his flesh. The only sound was the soft rush of air from his severed windpipe and then warm blood began to pulse from his opened arteries and veins. James held the man close, his knife hand pressed tight against the chest to hold the man still while he fought against encroaching death. The guard's thrashing ceased quickly, his blood drenching the front of his shirt and pants until his heart stopped pumping and there was nothing left to fight with. James sensed the man's surrender, coupled with the relaxation of his limbs. With the man becoming a deadweight James allowed him to slip down inside the enclosure, following him down so he could lay the body out of sight.

James wiped away the blood streaking his right hand, put his knife back in its sheath, then moved behind the machine gun, checking that it was loaded and ready for use. He took a look at the ammunition box fixed to the belt feeder on the left side of the weapon. Raising the cover, he made sure that the belt was settled in the feedway, then closed the cover again.

Reaching over his shoulder, James pulled his slung M-16/M-203 combo over his head and rested it against the side of the enclosure. He had a selection of 40 mm grenades in his ammo pouches, along with extra mags for his M-16 and the Beretta 92-F pistol.

James clicked his com-link and informed McCarter he was in control of the machine-gun post.

DURING A PREVIOUS VISIT to Somalia, Hawkins had been forced to take defensive action during a rescue operation. Innocent villagers were being terrorized by a Somali warlord and his dozen gunmen. Hawkins was part of a UN team, under the command of a Swedish officer. Despite the obvious fact that the villagers were going to be killed, the officer had backed off and the villagers were left unprotected. Hawkins had stood alone against the warlord and when the man threatened him with a gun, Hawkins responded in kind and shot the man. On their return to UN headquarters in Mogadishu the officer who had backed off tried to threaten Hawkins with a murder charge. Hawkins, refusing to bow down to the threat, called the officer's bluff and suggested they inform the media about what had really happened. After various heated arguments back and forth, the incident became a closed book. Hawkins resigned from the Army with an honorable discharge.

Now he was back in Somalia, only this time there would be no fudging the issue. The guilty would be dealt with in the only language they understood. The innocent people on the 747 wouldn't be abandoned to the wolves.

That thought was uppermost in Hawkins's mind as he rose from the darkness behind the machine gunner, his combat knife rising and finding its unsuspecting target....

RAFAEL ENCIZO KNEW the capricious nature of life only too well. The unexpected had a habit of turning things around and dealing out bad hands at the most awkward moments.

He had made his careful approach to the machine-gun emplacement, his movements slow and unobserved by the gunner manning the weapon. Encizo had seen no other likely individual in the area. The man he was closing in on sat behind his weapon with the intent of a rookie on his first sentry duty. He even went through the basic check and recheck of the ammunition belt, lifting the cover and peering at it, then closing the cover. He swiveled the gun back and forth, tilted it skyward. His movements kept his attention on the machine gun, which was helpful as far as Encizo was concerned. It was also a little fascinating to the Cuban. He couldn't help but wonder why the man was so attentive. Unless he was nervous. Perhaps overreacting to the possibility of an attack? Encizo considered the options. Whatever they were it would make no difference to the outcome.

The little Cuban was aware of the implications of Abrim Mansur's threatened strike against New York. The outcome of such an attack would leave the city and the nation reeling. He was also aware of the cold and deliberate intent behind the threat. Mansur, regardless of his personal attitude toward America, was a mean son of a bitch in Encizo's opinion. He was getting a little tired of hearing the justification these people gave every time they orchestrated atrocities. As far as Rafael Encizo was concerned, they were cowards who sat in safety while their followers were sent out to die. They showed little courage themselves, hiding in the shadows, moving from place to place, inciting others to risk everything.

This time at least Phoenix was in the position where they could hit back, take out the terrorists *before* they pressed the button.

Ready to make his move, Encizo reached down for his Cold Steel Tanto knife. Drawing it from the sheath strapped to his thigh, the Cuban pushed up off the ground, grabbing a handful of the machine gunner's hair, and dragged the man back across the top layer of sandbags. The gunner gasped at the sudden attack, his eyes wide and staring up at Encizo's face. It was the last thing he saw before Encizo made the fatal cut, the chill, honed steel biting deep into the man's naked throat. The gunner's body went into a massive spasm, his legs kicking out. Blood sprayed in wide arcs as the man's furiously beating heart pumped away his dying moments. Arms flailed, fingers tearing at the coarse material of the sandbags.

A shadow fell across the gunner's body, blotting out his contorted features. Encizo sensed the close presence, as the newcomer began to take aim with his Kalashnikov. He had no time to even wonder where the guy had come from, or how he had missed him during his approach. Encizo swiveled and dived in low, spoiling the man's aim. The muzzle swung skyward as the guy recovered his balance. The butt end of the Kalashnikov struck the sandbag inches away from Encizo's head. He dropped to the ground, twisting his upper body to get a good look at his attacker. The guy was tall, lean, his black skull shaved. His lips peeled back in a feral grin as he hauled himself around for a second strike at Encizo, the autorifle lashing out with unexpected speed.

Encizo felt the sting of pain as the blow glanced off his shoulder. He was still moving, regaining his balance as he gathered his legs beneath him and sprang forward and up. His left hand batted away the descending AK, his right streaking in from waist height, the Tanto fighting knife held with the cutting edge uppermost. It sank into the target's body just above the navel, propelled by every ounce of strength in the Cuban's arm. The blade penetrated to the hilt, the target gasping in shock as Encizo yanked upward, flesh parting to open a deep cavity. There was a warm rush of soft intestines and blood. The stricken target fell back, dropping his rifle to clutch at his organs, sinking to his knees with a moan that came from his very soul. He sank to the ground, his body seeming to deflate as it settled on the bloody earth.

Encizo leaned back against the wall of sandbags, taking a moment to breathe deeply before he keyed his com set and informed McCarter he was in control.

THE BRITON ACTIVATED an open channel, speaking to his three team members at the same time.

"We're going to move in toward the control tower. Disable those machine guns then head for the plane. Gary and I will cover your backs from this side."

McCarter clicked off transmission. "You set?"

Manning nodded.

They broke cover, moving at an angle across the open ground between them and the control tower. As they covered the final section, they were able to see a faint light in the glass-fronted control room on top of the tower.

Manning suddenly caught hold of McCarter's sleeve, guiding him to one side, where they crouched in shadow by a stack of discarded oil drums.

Approaching footsteps heralded one of the patrolling sentries. Manning reached inside one of his belt pouches and withdrew a wire garrote. He handed his Uzi to McCarter and circled the stack of drums, coming up behind the sentry as the man stepped by. McCarter heard very little of the attack, only a brief scuffle and a few seconds of harsh breathing as Manning's target fought the encircling strand of steel wire before it sank in deeply and cut off his air supply. The silence that followed was more acute than before. A dragging sound reached McCarter's ears, and he turned in time to see Manning drag the lifeless body behind the stack of oil drums.

Manning took his Uzi back.

"I guess the others should be well into their move on the plane by now," he said.

THEY WERE CROUCHING in the deep shadows beneath the 747's fuselage.

"The main passenger door is open," Hawkins said. "They have an access platform in place. Saw it when I moved in."

"That's handy," James said.

"What's not so handy is the armed guy standing at the top of the platform."

"See what you mean."

"So?" Hawkins persisted.

"Okay," James said. "We don't have time for fancy plans. We work our way around to the base of the access platform. T.J., you and me. Stun grenades ready. Rafe, you hit that guy at the door. The minute he goes down T.J. and I go up the steps and inside and toss the grenades. Once they go off we move into the cabin and you follow like your ass is on fire."

"We get any opportunity to assess the risks here?" Hawkins asked.

"Hell, no," James said.

"There goes democracy out the window."

"This doesn't have a damn thing to do with democracy. I'm older than you, and Rafe is older than both of us."

"So how come I don't have a say?" Encizo asked.

"Because you are way too old to be allowed to make decisions like this."

"Shit," Hawkins said, "I got lost around chapter three."

They moved along the 747's length, making for the front of the huge aircraft. Concealed by the front undercarriage wheels, they prepared themselves for the coming assault. James and Hawkins held stun grenades in each hand, the pins pulled so they held the spring-loaded levers down themselves. Encizo set his Uzi for single shot, locking and loading before they walked silently from beneath the underbelly of the plane and down the side of the access platform.

Encizo moved to the lead, peering around the edge of the platform so he could see the passenger door and the armed guard leaning against the frame. He took a long, heavy suppressor from his backpack and screwed it to the threaded muzzle of his Uzi. Shouldering the weapon the Cuban targeted the guard, squeezing back on the trigger. The shot punched out with a low thud. The 9 mm bullet hit the guard over his left eye, spinning him away from the open doorway. As he tumbled back inside the plane, James and Hawkins sprinted up the steps, entered the plane and threw their stun grenades into the cabin area. The moment they had released the grenades they pulled back and stepped outside, turning their backs on the open doorway, clamping their hands over their ears.

The windows of the 747 lit up with the blinding light from the detonating stun grenades. The light flash was accompanied by the harsh crack of the explosion. Within the confines of the 747's body the effect would have been dramatic, affecting anyone in the main cabin.

Removing the suppressor, Encizo ran up the steps and joined James and Hawkins as they went back inside, weapons up and ready.

The interior was misty with smoke from the grenades. In the half-light passengers were either slumped in their seats or staggering along the aisles, clutching their ears, eyes unseeing from the brilliant light emitted by the stun grenades.

The Phoenix Force commandos ignored the passengers, who were easily identified by their appearance and clothing.

Hawkins spotted one hijacker, clad in tan clothing and wielding an AK. He was pushing his way through the milling passengers, lashing out blindly with his rifle. Despite his inability to see fully, the hijacker struck a couple of the passengers before Hawkins put him down with a single shot from his Uzi. The bullet hit the target in the side of his head, knocking him off his feet.

Encizo, recalling the photographs of the two men identified as being part of Mansur's group, searched the faces of the passengers as he eased his way along the aisle. The man would be even more determined not to be spotted now that the hijack had been compromised. He would be doing his best to slip away unnoticed, possibly hoping to be reunited with his fellow hijackers on the outside for protection.

He might have got away with it if he hadn't been moving in the wrong direction. The standing passengers were all struggling to reach the front of the plane, except for one man, his back to the rest as he pushed toward the rear.

Encizo caught sight of the man and increased his own pace, pushing aside the throng of passengers as he went after his man. The man broke clear of the main group of passengers. In the clear he suddenly realized he had exposed himself and turned to look back at his pursuer.

Yusef Kasim.

Encizo recognized his face from the downloaded images he had seen on *Dragon Slayer's* computer.

"Kasim," he called out.

Kasim ignored the challenge. He reached under his jacket for the handgun Hanni Amir had covertly passed to him before stepping off the plane following its landing. He turned quickly, raising the weapon, and felt the stunning impact of the burst of autofire from

Encizo's Uzi. The burst drove him across the aisle and he fell across a row of seats, the handgun slipping from his fingers. He tried to untangle himself from the seats, but his strength was slipping away fast. He had time to raise his head and see the man who had shot him moving along the plane. He saw the man lift the Uzi again, angling the muzzle down at his body. Encizo tripped the trigger a second time, and Kasim's body jerked under the impact of the burst.

A flicker of movement off to his left brought Encizo around, his Uzi tracking ahead of him. He held his finger clear of the trigger when he recognized the figure of a young woman in the uniform of a flight attendant. She was blond and attractive, and looked terrified.

"I'm not going to hurt you," Encizo said.

He reached out with his left hand, the young woman grasping it tightly. She had been standing in the alcove of the 747's galley section. The wall of the galley had protected her from the flash of the stun grenade, though the sound had dulled her hearing.

"Do you know where the passenger called Hanni Amir is?"

Susan Morris studied Encizo's lips. Part of her training as an attendant had been to study and learn to read lips. It often helped on flights when there could be a degree of noise from other passengers.

"Oh, him? He was the one who took over the plane. Threatened us with a bomb. He got off the plane when we landed," she said. She indicated Kasim's bloody body. "Was he one of them?"

Encizo nodded.

"Have any more terrorists come on board?"

Susan shook her head. "Only the other one you shot when you came in. There was one in the doorway. Did you…?"

"Yes. Have they taken any of the crew off the plane?"

"The captain, Percy Dexter. He was taken off after we landed. I watched through one of the windows. They took him to the control tower. We haven't seen him since."

"Rest of the crew?"

"On the flight deck."

"Passengers on the upper deck?"

Susan shook her head. "Just what you see down here. We run a lot of half-full flights these days."

Encizo picked up the gun Kasim had dropped.

"Had any training with one of these?"

"A little."

Encizo handed her the pistol.

"When we leave close the main door and secure it. Keep it that way until you get the all clear."

"How long is that going to be? These people need to get outside. You've probably noticed it doesn't smell too good in here."

"Sorry, but you'll have to wait a little longer. Try to settle the passengers and let the effects of the stun grenades wear off."

"I understand."

Encizo moved along the plane, pushing his way through the milling passengers. He encountered James and Hawkins at the front.

"Yusef Kasim is dead. The other passenger, Hanni Amir, walked off the plane after it landed."

James activated his com set and gave McCarter a quick rundown of their move on the plane.

"The pilot, name of Percy Dexter. He was taken off the plane and taken to the control tower."

"Okay, we're moving in now."

THEY HAD ALMOST REACHED the control tower when the flap of one of the tents was thrown open and a man stepped outside. He was still buttoning his shirt, peering around the site. He wore a holstered side arm.

"Jesus," McCarter muttered under his breath.

The newcomer turned and looked directly at the Phoenix Force duo. Whether by accident or design, no one would ever know. But that simple act wiped away the element of surprise.

The hijacker went for his hand gun, most probably aware that he was at a disadvantage.

Manning swung around the muzzle of his Uzi and hit the guy with a short burst that put him on his face.

"Here we go," McCarter said. He clicked on transmit and gave the general command to the rest of the team. "Cat's out of the bag. Let's do it."

He slid his M-16 A-2 off his shoulder and plucked an HEDP round for the underslung M-203 launcher from one of the pouches on his harness. Snapping the round into place, McCarter followed close behind Manning as they started toward the control tower.

The Uzi burst had alerted the encampment. Figures were starting to emerge from the cluster of tents.

Lights went on in the control tower and the adjoining buildings.

An AK-74 started to crackle, bullets smacking the ground just short of McCarter and Manning. Someone would find their range in short order, McCarter realized. He turned and aimed, triggered the launcher at the standing trucks. The round struck the closest truck, the resultant explosion blowing the vehicle apart. Fuel detonated a couple of seconds later, spraying in all directions. The destruction of the first truck had a ripple effect, heat and concussion reaching to the next vehicle. The second fuel tank blew, lifting the rear of the truck off the ground and bouncing it against the last truck in the row.

The suddenness of the powerful detonations caught the hijackers' attention for long seconds, allowing McCarter and Manning to reach the base of the control tower.

With their backs to the wall the Phoenix Force pair was able to turn its weapons on the exposed hijackers.

They took out three of the armed hijackers as the men snapped out of their momentary hesitation, dumping them on the ground.

Manning picked up a rush of figures from his left. The crackle of autofire preceded the snap of slugs peppering the wall close by. He felt concrete chips hit his sleeve. Manning turned, bringing his Uzi around, and triggered twin bursts, catching his targets on the move. The hijackers went down hard, raising dust as they hit the ground.

Triggering shots at anything that moved in their direction, McCarter edged closer to the door of the control tower. He used a booted foot to kick the door open, ducking inside. Movement at the foot of the access stairs drew McCarter's attention. A figure lunged at him, a knife in his right hand. McCarter used the M-16 to parry the man's thrust, then swept the butt around to catch the side of his opponent's face. The blow snapped the guy's head back, blood spraying from a split in his cheek. The pain failed to halt his attack and he made a wild slash with the knife, slicing open McCarter's left sleeve and catching the flesh of his upper arm. The Briton swore as the keen edge of the blade sliced his flesh. He backed off, his opponent mistakenly thinking McCarter was retreating. Instead the Phoenix Force leader came to a dead stop, reversed the M-16 and drove it directly into the man's face, putting all his strength behind the blow. Under the impact the guy's face caved in, teeth smashed from his gums and his nose flattened. Blood squirted in streams. The man stumbled back against the wall, the knife dropping from his fingers as he reached up to cover his crushed face. McCarter pulled the M-16 back online and put a single shot into the man's head.

Manning barreled in through the door, turning to fire as he did.

"Cover me," McCarter yelled and went up the stairs two at a time. He clicked on his com-link and snapped out the order to Jack Grimaldi. "Pickup time, flyboy. Whenever you're ready."

JACK GRIMALDI HEARD the terse command from McCarter. He leaned forward to fire up *Dragon Slayer*'s engines. As the power started to build, he checked his computer readout, affirming that his course was logged in and ready to guide him to the target. He pulled on his helmet, activating the slave system that locked him into the helicopter's weapons array. The integrated system allowed him to target the aircraft's weapons simply by eye contact with the display on his visor. A touch of another button on his console brought all weapons systems, chain gun and missiles clusters on line.

Dragon Slayer rose at his touch. Grimaldi took the helicopter to altitude, then brought it on course. He upped the power, the sleek machine streaking over the Somali landscape.

Off to the east the sky was starting to show pale light....

THE SUDDEN ERUPTION as the trucks exploded told James, Hawkins and Encizo that their two partners had committed them fully.

They were on the ground, cutting across the strip in the direction of the main encampment. On the tail of the explosion they heard the crackle of autofire.

They were coming up on the area when McCarter's call to Jack Grimaldi came through their com-links.

"Clean-up time," James said into his mike.

He snapped an M-397 round into his M-16/M-203 combo and tailed off from Hawkins and Encizo as he caught sight of a tight group of armed men heading in his direction. The black Phoenix Force commando stood his ground as the group raised its weapons and opened fire on him. James felt something snap through the material of his jacket. He leveled the M-16 and triggered the grenade.

The M-397 round, designated as a BFR, arced through the air to drop in front of the advancing hijackers. It struck the ground, giving the impression nothing was going to happen. Moments later a small internal charge threw it back into the air, and as it reached its height from the ground the grenade exploded. The blast tore into the advancing hijackers, hitting them in the upper bodies, shredding flesh, replacing confusion with pain, and in a number of instances causing death.

Hawkins had cut off toward the collection of tents as armed figures began to emerge. His Uzi crackled in short bursts as he used his ammunition carefully. He coolly locked onto each target, making certain he had acquisition before he touched the trigger. His targets went down under the calculated fire. Plucking a fragmentation grenade from his harness, Hawkins armed the bomb and tossed it in toward the tents as he got within range. The grenade exploded, distributing its deadly fragments through the tents. Scorched cloth burst into flame.

As Hawkins moved by the tents, he heard an AK-74 crack and felt the 5.45 mm slug pass through his backpack. The force turned him half around, and Hawkins found himself facing his attacker. The hijacker, bloody and scorched from the grenade blast, had his Kalashnikov to his shoulder as he aimed for a second shot. Hawkins let himself drop, rolling as his body struck the ground. Flat on the ground the American commando pushed his Uzi forward and fired be-

fore the hijacker could adjust his aim. The burst of
9 mm autofire caught the guy in the groin and lower
body, kicking him off his feet, his rifle bouncing from
his hands as he landed, dark sprays of blood following
him down.

One of the smaller buildings had attracted a number
of the hijackers. Rafael Encizo had noticed the men
moving to the building and slipping inside. He saw
they were collecting additional weapons. Two of the
hijackers emerged, one carrying an RPG rocket
launcher, the other man toting a number of the missiles
for use in the weapon.

Encizo didn't know what they intended to do with
the launcher. He decided whatever it was there would
be no gain for Phoenix Force. The Cuban ran toward
the two men, bringing himself within range, and pulled
the Uzi into target acquisition. He triggered a burst,
arcing the SMG between the pair of hijackers. Encizo
maintained full control over the Uzi, laying down his
fire with accuracy. The 9 mm slugs ripped into the
two men, knocking them off their feet. One stumbled
against the wall of the building.

Still on the move, the little Cuban freed a fragmentation grenade, pulled the pin and tossed the grenade
in through the open door of the building.

The resulting blast indicated the building had held
a significant supply of munitions. The explosion blew
the structure apart, sending a burst of flame into the
sky and hurling men off their feet as the concussion
spread. Debris filled the air, amid a cloud of thick dust
that billowed out from the blast site. Shattered stone
sailed through the air. Encizo, on his knees, bent his

head down into his chest as the cloud of dust washed over him.

As soon as the dust cleared, he pushed to his feet. He could see Hawkins and James moving forward as they drove the hijackers away from the cover of the buildings and out onto the open strip. The Cuban replaced his spent magazine for his Uzi, cocked the weapon and moved on to join his partners for the final assault on the hijack force.

THE BLAST from the munitions building shattered windows in the control tower. Sadiqi threw up his arms as the glass imploded, showering the occupants of the room with keen slivers.

Hanni Basur, the passenger on the 747 known as Hanni Amir, was hit in the face by a number of fragments and stumbled away from the windows, his hands raised but not touching his bloody face.

The 747's pilot was seated a distance away from the front of the control room, so he escaped serious injury. He received a couple of minor facial cuts before he threw himself to the floor.

The other hijackers in the room were also at a safe distance from the flying glass.

The combined effect of the explosion and the shattering glass caught the occupants off guard. It left them briefly vulnerable, and it was during that time that David McCarter and Gary Manning burst into the control room.

As the Phoenix Force pair entered the control room, the hijackers reacted, but with less speed and coordination than required.

The M-16 in McCarter's hands fired as he caught a glimpse of the trio of hijackers on the far side. They had reached for their weapons, bringing them to bear as McCarter and Manning showed.

McCarter raised his M-16 without pausing to change direction. His finger worked the trigger, and the assault rifle punched out 3-round bursts, the 5.56 mm rounds effectively taking them down in rapid succession.

Sadiqi was Manning's target. The hijack commander, bleeding from face and hands, snatched his pistol from the holster on his belt. He sleeved blood from his eyes and turned to face the attackers, and found himself facing the muzzle of the Uzi SMG in Manning's hands. Sadiqi tasted blood in his mouth from the cuts on his face. He kept on lifting the pistol, knowing he was doing it very quickly, and for a moment he believed he was going to win. Then the Uzi crackled, sending a burst of 9 mm autofire into Sadiqi's chest. The impact knocked the man back against the air control desk. As he fell, his body racked with pain, all he could hear was the sound of battle coming from outside the control tower, and even that faded away to complete and utter silence.

Someone lurched in Manning's direction. The big Canadian sensed his closeness and he turned, bringing up the Uzi in a defensive action. He stared into the glass ravaged face of Hanni Basur. The man had slivers of glass protruding from his face, and he was bleeding profusely. Manning fired in reflex, the Uzi's burst knocking Basur off his feet and dumped him in a bloody heap on the floor.

McCarter had Percy Dexter back on his feet.

"You all right?" the Briton asked.

Dexter nodded. "Tired of sitting around here, but apart from that okay." He stared at the Phoenix Force pair. "What about the plane?"

"We took it back."

"Who are you guys?"

"Don't ask 'cause we can't tell," McCarter said. "Can you get that 747 back in the air?"

Dexter grinned. "Can a hog make bacon? Damn right I can. That runway is a tad short, but I'll get her up. Just give me the chance."

"You'll get it, mate. Just give us a little time to clear up this bunch of bloody hijackers."

"Before the windows blew in the guy called Sadiqi got on the radio. Sounded like he was calling for backup. You might have visitors on the way."

"Bugger it," McCarter said. He clicked on his comlink and spoke to Jack Grimaldi. "We've just heard there may be reinforcements on the way, Jack. Can you check it out for us?"

"Will do. You guys okay to hang on while I divert?"

"Yeah. But make it snappy, flyboy."

GRIMALDI PUT THROUGH a call to Stony Man, asking for help.

"You got us on satellite?" he asked.

"Clear as day," Kurtzman said.

"I just had a call from Phoenix advising they might have unfriendly visitors on the way in. Can you see anything heading our way?"

"Give me five and I'll come back to you."

Grimaldi boosted *Dragon Slayer,* taking the combat chopper to a greater altitude so he could oversee the area around the airfield. The day was brightening around him. The pilot was able to make out details on the ground now. He turned north and checked out the terrain. The land was sandy, with a scattering of skinny trees and patches of sparse brush. Grimaldi spotted the thin meandering of a watercourse.

"Got you a contact," Kurtzman said through the satellite link.

He sent the coordinates through to *Dragon Slayer*'s integrated computer.

"Three vehicles coming in from the northeast. If they stay on their present heading, they'll hit the airfield. We identified them as Land Rovers. Open backs. Number of passengers on board."

"Roger that," Grimaldi said. "I'll go take a look."

"We can get another ten, maybe twelve minutes before this bird logs out," Kurtzman stated. "Any joy and I'll be back, as Arnie what's his name says."

Grimaldi locked into the coordinates Stony Man had sent him and *Dragon Slayer* banked sharply and put herself on the heading. Making contact with Phoenix Force Grimaldi relayed the information he had.

"I'm going to check those vehicles out. See the kind of reception I get."

"Thanks, Jack."

On the monitor the location grid informed Grimaldi he would be over the convoy within the next sixty seconds. He took the helicopter down until he was leveling out at a couple of hundred feet. The ground flashed by in a sandy blur.

Grimaldi spotted the three long wheelbase Land Rovers. They were bumping their way along a narrow, defined track, clouds of dust in their wake. He swung *Dragon Slayer* in a banking turn, easing off the power so he could get a good look. The men in the open backs were carrying an assortment of weapons. As Grimaldi flew in toward them, he saw the passengers staring up at him.

And then without warning they starting shooting, mostly autorifles. He was out of range, but that didn't stop them. The Land Rovers all drew to a halt, more dust boiling up from beneath their wheels. As it cleared, Grimaldi saw that a number of the men had climbed out of the Land Rovers and were milling round in groups.

He realized why when he saw one of them follow *Dragon Slayer*. The man had something resting on one shoulder.

"Son of a bitch," Grimaldi said.

He took *Dragon Slayer* in a sideways slide, a fraction of a second before the man on the ground let go with an RPG rocket launcher. The missile shot from the tube, curving up at where the combat chopper had been only seconds before. Grimaldi saw the missile as it hurtled past.

"Okay, boys, if that's the local greeting, here's my reply."

Grimaldi arced *Dragon Slayer* around and lined up on the Land Rovers. He activated the stub-wing pods and fired off a heat-seeker. It streaked toward the parked vehicles, a white trail following it. It hit the center vehicle and took it out in a mushroom of fire and smoke, kicking the Land Rover onto its side. Men scattered. They left some of their company on the ground. Bringing the chopper back for a second run, Grimaldi saw that the armed crews had deserted the vehicles and were making for cover in the surrounding terrain. He hit the rear vehicle, then returned a third time to demolish the remaining Land Rover.

Standing off, Grimaldi laid down a few bursts of fire from the chain gun, the 30 mm shells kicking up large gouts of earth as they chopped their way across the ground. His fire took out a number of the scattering men, the 30 mm shells doing considerable damage to flesh and bone. Grimaldi stayed around for a while, making his presence felt as a silent warning to any of the others.

When he finally moved off, he left the three Land Rovers smoking wrecks and their surviving crews debating whether to continue to the airfield, or stay away and let Mansur's people handle whatever had happened.

Kurtzman came back on the satellite link.

"You have a chopper coming in toward the airfield. Good way off but staying on a direct course. I'd say another forty minutes if she stays on line."

"Okay, we'll keep our eyes open."

WHEN MCCARTER AND Manning emerged from the control tower, there was a lull in the fighting. In fact, the fighting was over. Mansur's force had been reduced to a few wounded men. The rest were dead. All the survivors had been disarmed.

James, Hawkins and Encizo had leveled the site, except for one of the buildings. The only other untouched object was the fuel tanker they had spotted on the far side of the field. Even the helicopter had been put out of action.

They stood watching over the surviving hijack terrorists.

"T.J., go and check that tanker," McCarter said. "If there's aviation fuel on board, we can pump it into the 747."

Hawkins turned and started across the strip toward the tanker.

"Dexter, you get back to your plane. Fire her up. The sooner you're out of here the better."

Dexter nodded and left them.

"Let me guess," McCarter said. "You didn't torch that building over there because you found something inside?"

"They didn't make you bossman for nothing," James stated.

He led the way across the building and pushed open the door. They stepped inside, feeling the cool temperature from the air-conditioning unit, which was still running.

On the bench was the nuclear device that the late Jeffrey Hardin had built. Next to it was the control device. Neither that, nor the power pack fixed to the bomb itself was switched on. McCarter walked around the bench, examining the bomb. Sitting there on the bench, inactive, it was nothing more than a hunk of metal. When the Briton thought of the terrifying potential within that hunk of metal, he experienced a chill that had nothing to do with the air-conditioning.

"Okay. Go through this place. Collect any paperwork you find. That laptop on the bench and any disks. When we leave we take that thing with us to the carrier and hand it over. Let the Navy specialists deal with it. Jack can plant a couple of missiles into this place."

Manning and Encizo stayed inside to go through the contents, while James followed McCarter back outside. As they left the building the fuel tanker rolled to a stop, Hawkins at the wheel.

"Aviation fuel," he said, leaning out the cab window.

"Get it over to that plane," McCarter said. "Get Dexter's help to pump it into the tanks. I want that bloody 747 out of here as soon as possible."

Hawkins raised a hand and rolled the fuel tanker across the strip toward the waiting airliner.

"You have any objections if I go and check out those wounded men?" James asked.

McCarter grinned. "You'll only pull faces if I say no."

He watched the tall black man make his way across to the injured men.

First we go all out to kill them. Next minute we're giving them medical treatment. McCarter shook his head at the pure craziness of it all.

LESS THAN AN HOUR LATER Phoenix Force stood and watched as Flight 291 pulled into the sky. The 747 rose with seeming slowness until it vanished from their sight. All that was left were a couple of pale vapor trails.

"You guys ready now?" Grimaldi asked.

Once he had arrived, the nuclear device had been loaded on board *Dragon Slayer* ready for the flight to the coast and the U.S. carrier waiting for them on the Indian Ocean. They had also loaded all the data they had found within the workshop.

Grimaldi had reported his clash with the incoming force and his destruction of their transport and the dispersal of the crews. He had also mentioned the possible arrival of a helicopter.

Stony Man had been informed on the outcome of the mission and Phoenix Force had been told about Able Team's success with the hijacked submarine. They were winding up their operation back in Govograd, liaising with the Russian undercover team.

"Let's go, Jack," McCarter said.

It was then that the beat of a helicopter's rotors broke the calm of the airfield. It swung into view from behind the control tower, easing across the strip to hover twenty feet from where Phoenix Force stood. The machine was an SA-341 Gazelle, French-built and capable of carrying missiles along with its gun pods. This particular machine had no missiles, but its machine guns could be clearly seen. Apart from the pilot there appeared to be only one passenger.

He sat staring around the airfield in disbelief, at the leveled buildings and the dead and wounded men on the ground.

"Now we've got it all," Hawkins whispered. "You know who that ole boy is?"

"Abrim Mansur," McCarter said.

"That's right, boss."

"Come to check out his investment," Grimaldi said. "I have the feeling he ain't going to be best pleased with us, fellers."

"I'm not too happy about those damn machine guns pointing in our direction," Manning observed.

Behind the Canadian there was the sound of a weapon being loaded. Manning realized that someone was putting a round into an M-203 grenade launcher. He heard the click as the weapon was closed, locked and cocked.

"If you want 40 mm of HE up your ass, stay put," Calvin James said softly. "If you want your ass to remain part of you, just give me room."

"Now?" Manning asked.

"Now," James yelled.

Manning leaned to the right, shouldering McCarter aside, giving James his clear shot.

The M-203 smoked as James pulled the trigger. The M-406 high-explosive round closed the gap in a split second, impacting against the helicopter's canopy. It detonated with a loud crack, shattering the canopy and filling the cockpit with 325 red-hot fragments. Within the confines of the cockpit there was nowhere for Abrim Mansur or the pilot to go. They died in the blast, bodies shredded and pulped. The helicopter's canopy blew out, Mansur's shattered and bloody corpse hanging out over the metal frame. The helicopter, with no hand controlling it, spun around, crashing into the base of the control tower. The deadweight of the chopper dragged it to the ground, where leaking fuel added fire to the already demolished aircraft.

McCarter glanced at the burning Gazelle, turned to look at James.

"I believe that is mission accomplished, gentlemen. So let's get the hell out of here and go home."

The last thing Grimaldi did before putting *Dragon Slayer* onto the set course for the U.S. Navy carrier was to lay down a couple of HE missiles, taking out the control tower and the workshop where they had located the nuclear device.

Dragon Slayer settled on its easterly course, out across the Somalia coast and over the glittering expanse of the Indian Ocean, heading directly for the waiting carrier.

EPILOGUE

War Room, Stony Man Farm, Virginia

Hal Brognola held up his hand to stem the conversation in the room.

"This one is going to rumble around in the background for a while. A lot of people got their feathers ruffled, and they're still bitching, but there isn't a damn thing they can do about it. We've had diplomatic complaints from Afghanistan about U.S. incursions without prior consultation. This is just someone stirring the pot because they got their rear ends kicked."

"You mean Mansur's group, Afghanistan chapter?" James asked. "Comes down to them being bad losers is all."

"The right word in the right ear causes ripples in the diplomatic pool," Brognola said. "We didn't play their game."

"If we had, that nuclear bomb would have ended up being flown into JFK," Hawkins said. "The day we let diplomatic protocol run us we might as well shut up shop and go home."

"The kind of people we're up against don't wait for

territorial decisions to be made,'' Carl Lyons said.
''They decide to do something, they go right ahead.''

''Lucky for us the President was fully on board,''
Brognola said. ''He had no intention of letting Mansur
carry through his operation. He said no quarter and
stuck to his promise when the flak started to fly. He
refuses to stand by and let anything like September 11
happen again if it can be prevented, and to hell with
hurting international feelings. Unofficial sources tell
me he's handed out a few harsh words to some of his
own people when they questioned his decisions on
this.''

McCarter shook his head. ''Even though there was
the chance of a nuke being exploded at JFK? Bloody
idiots would still expect us to consider the options.
What options? You stop them, or you let them wipe
out a whole city. Where's the choice?''

''There are certain factions, interested groups, so-
called intellectuals, who would sit and argue the point
all day,'' Barbara Price said. ''They have the notion
that you don't combat evil by opting for their violent
conceptions of life. Human rights violations. Territorial transgressions. The breaking of religious codes.
They all have to be considered before you act against
any international threat.''

''What about those issues on behalf of the people
living in and around New York?'' Blancanales asked.
''How do their human rights stack up against someone
like Mansur shipping in a nuke to turn them all into
dust? Jesus, Hal, I wonder sometimes who we're fighting for. And why.''

''For what it's worth, Pol, the President sent his

thanks for what you all did. On behalf of the nation. Most likely the general population will never know what went off over the past few days. The passengers on Flight 291 were involved in a hostage situation. They won't be told why Mansur had them hijacked."

"So the unsung heroes slope off into the sunset once again," James said. "Or do we get a pay raise in lieu of national recognition?"

"What do you think?" Brognola asked. "You did great, all of you. This was a shitty mission from day one. Picking up intel as we went along, poking around in the dark. Working on gut feelings and hunches. Especially Aaron."

"Hey, you got a mention," McCarter said.

"Don't knock it," Brognola said. "If we think back, it was Aaron who initiated this whole thing. Intuition and scraps of data picked out of the airwaves. That's what gave us our first leads. As far as I'm concerned he can keep right on doing that for us."

"Okay," McCarter relented. "Go on then, I'll buy you a drink next time I meet you in a pub."

Kurtzman laughed. "What do you mean next time? I'm still waiting for the *first* time you buy me a drink."

"We'll talk about that another day."

"The Russians were pleased to get their submarine back," Brognola said, "despite some damage that occurred."

"They were lucky we didn't sink the thing," Schwarz said.

"The Russian president acknowledged the assistance he received from the U.S. If those missiles had been fired on the oilfields, he wouldn't have been so happy. Taking them out of terrorist hands also allowed our military people to breathe easier.''

"We get any feedback from Lipov's team?'' Blancanales asked.

"What he means is did he get any mention by a young lady named Danielle,'' Lyons said.

"He up to his old tricks again?'' McCarter asked.

Schwarz smiled, shifting in his seat to accommodate his bandaged arm and shoulder. He was still wearing a sling, which he didn't like and wore under protest. "And some,'' he said.

"We were only there a few hours,'' Blancanales protested. "I hardly had a chance to say a word.''

"After you left on the *Red Star,* Lipov and his team called in their backup and went through Govograd like a hurricane. They rounded up all the local undesirables, including the top man.''

"Bortai?'' Lyons asked.

"That's him. Govograd is a quiet town now.''

Barbara Price picked up a printed sheet.

"A certain Somali warlord by the name of Numbar raised a stink, saying some of his local, unarmed, people were the subject of an unprovoked attack by an American military helicopter.''

"He's lying through his teeth,'' Jack Grimaldi said. "*Dragon Slayer* doesn't carry any kind of identifying markings.''

"Oh, he knows it and so do we,'' Price said. "When he was asked about an American airliner being held on his territory, he said it was a fabrication. So he was sent copies of satellite photos showing that very airliner on an airfield clearly situated on Somali territory and asked if he wanted to take the matter further. He decided to play dumb after that.''

"We got a curt note from the Iranians," Brognola said. "A strained thanks for the return of Waris Mahoud's body with a suggestion that this doesn't mean we should imagine they're in any way pleased with our handling of the Mansur incident, or that we are about to become best buddies.''

"Some people are just hard to please," McCarter muttered.

"So, Mansur and most of his top people are dead," Manning said. "That still leaves followers and some shady backers alive and probably not too pleased with the outcome. They don't just forget their beliefs, or turn the other cheek. How do we know they won't try again?''

"We don't and they will," Price said. "Which is why we can't sit back and feel too complacent. There are other Mansurs out there. Sitting somewhere, brooding about what happened this time. Angry because their genuine feelings about this country are still being ignored. That the injustices they believe are directed at them alone go unpunished. With that frame of mind it isn't a big step from contemplative thought to a perceived righteous deed.''

"The lady isn't wrong," McCarter said, sitting upright. "We're in this for the long haul. A very bloody long haul.''

Hellbenders

Available in March 2004
at your favorite retail outlet.

Emerging from a gateway into a redoubt filled with preDark
technology, Ryan and his band hope to unlock some of the
secrets of post-nuclear America. But the fortified redoubt is
under the control of a half-mad former sec man hell-bent on
vengeance, who orders Ryan and the others to jump-start his
private war against two local barons. Under the harsh and
pitiless glare of the rad-blasted desert sun, the companions
fight to see another day, whatever it brings....

GOLD EAGLE®

GDL65

James Axler
Outlanders

MAD GOD'S WRATH

The survivors of the oldest moon colony have been revived from cryostasis and brought to Cerberus Redoubt, leaving behind an enemy in deep, frozen sleep. But betrayal and treachery bring the rebel stronghold under seige by the resurrected demon king of a lost world. With a prize hostage in tow to lure Kane and his fellow warriors, he retreats to the uncharted planet of mystery and impossibility for a final act of madness.

Available February 2004 at your favorite retail outlet.

Or order your copy now by sending your name, address, zip or postal code, along with a check or money order (please do not send cash) for $6.50 for each book ordered ($7.99 in Canada), plus 75¢ postage and handling ($1.00 in Canada), payable to Gold Eagle Books, to:

In the U.S.	In Canada
Gold Eagle Books	Gold Eagle Books
3010 Walden Avenue	P.O. Box 636
P.O. Box 9077	Fort Erie, Ontario
Buffalo, NY 14269-9077	L2A 5X3

Please specify book title with your order.
Canadian residents add applicable federal and provincial taxes.

GOUT28

THE DESTROYER
POLITICAL PRESSURE

The juggernaut that is the Morals and Ethics Behavior Establishment—MAEBE—is on a roll. Will its ultra-secret enforcement arm, the White Hand, kill enough scumbags to make their guy the uber-boy of the Presidential race? MAEBE! Will Orville Flicker succeed in his murderous, manipulative campaign to win the Oval Office? MAEBE! Can Remo and Chiun stop the bad guys from getting whacked—at least until CURE officially pays them to do it? MAEBE!

Available April 2004 at your favorite retail outlet.